To

This is Lauren Henderson's ~~second~~ anti-heroine, Sam Jones, all seven of which have been translated into several languages. With Stella Duffy, Sparkle Hayter and Katy Munger, she runs a website, www.tartcity.com, devoted to Tart Noir, their brand of girls-behaving-badly crime novels. Together with Stella Duffy, she is editing a Tart Noir anthology of short stories.

Lauren divides her time between Italy and New York, and, when not cocktail-tasting, writes full-time.

Praise for Lauren Henderson:

'The pleasure of reading Henderson's books lies not so much in the plots that she unravels as in the wit and sharp modernity of her dialogue, and the delightful irrepressibility of her character Sam, even when in pain and danger'
Marcel Berlins, *The Times*

'Plenty of action and good fun . . . Sam makes an admirable 21st-century heroine' Susanna Yager, *Sunday Telegraph*

'Camden Town heroine Sam Jones really struts her stuff . . . this lady has the kind of style and chutzpah of the rare kind of "alternative" comedian who actually makes you laugh'
Mail on Sunday

'Neatly handled and cleverly paced . . . an exuberant celebration of nineties woman at her most hedonistic and sexy. But underneath there is a noir edge that Lauren Henderson never lets her readers forget . . . stakes her claim to be one of Britain's rising dark stars' Val McDermid, *Manchester Evening News*

Too Many Blondes

Lauren Henderson

ARROW

Published by Arrow Books in 2002

1 3 5 7 9 10 8 6 4 2

First published in the United Kingdom in 1996 by
Hodder and Stoughton, a division of Hodder Headline PLC

Arrow Books
The Random House Group Limited
20 Vauxhall Bridge Road, London SW1V 2SA

Random House Australia (Pty) Limited
20 Alfred Street, Milsons Point, Sydney
New South Wales 2061, Australia

Random House New Zealand Limited
18 Poland Road, Glenfield
Auckland 10, New Zealand

Random House (Pty) Limited
Endulini, 5a Jubilee Road, Parktown 2193, South Africa

The Random House Group Limited Reg. No. 954009

www.randomhouse.co.uk

A CIP catalogue record for this book
is available from the British Library

Papers used by Random House are natural, recyclable
products made from wood grown in sustainable forests.
The manufacturing processes conform to the environmental
regulations of the country of origin

ISBN 0 09 941514 3

Printed and bound in Great Britain by
Cox & Wyman Ltd, Reading, Berkshire

To my grandmother, who found the first book
'very interesting and instructive'.

Acknowledgements

With many thanks to Andrew, exercise teacher and bouncer extraordinaire, who kindly allowed me to pick his brains without wincing too visibly. Any mistakes in the book are of course all his fault and nothing to do with me.

And to the usual suspects: Caroline (editor manqué), Francis, Jenni, Lisa and Sandy – I hope being closed in a room with the first draft and not allowed to come out until they had prepared a book report didn't ruin their holidays. To Kate, and also to Giacomo, despite his not having read this one either. Bastard.

1

Any friendly atmosphere that had once existed at the Chalk Farm gym was on the wane, to the point where most of us who worked there thought that 'community spirit' meant the brandy Lou kept for emergencies in the bottom drawer of a filing cabinet. The tension in the air was so thick you could have cut it with a rusty chainsaw. But we weren't expecting murder. Even for the more hardened souls among us, that came as something of a shock.

Luckily, the police didn't know about my fundamental prejudice against blondes; it would have counted against me. Because by any standards of normality or decency, there were simply too many blondes at that gym. If one of them had died in less suspicious circumstances I would have put it down to Darwin's theory of natural selection.

Only the way this one happened to die was about as natural as the colour of her hair.

*   *   *

Closing time on Saturday night, and Camden Town was as packed with people as rush-hour down Oxford Street. Swaying drunks, groups of boys elbowing their way noisily through the streets, painted white Goth faces with purple lips above layers of black-fringed clothes, the road black and wet with rain and the traffic lights at the big intersection outside the tube station blinking into the puddles, green, yellow, red, ignored by everyone except the honking cars: this was where I lived, and I loved it. I'd never felt more at home than I did here.

Tom wasn't so sure.

'Where did you say we were going?'

I sighed. 'It's an indie club called Silver. You probably won't like it very much. But it's free, so if you hate it you can always go to the jazz room at the Electric Ballroom, OK? It was you who wanted to come in the first place.'

'That was only because I didn't have anything else to do—'

I had bumped into Tom earlier that evening at his favourite pub, the Freedom Arms, just a few steps down Camden High Street, having dropped in there for a quick one or two before going dancing. Tom was drinking alone and looking rather miserable, so I had offered to take him along with me. He's one of my oldest friends. I did warn him that it wouldn't be his type of music but I could tell he wasn't listening.

We reached the club, which is opposite Camden Town tube, below a pub that used to be excellent before they opened it up to make room for the tourists and would-be yuppies and ruined its atmosphere. There was already a queue stretching round the side but I ignored it, walking straight to the entrance and past the first pair of bouncers. I waved at James, who ran Silver, from behind a pillar.

'Hi, it's me. Can I bring someone in with me?'

'Sure. She's OK, man,' he said to the bouncer next to him, and to me: 'Down you go, Sam.'

I used to thank James profusely for letting me in, but he had always ignored it and now I didn't bother any longer. As far as I was concerned he was being very generous – I used to date a friend of his and we'd met a couple of times at gigs. I didn't see why that should necessarily entitle me to get in free to his club, but if he wanted to take that attitude it was fine with me. I just hoped Tom was suitably impressed.

I pushed open the doors at the bottom of the stairs and stood for a moment breathing in the atmosphere. If I had a sense of belonging to Camden Town, it was centred around this place. Papered with flyers from old gigs, it was wooden-floored, with a big central bar and wall-to-wall low-lifes, smoking and drinking far more than was good for them. The music pumped out from overhead speakers. It was early yet – hardly anyone would be dancing. I was charged up and felt like I owned the world.

I turned to Tom. 'Do you want a drink?'

It was a stupid question, really. I bought him a whisky and a lager for myself and we stood at the bar, checking out the talent. Well, I was; these were not the sort of types among whom Tom would look for a paramour.

Tom was in a gloomy mood. He's a not very successful poet who's always threatening to chuck it all in and become a primary school teacher. I realised I might have made a mistake bringing him here; it really wasn't his kind of music. He's an ex-soul boy. Also he was the only person there in an Aran sweater and corduroys, and he was probably feeling self-conscious.

'What do you think?' I said brightly. He grimaced.

'Everyone's wearing *black*, Sam,' he said. 'Isn't that out of date by now?'

'This kind of black is timeless,' I said firmly. 'Look at her, for instance.' I indicated a girl across the bar from us who, while only seventeen or so, looked like a dead ringer for an early Siouxsie and the Banshees fan: hair black as coal, skin the necessary, almost putrid, white, mouth painted on with prune lipstick and little regard for the original contours.

Tom shuddered. 'I'd rather not.'

Since his taste only runs to pallid blondes, I wasn't very sympathetic.

'Well, I'm wearing all black,' I pointed out. Little black dress, fishnets and my big black boots with lots of zips and laces: basic dancing wear.

He looked at me. 'You're different,' he said. 'You look essentially healthy and clean.'

'How *dare* you.'

'I mean,' he said hurriedly, 'you look too glamorous to fit in, in a way – I mean, you're dressed up like a vampire, but you look like Gina Lollobrigida dressed up as a vampire – you look like someone one could actually want to have sex with, unlike most of the women here, who I feel I would catch some primitive, testicle-rotting eighteenth-century disease from—'

I felt it was time to change the subject before the women to whom Tom was referring so disparagingly overheard him, karate-chopped him to the ground and kicked him accurately in his floppy parts. Most of them looked as if they had been on the

11

requisite council-sponsored courses and would welcome a chance to practise their technique. 'Oh, look,' I said swiftly, 'it's Derek.'

'Who?'

'Derek. He teaches weights at the gym. I wonder what he's doing here? I wouldn't have thought it was his kind of place.'

I pointed him out to Tom. Derek wasn't difficult to spot; practically everyone here was a cadaverous shade of white and dressed in black, while Derek was the opposite. He was also over six foot and in superb physical condition, which on its own would have caused him to stand out among the bar-propping, non-dancing section of the club's habitués. They were the kind of people who considered tapping another cigarette out of the packet an over-strenuous activity.

'Who's that he's talking to?' Tom said, perking up for the first time that evening. The woman to whom he was referring was pretty and indubitably blonde, her fair hair gathered up in a high ponytail and cascading down over her face. She was much smaller than Derek, who made her look fragile by contrast. Definitely Tom's type.

'Not the faintest,' I said. 'Want an introduction?'

'No,' Tom said despondently. 'What chance have I got next to that guy? His pecs must be bigger than Arnold Schwarzenegger's.'

Tom is very large and adequately muscled himself; he should be, since he works as a labourer when his latest Arts Committee grant has run out. However he was currently sporting an extra layer of subcutaneous fat which had the effect of blanketing his not unimpressive muscular development. If he stopped drinking he'd probably lose it in a month.

'*Conan the Destroyer* with Grace Jones, the only film where the hero's breasts are larger than the heroine's,' I said flippantly.

'Actually Derek isn't too pumped-up. He does a lot of basketball.'

Tom gave me a withering look. 'Is that supposed to reassure me?'

'What I'm wondering,' I said thoughtfully, 'is whether his girl-friend knows he's out with another woman on Saturday night. Linda's not likely to be happy about that. He'd better hope she doesn't find out.'

'Is she very jealous?'

'Yes. But I wouldn't be worried about that if I were him, so much as the fact that she happens to be the manager of the gym.'

'Oh.'

'Derek does have a rather Stud-U-Like reputation—'

'Well, if I looked like him I would too!' Tom said bitterly.

'Shall we go and have a dance?' I suggested. I always try to steer the conversation down a happier path when Tom becomes maudlin, otherwise he drags me down with him into his personal slough of despond, and it takes ages to clean that kind of stuff off your clothes.

'You dance,' he said, turning up his nose at the track currently throbbing forth from the speakers. 'I'll watch you.'

We threaded our way through towards the dance floor. The club is sometimes used for gigs and so there's a little stage at the back where the exhibitionists dance, with the main dance floor below it and a balcony running round two sides. The last side is the DJ's platform. I was aching to dance, but I was also carrying my new ankle-length leopardskin coat with big lapels – seventies, second-hand – and I was loath either to put it down or trust it to the cloakroom. Tom, however, swore he would guard it with his life, and he was usually reliable. So I left him propped up against the balcony with the coat over his arm and plunged down the stairs into the seething maelstrom, clearing out, by dint of my elbows, a space where I could throw myself around in comfort.

They play my favourite kind of dance music here, very loud with good tunes and plenty of thrashing guitars. Groups of boys linked arms, shouting the lyrics of the cheerier songs; when anything more gloomy and noisy came on they changed mode and threw themselves into each other, yelling raucously. Luckily I had my boots on and anyone who bumped into me got such a kick on the shins that they didn't come back. You can always tell the well-brought-up boys – they're the ones who apologise to you as they limp away with your toecap imprinted on their lower leg.

After about an hour James put on 'Touch Me, I'm Sick', which is particularly exhausting, combining as it does a throbbing rhythm with the convention that everyone stops dead to shout the chorus – which with praiseworthy simplicity consists solely of the title – each time it's repeated. After all this I was quite drained and most of my hair had fallen down, so I went in search of Tom. He was back at the bar, and I was glad to see that my coat had accompanied him.

'What was that last song?' he said with the air of an anthropologist who has discovered a particularly distasteful tribal ritual and isn't looking forward much to writing it up.

'It's by Mudhoney – "Touch Me, I'm Sick".'

'Mm. Someone here was shouting something a bit different—'

'The last time they sing it it changes to "Fuck Me, I'm Sick".'

'Yes, that was it.' He shuddered slightly. 'Can I have another whisky?' he said to the barman. 'I need it. And half a lager for my lady friend.'

He pushed my drink over to me.

'I think your mate just left,' he said, 'with that girl. They looked quite friendly.'

'Derek?'

'Mr Throbbing Gristle, yes.'

Someone tapped me on the shoulder.

'Hi, Sam, how're you doing?'

It was Lucy, a pudding-faced girl who was a researcher for a cable TV programme on indie music. With her was a man she introduced as a producer she worked with, and a singer who had named himself after his struggling grunge band. The producer looked interesting, by which of course I mean attractive, but he disengaged himself almost straight away to go and chat to the guitarist of a reasonably successful band who was posing at the end of the bar, pelvis jutting out provocatively. He was so fashionably thin his hipbones had worn holes through his jeans.

The singer I knew already.

'Hi, Leggo,' I said. 'How's it going?'

'All right,' he said.

This was positively loquacious for Leggo who, though very beautiful, wasn't much for making conversation. Lucy, the diametric opposite, launched into an unsolicited run-down of how exciting her week had been. She was a good example of the precept that whenever you start a sentence with the words 'It was really fascinating' your audience will invariably be bored to tears. I listened patiently nonetheless, choking back the yawns, because she had been promising for ages to feature me and my metal sculptures on the programme's two-minute slot covering artistic happenings. Though only a slender opportunity for stardom, it was so far the one prospect I had.

'You must come round and look at my new stuff,' I said hopefully, when I could get a word in edgeways. 'I've done this new mobile which looks really stunning.'

'Great,' she said, 'you must give me a ring some time.'

I wasn't a media expert but I still knew that this meant no. I brooded gloomily, trying to decide whether she and Leggo were an item. I had tried to chat him up a while back but he had been too out of it to respond. I wondered if he were one of those men who, rather than taking the initiative, prefer to be clubbed over the head and dragged back to your cave by their hair. Plenty of those around: why else do you think they grow their locks so long and flowing nowadays?

I introduced Lucy to Tom, which was not a good move; he asked her why there wasn't more poetry on TV and she in response pointed out that they had featured a reading of Jim Morrison's oeuvre on the programme only last week. At this point I left hurriedly; Tom's aesthetic principles are rather rigid and I doubted that he would count that as poetry. I didn't want to be around for the explosion.

*   *   *

'I think that guy wants to talk to you.'

I looked up, cross at being interrupted. It was about an hour and a half later and I was tucked away in as quiet a corner as the club could offer, staring into the eyes of a very attractive man with whom I hoped to spend the night.

'Where?' I said irritably. 'Oh. Hi, Tom.'

'I'm off now,' Tom said, raising his eyebrows in a conspiratorial, Roger-Moore-acting kind of way. 'Do you need a lift?'

We've honed this routine down to a fine art by now. Ideally the person to whom I (or Tom) am talking then offers me (or Tom) a lift too, which sorts out his (I can't be bothered to keep putting the other bit in) intentions towards me. If he remains silent, I leave with Tom; and if he does offer a lift but I don't want to go with him, I can decline gracefully by pleading a prior obligation to a friend.

'No problem,' my companion duly said to me, 'I'll see you home. I've got my car outside.'

'Yeah, I wouldn't mind staying a bit longer,' I said in my best cool voice, as if the thought had just occurred to me. 'It's OK, then, Tom, but thanks.' I retrieved my coat, taking the opportunity to make a Leave Me, I Would Be Alone face at him.

'No sweat,' Tom said, dutifully following the routine. 'Catch you later.'

He backed away to a position where only I could see him and started mouthing something at me which I couldn't catch. His eyebrows were waggling like windscreen wipers or Roger Moore again, this time trying to indicate surprise. I waved him away impatiently and turned my back. I didn't want to mess this one up through any indiscretion of Tom's.

'I hope you're not going to have to go out of your way to take me back,' I said politely.

'Wherever.' He looked straight into my eyes. I felt my stomach melting. 'No problem at all.'

He wasn't a stranger. Or, in other words, I wasn't behaving like a complete idiot. And though I didn't know him all that well, I intended to improve the terms of our acquaintance as soon as possible. From the way he was looking at me he had much the same sort of thing on his mind.

Just then the music stopped dead. A groan went up. Then the first strains of Crystal Gayle's 'Don't It Make My Brown Eyes Blue' rang out; this was always the last song of the night, James's way of signalling that it was time to wind down and go home.

'Feel like a dance?' he said, looking into my eyes and nearly melting me down in the process.

'Are you serious?' I said incredulously. Why, this was country music, forsooth. Not his kind of thing at all.

'Sure. Look, there're a couple of others already.'

I was about to say something cutting along the lines of, 'Yeah, sad losers,' but he forestalled this by taking my hand and leading me down the stairs to the dance floor. As soon as he touched me I would have followed him to most places I could think of; his hand was warm and dry and brooked no refusal. He swung me to face him and put his hands low on my waist, pulling me against him. I slid mine up to his shoulders, then round his neck. He was so relaxed, so confident that it became very easy for me to follow his lead, abandoning myself to whatever might happen, no need for choice. At the moment that idea was very seductive.

His eyes were very dark. He bent his head and kissed me, not a tentative kiss but a sure, deep one, absolutely confident of himself and his attraction, his whole body pressed tight against mine, leaving no space for anything but assent. For an instant I hesitated, reasons tumbling over themselves as to why this wasn't a good idea; then the whole scene, the corny appeal of the slow dance at the end of the night, his hands on my bottom grinding his body into mine, the heat and sweat of the atmosphere, all pulled at my senses and I let myself go, falling into it, my hands burying themselves in his hair, my body relaxing against his. I didn't come out of it till he lifted his head. The centre of my body was throbbing so loudly I didn't realise for a few seconds that the music had stopped.

I took his hand and led him out of the club, pulling my coat around me as the cold air hit. His car was unexpectedly smart and he drove it smoothly through the night streets, soul music on the stereo; we hardly spoke, only enough for me to issue directions to where I lived. We pulled up outside my studio and I could see that he didn't like the idea of leaving his nice car here in this back street lined with dingy old warehouses. Still, he made the sacrifice. I just hoped he'd consider me worth it.

He lost no time in putting this to the test. Two seconds after we were inside my studio and I had barred the door behind us, he had me up against it, perched on the big cross-bar with my legs round his waist and my skirt rucked up round mine, holding me up effortlessly with one hand while he busied himself with the other so effectively that I had to hold on to him tight to stop myself collapsing in a pool of pleasure. Then I hit a wave and had to hold on to him even tighter for a while. He didn't seem to mind.

He was very strong and very good and very inventive, and what with one thing and another I didn't get much sleep till dawn, when he left me tucked up in bed and climbed back down from my sleeping platform to the main studio. He was so smooth that, descending the ladder, he didn't even get his hair caught in the giant sculpture that dangled smugly from the ceiling on a thick length of chain. I find it hard to avoid bumping into the wretched thing myself, and I hung it there.

I waited till I heard he had shut the door firmly behind him, then turned over, yawning, released, and curled into a ball, glad to be alone. I hadn't thought he'd want to stay but I can never manage to throw people out after sex – it seems so rude, even if you know you'll both be grateful for it later on. He had perfect manners: he kissed me, whispered: 'See you around,' and left me to get some sleep. After all, we both knew we'd be bumping into each other again. Camden is a small place.

No, he had been perfect from start to finish. He knew all the buttons to press and which order to press them in; his moves were choreographed down to the last exquisite detail. It wasn't his fault that I prefer things a little more uncontrolled. Even when I was writhing in ecstasy, part of me had been detached, as if I were watching our bodies projected on a giant screen. It's impossible to lose yourself completely in sex when you can practically hear your companion's mind ticking away, appreciating what the two of you are up to and working out what you're going to do next.

But he had made it clear that he liked to run things, and I was having such a good time I didn't feel like making an issue of it. Besides, I sensed that I would have ruined it if I had. Sex was sport for him and he liked it played his way – not that his fellow player lost out. God knows he had been considerate enough.

It was exactly what I had needed. I was still recovering from a big, sad love affair which had finished rather unconventionally six months ago, and it was nice to find that I hadn't forgotten how all the bits fitted together. I wasn't currently capable of any kind of involvement more serious than this; I was feeling about as ready for commitment as a female praying mantis.

Pale dawn light filtered through the dirty, dusty skylight above my head. Smiling to myself, I turned over and went to sleep.

2

I was a few minutes late for Rachel's exercise class. Lou, the receptionist, wanted to check my schedule for that week, and when Lou wants to ask you something, you let her. As I pushed open the double doors to the gym the thick, moist air inside slapped me in the face like a hot towel. Lines of gyrating bodies, nearly all female, stretched up and down in front of Rachel's tall, slender figure. It looked like the parade ground for a new model army. I waved at Rachel and buried myself on the far side of the room. She nodded at me briefly but her expression didn't alter for a moment, remaining concentrated and serious.

It was like being inside a hothouse – green, humid and full of bright colours – only no one asks exotic orchids to do twenty jumping jacks on each side. The gym was huge, the size of three badminton courts laid side to side, and we were using two-thirds of it; screened off next to us were the thuds and grunts of a football practice. Everything was painted green, from the floor right up to the iron latticework of struts and gantries which criss-crossed the ceiling beneath the skylights set into the vaulted roof. The colour was chipping away in places to reveal the depressing shade of mustard which the green had covered up. This wasn't a yuppie gym with the membership subscription running into hundreds of pounds a year; it was owned by Chalk Farm Council and run on a fashionably minimalist budget. The decorators who had done the job were probably someone's brother and his mate with a few pots of paint that had fallen off the back of a lorry.

Still, the effect was cheerful and the atmosphere, at this

moment anyway, was uplifted by the loud, repetitive techno music which pounded out of the speakers. Everyone was breathing fast and some of the more unfit aerobicisers were already as pink-faced and damp as accountants on a stag night.

Rachel seemed to be the only one unaffected. She was moving on the beat as crisply as ever, limbs rising and falling like parts of an automaton. Her hair was pulled back into a ponytail, smooth to her scalp then kinking out beyond the elastic into a black waterfall. She wore a black leotard over mauve printed leggings, and through the crowd of sweaty, straining bodies her lavender legs flashed up and down as if pulled by strings. The leggings finished at mid-calf; beneath them her calves and ankles were the colour of *café au lait*, sculpted like polished wood. Her thighs were impossibly long and slender, her face distant, beautiful and fierce. If Rachel were a general I would enlist in any army she commanded.

The clapping at the end was deafening; I suspected people were applauding out of relief that they had survived without ripping anything irreparably. I was soaked in sweat as if all my joints had been lubricated. Knowing Rachel as I did, I could tell that she'd been in a bad mood when she started the class and had put us all through a punishing workout to exorcise it.

I looked over at her. She was towelling her face down. Pulling the elastic off her hair, she shook the resulting shock of fine black electrical wires around her face and gave them a rub with the towel as well. I took a cup of water from the dispenser, knocked it back in one go, refilled it and wandered over to where she was standing.

'That was some going-over you just gave us,' I said.

She smiled up at me over the towel.

'Bit too much for you, was it?'

She looked infinitely more relaxed now. Exercise will do that for you. I was on an adrenaline high myself.

'Piss off,' I said with the deft wit that one day will make me famous as the Dorothy Parker of Camden Town. 'I can keep up with you any day.'

'You're only part-time,' Rachel said, waving a long, elegant finger at me. 'So don't you get fresh with me, girl.'

I didn't have to take this kind of vulgar abuse.

'Why does your music all sound the same?' I said sweetly. 'Would you like to borrow some tapes with tunes on them?'

She narrowed her eyes.

'Right, that's it. You can buy me a drink to apologise.'

'Sure. Coming down to shower?'

'No, I'll go home. See you in the Pheasant in half an hour?'

'OK.'

I collected bag and coat and wandered out into the hall, wanting to give the crowd showering downstairs another five minutes to thin out, so I could enter the changing rooms without using a shoehorn. There was usually a rush after an evening class. People wanted to get home as soon as possible and flop in front of the TV, having earned their rest.

Linda, who ran the gym with an iron hand in a chainmail glove, was pinning a notice to the big board that ran along one side of the reception area. I would have backed away, but she had seen me already, and she had the kind of stare that fixed you to the wall. She was my height, and her eyes bored straight into mine. In a flash of empathy, I knew exactly what a butterfly feels like when the pin goes through its tummy and into the cork board.

'Oh, Sam,' she said briskly, 'I'm glad to see you. I wanted to know if you'd seen the new exercise bands? They were in a blue bag in the office and they've completely disappeared. I was looking for them just this afternoon.'

'Can't help, I'm afraid. I don't use them for my classes and I didn't notice the bag last time I was in there.'

'And when was that?'

'Friday.'

'Hm.' Linda stared at me even harder to let me know that I wasn't exempt from suspicion. 'Well, if you do see them I'd like to know. They were very expensive. I ordered them specially.'

'Sure.'

I looked at the notice that she had pinned up.

'Oh, that doesn't apply to *you*,' she said with her customary dismissive air, the one specially calculated to endear her to her employees, 'it's only for contracted, full-time staff members with voting rights.' Her implication was that she failed to understand my delay in slitting myself open with a ceremonial sword in the middle of the hall with a sign around my neck explaining that I was doing this out of shame for not having secured a contract of employment at the Chalk Farm Gym.

'Can I read it? Or is that a sackable offence?'

She shrugged and walked off. Sophisticated as always, I stuck out my tongue at her back. Lou, who had heard the exchange, shot me a sympathetic glance, then busied herself at her desk as Linda went into the Plexiglas reception cubicle and started flicking through some leaflets.

That Linda made a very good gym manager, no one would deny: she possessed a robot-like efficiency and an equally inhuman capacity for hard work, always the first to enter and the last to leave the gym each day. Behind her back I referred to her as Helga, and that was in an attempt to be friendly. My acquaintance with Linda was comparatively recent: until a few months ago, I hadn't been teaching here regularly, only filling in for others when they were ill or otherwise engaged. Since one of the part-time weights teachers had left, however, I now taught four classes a week. I was making a concerted effort to be fit enough to live up to the expectations of my acolytes and thus was spending quite a lot of time in the gym. It had always been Lou who arranged the class schedule and rang me for occasional work before. I hadn't really rubbed up against Linda, who considered herself rather above dealings with the human race in general and fill-in teachers in particular.

She did some teaching, mostly Level Three aerobics classes (Advanced. Initiates Only) that combined a Germanic precision of movement with an equally Teutonic disregard for pain levels and had a higher than usual proportion of male attendance, probably because no one could call you a sissy for doing aerobics the way Helga taught it. Her circuit training classes were only suitable for people who by normal standards were super-fit already.

I looked over at her. She had a small, pale, carefully made-up face which possessed a certain rat-like prettiness, though this was spoilt by the compressed line of her mouth, which softened only for Derek. Her small eyes were enlarged with mascara, and her blusher always stayed in place, no matter how hard she was working out. Today her hair was in a top-knot and she was modelling a tiny black zip-front top over a navy Lycra catsuit. It was an outfit designed to show what a good body she had: and it was good, if you liked women whose skeleton is so lightly covered with flesh that you wonder why they bother with it at all.

It went down well with Derek. While only too happy to engage in sexual congress with any attractive woman he happened to meet, he preferred his girlfriends thin, blonde and smartly dressed. Like Linda – and like the girl I'd seen him with last night, in fact. Ideally, they had also to understand that he considered himself free to have the above-mentioned flings, as long as he made sure that the flingees were aware he had no serious intentions towards them. Keep things light, have some fun, stay friendly afterwards, that was Derek's philosophy, and honourably enough he didn't seem to consider his one-night stands as sluts; in fact he was more affectionate to them afterwards than before, as a sultan might be with members of his harem. A lot of girls positively enjoyed this treatment and would banter with him teasingly, but I didn't think Linda much relished being cast as the Chief Sultana.

Written in her best management-course jargon, Linda's notice called a meeting in a few days' time to discuss the proposed re-targeting of the gym's membership structure and regally required all voting members to attend. It was signed 'Linda Fillman, Gym Manager'.

I strolled over to the reception cubicle. Linda had gone by now, probably to align all the floor mats at ninety-degree angles and count them to see if any were missing. Sticking my head round the door, I said to Lou in an affected voice: 'Linda Fillman, Gym Manager.'

Lou pulled an expressive face. She was our authority figure, being about fifty, though she didn't look it, managing to pull off the difficult feat of appearing both voluptuously gorgeous and motherly. Lou had been working at the Chalk Farm Gym and Leisure Centre for ever, and had little time for what she called Linda's airs and graces. She was always a splash of colour against the white background of the reception area, like a Matisse hanging on the wall; she wore her hair in a smart straightened bob and usually wrapped bright scarves over it, pinned into place with big gold brooches. The turban *du jour* was composed of red and green swirls and went well with her red dress. Her earrings were huge gold hoops and her shiny fingernails, each one longer than all of mine put together, flicked lightly over the keys of her computer, like tap-dancing birds. She said: 'Why don't she just put "Linda"? Everyone knows who the hell she is. I tell you, her hovering over me every minute's enough to give me a heart attack. As if I couldn't do my own job and hers too without getting all hot and bothered like she does. Hah! She's nothing but a scraggy chicken, if you ask me. Don't know what Derek sees in her.'

I went downstairs grinning. Lou always cheers me up. The stairs were clogged with dressed and made-up women heading purposefully in the other direction, and I was pleased to find the showers nearly empty. Two girls were talking animatedly under the stream of water; one was very dark-skinned and would have been pretty, in a florid way, without the sulky expression that seemed as much a part of her face as the features themselves. She was saying: 'No, he likes me, man, I'm telling you! Should have seen the way he was looking at me today in class. He was really staring, you know?'

The other girl, colourless except for the parts she was loofahing, which were bright pink and cellulite-pocked, said impatiently, 'Honestly, Naomi, you can be so st-*you*-pid!'

'What do *you* know about it?' Naomi snapped.

'They say he's had everyone here already, didn't you know that? Probably carrying more disease than Typhoid Mary!'

I couldn't help grinning. The girl called Naomi opened her mouth to retort but then she caught sight of me and changed her mind, happy to wash her inner thighs but not her dirty linen in public. By the time I was undressed and in the shower, she was bringing her friend up to date with what had happened on *East Enders* the night before.

They left before I did and I washed myself at a leisurely pace, knowing that Rachel would be a little late. Her flat wasn't far away, but thirty minutes for her to get home, change and leave again was pushing it. I checked out my nude body in the mirror, reasonably pleased by what I saw. I was OK for twenty-six, even if I'd never have the musculature I wanted in my upper arms without working out six days a week.

Still, everything was under control, particularly my natural tendency to an hourglass shape. That was what Tom had meant by his Lollobrigida comment last night. But as long as I was a size twelve I was happy – there's only so much you can do with the raw material. Rachel had my idea of a perfect figure, tall and slim while avoiding Linda's excessive thinness; though, discontent being an essential part of the human condition, she considered that her bosom was too small and had invested in a large collection of padded bras to compensate. In this she reminded me of Mrs Smiling in *Cold Comfort Farm*, whose obsession was tracking down rare brassières.

I dropped into the downstairs office on my way out. This was a cubbyhole near the foot of the stairs which had become a sort of *ex officio* staff room when Lou had thoughtfully installed an ancient kettle and a jumbo box of teabags. There was a small table and a few chairs, but the rest of the contents were ancient filing cabinets and some weights that needed repairing. The main advantage of this office, apart from the ease with which one could make a cup of tea on demand, was that since Linda had her own office upstairs her character could be torn to pieces in safety down here without the risk of her overhearing. This was facilitated by the convenient fact that from waist height up the walls were Plexiglas, which allowed one to check out who was inside before entering and thus avoid the duller members of staff. Equally, if you were sitting down with a cup of tea and passing an idle moment by bitching about someone, there was plenty of time to spot them coming down the corridor and change the subject in advance to something on which everyone could agree. Like Linda.

The occupants of the staff room at that moment were Derek and Jeff, the former propped nonchalantly against a filing cabinet, talking to the latter. Derek never simply stood or sat; he reclined or leant or propped himself against something. He flashed me a friendly smile.

'Hi, Sam, how's it going?'

'Fine, thanks.'

I grinned back at him. His ease of manner was contagious; Derek had a natural ability to cheer most people up just by being himself. There were plenty of good-looking guys with perfect bodies in the gym, but Derek took the prize for his handsome face and air of total relaxation. Nothing was a problem for Derek, and probably nothing ever had been. Women near as dammit ripped off their G-string leotards and threw them at him screaming: 'Take me, take me'; he kept in excellent shape without having to put in the hours every day in the gym, as some less naturally muscular types had to do; and his friendliness won over most of those who might have been inclined to be jealous of him. You couldn't even blame him for his promiscuity; he was so open about it, so take-it-or-leave-it, that's-the-way-I-am. He genuinely admired Linda, her drive and resolution; he liked the idea that his girlfriend was not just another witless bimbo but a gym manager. Though perhaps it would have been pushing the envelope to call Derek a feminist.

Jeff, however, was one of the few people immune to Derek's charm. You could tell that just from his body language: right now he was sitting straight up at the table with his arms folded over his chest, stiff as a board, while Derek lounged against the cabinet, the picture of self-assurance and health in his white T-shirt and tracksuit bottoms. It wasn't his fault that he made Jeff look pale and scrawny by comparison, but Jeff held it against him just the same.

There is always an unspoken gym hierarchy, because body-builders are so competitive. Jeff, as an aerobics teacher and skinny to boot, was at the bottom of the scale. Male aerobics instructors came in for a lot of grief. Some steroid freaks would call them ponces – very reconstructed – and try to intimidate them by staring them down in the corridors (if nothing worse). Jeff worked out two hours a day, and despite that was often teased for teaching classes where he jumped up and down in front of a load of girls.

Chalk Farm, with all its commitments to equal opportunities, was better than most gyms; it had already kicked out members for that kind of behaviour. It was a twist of irony that Jeff's particular dislike was reserved for Derek, who never participated in any of the teasing, being much too busy eyeing up every new female rear end which sauntered through the gym. But life isn't fair and men – particularly ones who gather together in front of floor-to-ceiling mirrors in an effort to pump up their bodies like balloons – are in general about as rational as a group of five-year-olds squabbling over who gets next go on the Game Boy.

'Have either of you guys seen a blue bag with some exercise bands in it kicking round here?' I asked. 'Only Linda's been on my case about it.'

Jeff shook his head. 'She asked me about it, too.' He and Linda were always at daggers drawn and I could tell he would have added something derogatory if Derek hadn't been present.

'Linda worries too much, that's her problem,' Derek said easily. 'She's a bit stressed at the moment. Don't take it personally. It'll turn up.'

'I'm sure it will. Well, see you around.'

'Are you off?' Jeff asked.

'Yeah, I'm meeting Rachel down the Pheasant.'

'Oh? Might join you later,' he said.

Bollocks. I had made a fatal blunder. Jeff was the gym leech; he clamped on to you with his powerful suckers and bored you senseless, draining you of energy till you were limp and fit for nothing apart from watching the kind of Australian soap operas they show just after lunchtime when you are sleepy and digesting and consequently less demanding of your entertainment. Rachel would curse me out for having, in a moment of distraction, let slip where we were going. I smiled politely and made my escape before he could pin me down to a definite arrangement.

As I closed the office door behind me, I caught a glimpse of Derek's face. He had straightened up, and his carefree manner was gone; he looked distinctly preoccupied. Maybe he had misplaced the exercise bands and didn't want Linda to find out. Her wrath was mighty. No, Derek could easily deal with that kind of trouble. I thought it more likely he was worried she would find out who he had been with last night.

*   *   *

The Cock and Pheasant is a trendified little pub in an alley off Camden High Street, all mint-green walls, gilded mirrors and polished floorboards, verging perilously on wine-bar territory.

I'm told that it's the best place in North London for picking up graphic designers. Still, one can't hold that against a pub where they have an excellent selection of draught lagers and baskets of the establishment's own little matchboxes scattered about for you to plunder. I love those things; they make me feel sophisticated.

Rachel, of course, wasn't there yet. I fought my way through the leather jackets and black plastic rucksacks to the fireplace at the far end, where I found two stools near the mantelpiece and sat trying to make my gin and tonic last longer than a couple of seconds. She arrived five minutes later, looking fabulous, her hair wound up into a bun on top of her head, a short black trenchcoat tied tightly round her narrow waist. Men and women alike stared at her covertly. She stopped at the bar to get a drink. I noticed bitterly that she didn't have to wait to be served and told myself it was merely because she was taller than I was. Dream on, dreamer.

'Hiya,' she said, perching on the stool next to me. She let out a sigh of relief. 'God, it's nice to be sitting down. It's been a long day.'

'Er,' I said nervously, having decided to tell her at once, 'I have a little bad news. Jeff may be joining us.'

'Shit, Sam! Why did you tell him where we were going?'

'It just slipped out. I'm sorry, I feel like a complete prat. Do you want to go somewhere else?'

She shrugged. 'No, I like it here. Besides, where are we going to find another place we can sit down? We'll just have to talk about feminine hygiene till he gets the hint and buzzes off.'

'Jeff thinks he's a feminist,' I pointed out. 'He's much more likely to tell us what he thinks of the new sanitary towel ads on TV and why they're demeaning to women. That's his idea of a chat-up line.'

'He's a sad fuck, eh.' Rachel took a long pull at her drink. 'Look,' she said more seriously, 'what did you think of the class? You haven't been in a while, have you?'

'It was very good,' I said honestly. 'We had a great time. But it shouldn't be down as Level One to Two. Linda will give you hell if she drops in to check up on you. That was definitely Two to Three.'

Rachel shrugged and drained her drink. 'It's usually easier than that,' she admitted. 'I was a bit wound up, you know?'

'I could tell. Want to talk about it?'

'Oh, shit. Man trouble, the usual thing. Said he might drop round and then he didn't, so what's new?'

For some time now – since before I had known her – Rachel had been having an affair with a married man. There's nothing much you can say to this, and I had duly said nothing much when she told me. They were conducting it according to strictly classical lines: he made promises and broke them; she twiddled her thumbs at home whenever he failed to show up as agreed, despite being well aware that the actual timing of his visits bore little relation to any arrangement he might previously have made with her.

'You should date more,' I said, trying to refrain both from criticism and from sympathy, neither of which I considered particularly useful in the circumstances.

'Oh, I do, from time to time. But they never live up to him. God, what a nightmare.' She shrugged. 'He did get in touch today. He had to take his wife out last night – apparently she was feeling a bit low.' Her voice was as flat as unleavened bread.

'Bet that made you feel better about it. Do you want another drink?'

'No, I'll get them.' She made a gesture with her hand, as if brushing away an upsetting subject. 'What're you on?'

'G and T, please.'

'Oh, very posh.'

Jeff still hadn't appeared by the time Rachel came back with our drinks. I was beginning to think we were safe.

'Helga put up a poster after you left,' I said, having remembered this during Rachel's absence at the bar. 'It was something about a meeting to discuss the membership structure. She had the nerve to tell me I shouldn't even be reading it because I'm not full-time. Can you imagine?'

'Pay no attention,' Rachel said dismissively. 'You know what she's like. Any pretty girl comes within a mile of Derek and she shows her claws.'

'I've hardly even talked to Derek!' I protested truthfully.

'All you need to do is say hello to him in passing. That's enough to get Helga wound up.' She sipped her drink. 'And I think I know what the meeting's about, despite that awful jargon she uses.'

'Oh yeah? Anything interesting?'

'You could say that. She wants to yuppify the gym. Double the membership fee and use the money to put in Jacuzzis and steam baths. Capitalism in action. It's a total betrayal of everything the gym's supposed to be about. She'll probably get a hefty rise in salary, but of course our wages won't go up. Management always does itself well and the workers come off worst. Welcome to Great Britain, plc.'

Though Rachel's elegant eyebrows were arched, her lips weren't moving; and even if she had been studying ventriloquism on the sly, the protest march vocabulary wasn't her style. Jeff's rather whiny voice wasn't hard to identify. I turned my head. He was standing next to me.

'She can't do that,' I said to him dismissively, thinking he was exaggerating. 'The council owns the gym—'

'She thinks she's got enough pull with a couple of people on the steering committee to put it through,' Jeff said. 'She'll tell them it's a rationalisation of services or some right-wing shit like that and they'll fall for it. They'll probably use it as a flagship to prove they're not the loony left-wingers they've been painted by the Tory-run press—'

I agree with most of what Jeff says, but I loathe the way he says it; he's one of those thin, white, unhealthy-looking, middle-class young men who dress in donkey jackets and put on fake working-class accents when selling copies of *Living Socialism* outside tube stations. Any minute now he would start waggling his finger and calling us comrades.

I looked at my watch and said: 'God, is that the time? I had no idea it was so late. I must get home.'

I stood up and started pulling on my leopardskin coat. Rachel took the cue.

'Yes, I should be off too,' she said, picking up her bag. 'Nice coat, Sam.'

I basked proudly. Jeff in the meantime was looking very disappointed.

'Oh, come on, stay for another drink,' he said plaintively. 'It's my round.' I noticed that though he addressed this to both of us, his eyes were fixed on Rachel.

'Sorry, Jeff, I'm really tired.' I scooped up a handful of pale green mini-matchboxes from the mantelpiece and stuffed them in my coat pocket. No one was looking. I filled the other one as well. Now I really did have Lollobrigida hips.

Rachel foolishly relented.

'Well, maybe just a quick one,' she said. 'I haven't got far to go, after all.'

Jeff was so happy to have company he didn't even notice my exit, which was sideways through the crowd. I was trying to avoid squashing the matches.

3

I didn't have any classes to teach the next day, so I spent it at home in the studio fiddling with my mobile, aka the Thing, of which I was inordinately proud. It was a sort of silver sphere, though very irregular, bound about with a thick steel cable which I had frayed and worked on till parts of it formed an intricate mesh through which the sphere glowed dimly. For a long time the wretched Thing had been the bane of my life, squatting on the floor of my studio like an ill-tempered toad with a bad case of the sulks; it knew it was unfinished and it wasn't happy about it. The trouble was I didn't know what it needed.

In the end it was a chance remark that gave me the idea of attaching a chain to it and hauling it over one of the beams in the ceiling. Immediately the Thing had cheered up; obviously it had known all along that it was really a mobile and had been waiting impatiently for me to realise this. Swaying majestically in the air like a newly discovered planet, it was extremely pleased with itself and me. The only trouble was that it was untethered, apart from the chain on which it hung, and so, though secure enough, it tended to sway dramatically in the breeze whenever I had a skylight open. I was trying to rig up a system to stabilise it, without much success so far.

Still, I was so happy to have finally cracked the problem of the Thing's true identity that I didn't really care if it swung like a pendulum. I had meant to ring Tom to see if he wanted to go out for a drink; but I became absorbed in sketching another mobile, Son of Thing, this one specifically designed to be suspended in mid-air rather than just happening that way by accident, and lost all track of time until my stomach informed me that it was ten-thirty at night and I was starving.

I rifled through the cupboards and produced a packet of Sainsbury's Potato Rösti with Red Peppers, which I heated up in a frying pan, wondering whether it counted as eating fresh vegetables if the pack had been vacuum-sealed. Somehow I doubted it. A while ago I had made a resolution to improve my fresh fruit and vegetable consumption, which in practice meant actually consuming some: so, rooting around in the vegetable bin, I found a solitary onion, which I fried and added to the rösti. If that wasn't a fresh vegetable I didn't know what was. Feeling virtuous and uplifted by this effort I turned on the TV and settled down in front of some American cops-and-robbers show with a heaped plate and a bottle of red wine. I only drank half the bottle. I'm on a health kick.

It was raining again. Tilting back my head, I surveyed the skylight above me, which was now so clogged with dirt and pigeon shit that a ray of daylight had to be pretty tough to fight its way into the studio. I would have to clean it sooner or later. Bob, the night watchman for the big adjoining warehouse of which mine had once been an extension, swore that his cat Fat Shirley kept the pigeons down, but we both knew that this was an old man's fantasy. London's pigeons had interbred with the rat population to create giant genetic mutations capable of seeing Shirl off with one scornful flap of their wings. And Bob didn't put down poison, not out of any animal rights scruples, but because Fat Shirley hadn't achieved her current, sensually rippling contours by turning down any free grub that came her way.

I sighed. Far from washing away the accumulated filth, the rain just seemed to pack it down harder into a solid layer of sludge and grime, dung and dirt and feathers – I would have to avoid thinking about this while eating. It was putting me off my food. One of the many problems my friend Janey and I shared was pigeon infestation; when she got back from holiday next week I would ring her and ask what she did about hers. Why had no one made a film about killer pigeons? Maybe Tom would know. He was the film buff. Or could I count *The Birds*?

I didn't think so. If those little fuckers had been pigeons, Tippi

Hedren would have been covered in their poo by the end of the film rather than just having her hair messed up.

*   *   *

Drums rolled, the Pogues struck up a jolly Irish jig and the unmistakable slurred tones of Shane McGowan, articulating as best he could through his four remaining teeth and the bottle that was tilted between them, started singing about someone called Jimmy who played the pipes. My back was to the mirrored wall and in front of me were nine women who, like me, had weights in their hands. Two were newcomers, one of them Naomi from the showers; they looked understandably surprised at the music issuing from the speakers. The others knew me already and were tapping along with their feet. I started rolling back my shoulders, one after the other, and watched as my movements were mirrored split seconds later by my group of acolytes.

Josie, as usual, was bang in front of me, wearing her habitual bright smile. Her leotard was pink and her tights were grey. Around her waist was one of those nasty narrow belts, grey, of course, to go with the tights; her lipstick was bright pink and her trainers were white with a pink flash. She smiled constantly, no matter what I said or did, tilting her head to one side to let her shiny bob swing out. These classes were really supposed to be inductions into how to use the gym, after which the novices graduated to working out on their own. Josie, however, had been attending them for a year now and showed no sign of wanting to leave. She scared the shit out of me. It was the big, artificial smile and the obsessively co-ordinated clothes. I was sure that some day she was going to flip and smash someone's head in with a free weight.

The tape switched to Van Morrison, who promptly started sha-la-la-ing. Van Morrison always raises my spirits: cheaper than Prozac and just as effective. By this time we were working on the triceps. No saggy lower arms for us, thank you. Naomi from the showers was in the second row. With her javelin-thrower's frame she looked more like a bodybuilder than any of the others, but she seemed disinclined to make any effort. Each time she lifted the weights she looked aggrieved, as if I were personally insulting her by conducting the workout.

After fifteen minutes I packed them off to go round the gym circuit, keeping an eye on my watch so I could tell them to switch machines every minute or so. I made sure I had Naomi in view. I didn't want her to do herself an injury and hold me responsible. A happy-go-lucky Cajun tune played in the background, jolly but not too fast. I didn't like working out with weights to fast dance music. It speeded you up and prevented you from sensing the right pace for each different exercise, so that you worked the muscles less efficiently. Besides, rushing an exercise could cause sprains or worse.

I gave up worrying about Naomi; she was too sluggish to do anything forcefully enough to hurt herself and was currently moving her legs backward and forward about two inches each way on the leg-press machine, looking irritated that the pedals wouldn't move any further. You have to push for that to happen.

I checked my watch and called another change. Josie jumped up gaily and bounded gracefully over to the next machine, her hair belling out. She flashed a smile at me as if to say how much fun she was having. I shuddered. God knows what she really made of my music and my frayed assortment of cut-off T-Shirts over cut-off shorts over holey leggings, all that particular colour of charcoal grey to which black fades when you keep washing it for years.

It was time for the warm-down. Laying out mats for them and me, I clapped my hands in summons. They left the circuit reluctantly, which was good; all, that is, apart from Naomi, who couldn't wait to plop her behind down on the mat and stare at me sulkily instead of tilting her head to the left and holding it there for a count of five. We stretched ourselves out to Aaron Neville's hauntingly beautiful voice singing 'Tell It Like It Is' and then the hour was up. I clapped them and they clapped me back. Hoping to freak Naomi out, I gave her a Josie-bright I-Am-An-Axe-Murderess smile, but she was too stupid to understand the horror that lay behind it.

'See you on Thursday, Sam!' Josie piped as she left. *Don't* use my name, I wanted to respond, it *frightens* me. Naomi thunked out of the gym, casting me a hostile glance for having made her suffer. Even her thighs seemed to be wobbling in dull resentment. I put on another of my compilation tapes and started my own workout. It always frustrates me to see other people exercise when I'm supervising them and can't do it myself.

For an hour and a half I was lost to the world. People came in and out of the gym, but I hardly noticed them. I have my own routine worked out by now – I don't use many machines, mostly free weights whenever possible because they demand a balance and concentration that machines don't. If you get careless or slack on a machine it will protect you to some extent. A weighted bar across your shoulders won't. And it's a damn sight better for your posture.

I don't do any weights work on my lower body; if I did I'd have thighs like a shot-putter by now. I put on muscle there very easily. But I could do tricep curls and bicep exercises all day and hardly see a bulge in my upper arms, more's the pity. I worked on my stomach, which is ever ready to burgeon if not supervised, and finished off with a long series of stretches. When I left the gym I felt pleasantly heavy, as if I had reached all the saggy parts of my body and zapped them into shape.

Showered, perfumed and dressed, I went to look for Rachel. I found her in the downstairs office, not yet changed into gym clothes, chatting to Lesley. It was not a conversation of any great moment; Lesley wouldn't have been up to it. Blondes didn't come any dumber than Lesley, unless they were actually mute.

'Anyone want to come out for a cup of tea?' I said.

Rachel looked at the clock on the wall.

'OK,' she said, 'I've got an hour. Coming, Lesley?'

The gym was situated in a little back alley off Camden High Street, nearer to Chalk Farm tube station than to Camden proper. Thus, if you wanted to enjoy all the amenities Camden offers, such as the eponymous market, a wide selection of craft shops and hippy-run vegetarian restaurants, and a selection of picturesque and importunate drunks begging outside the cashpoints, you could indulge yourself merely by strolling up the road. If, on the other hand, you weren't in the mood for crowds, litter, and foreign tourists gaping at people in tartan bondage trousers with seventeen holes pierced in their nose, you could visit the gym via Chalk Farm tube and leave again in relative peace, which is to say without having pieces of newspaper and plastic drinks cartons blown into your face by the air whooshing hotly out of the fetid underground tunnels of Camden Town tube station.

'That guy's waving at you,' Rachel said to me as we walked down the high street. I swivelled my head to catch Leggo's dreadlocks swinging back from his face as he turned to wave at me before he bicycled on towards Camden. Like I said, it's a small place.

'He's cute,' Lesley said with enthusiasm. 'Who is he?'

'He's a singer,' I said. 'Indie rock kind of thing.'

She pulled a face. 'I hate that kind of music, it's so loud! He's in good shape, though. And I usually go for black guys, actually. It must be the contrast, because I'm so fair.'

Rachel's eyes and mine met eloquently for a moment. Fortunately for Lesley, we were just approaching the railway bridge and had reached our current favourite little café, a dilapidated but cosy hole-in-the-wall that served a myriad different herbal teas. I was working my way through the selection and had got as far as Rosehip and Hibiscus, which I duly chose. It turned out quite nice, despite being pink.

From Monday through to Thursday, Camden Market and its environs weren't unpleasantly crowded – only at the weekend was it unbearable. There were plenty of tables free in the café, and the girl leaning behind the counter had the unmistakably bored look of a foreign student who would tell the boss to find someone else to do his shitty job just as soon as she had learnt the adequate vocabulary at her seedy language school off Oxford Street. The café was very rustic in a cosy, seventies kind of way: faded kelims on the walls, cumbersome wooden chairs and tables with pleasantly battered surfaces. We chose a corner table by the window and settled down, as is traditional for off-duty workers, to bitching pleasantly about our place of employment.

Lesley had only just started at the gym. She was young and enthusiastic – well, technically she was only a few years younger that I was, but next to her I felt old and jaded – with short fair hair, big blue eyes and a body like Ballerina Barbie's, whose long Indiarubber limbs looked as if she could twist them into any conceivable position while still smiling cheerfully. Despite these advantages, she had a naïvely puppy-like, tongue-lolling-out disposition which, combined with the emptiness of her head – to say she had goose down for brains would be an insult to duvets – allowed me to patronise her tolerantly rather than hating her for being taller, thinner and blonder than I was.

She had obviously been waiting for a chance to let off steam. Ignoring her herbal tea, she exclaimed as soon as we sat down: 'She's so possessive about everything, that's what I can't stand!' Neither of us needed to be told that she was talking about Linda. 'You'd think she owned the gym herself! And it's not just the gym she thinks she owns—' She broke off, blushing slightly.

'But Derek too,' Rachel finished drily. We had both noticed Derek and Lesley noticing each other.

'Well!' Lesley shrugged, blue eyes wide and innocent. 'If she can't keep him, she should let him go, shouldn't she?'

'She isn't being fair, right? She should let the other girls play with her nice toy sometimes? Derek isn't an Action Man doll who's been sitting at the back of Linda's toy cupboard collecting dust, Lesley,' I pointed out.

Lesley pouted, her usual response if she didn't quite understand what was being said to her.

'And she's such a bitch!' she continued unheedingly. 'Did you hear what she said to Jeff the other day? She told him that he should sue the people who make those bodybuilding drinks because he was still as skinny as ever and as far as she was concerned he might as well have cut out the middle bit and thrown the money straight in the toilet!'

'I didn't know Jeff was still drinking that crap,' I said.

'They cost a fortune, that's true enough,' Rachel said meditatively. 'Trust Linda to hit his weak spot.'

'Why does she hate him so much?' Lesley said, her blue eyes wide as saucers. Her fair hair was fluffed out round her head and she hadn't taken off her bright, shiny pink padded ski jacket. Après-Ski Barbie. Plastic glass of Glüwein is not included in purchase.

Rachel shrugged. 'Jeff wouldn't get along with anyone in authority,' she explained, 'he's a Living Socialist.' Before Lesley could go into spasm she added quickly: 'And it doesn't help that Hel . . . Linda's such a control freak. He keeps challenging her, even when what she's doing is quite sensible, and it drives her mad.'

I was grateful to Rachel for not calling Linda 'Helga' in front of Lesley. One of the side effects of the latter's head being empty was that information went into her ears and straight out of her mouth again without passing through any thought processes along the way.

'But she's rude to everyone!' Lesley said. 'She's even rude to Lou!'

'That's because Lou is just as competent as she is,' I said. 'Linda always has to be better than anyone else. The only person she's halfway human to is—'

'Derek,' Lesley finished. I could practically see the stars shining in her eyes as she said his name.

'Look, Lesley,' I said firmly, bringing my large reserves of maturity and worldly wisdom to bear on the situation. 'I'd steer clear of Derek if I were you – at least till you've been here longer than a few months and your job's more secure. Play it safe. Make a point of showing Linda you're not interested in him. Talk to her about your boyfriend.'

'But I don't have a boyfriend.'

'Why let a mere detail like the truth impede you?'

She stared at me blankly. When they were handing out brains, Lesley was probably too busy running about fetching sticks in her mouth to apply.

'Look, Lesley, it's your life and your job, OK?' Rachel said. 'But Sam's right. Steer clear of Derek. It's not worth the aggro.'

'But it's not fair!' Lesley protested. 'What's it got to do with my job if Derek chats me up?'

'Satisfy my curiosity on one small point, Lesley,' I said. 'Are you by any chance the spoilt only child of doting parents who indulged your every whim?'

'Mum and Dad have always been brilliant to me,' Lesley said enthusiastically. 'I've said I'll pay them back the flat deposit when I start to make some money teaching.'

'I thought so.'

'What did you mean about Action Man before?' Her forehead creased up with the effort of remembering something that had puzzled her.

I smiled at her gently, wondering if I should lean over and pat her hand. 'Don't worry your pretty head about it.'

'But—'

'Sam was just saying that there are people and feelings involved,' Rachel explained. 'It's not just a game. I mean, you can say that if Linda can't keep him she should let him go, but things don't usually work like that in relationships.'

Lesley pouted stubbornly. 'I don't see why not.'

I was tempted to lean over and insert my teaspoon up her nose; at least she'd have something rattling round inside her head. Make a nice change for her.

4

As Linda had already made clear to me, I had not been invited to the meeting that evening, which of course was precisely why I attended. Usually the only way to drag me to a meeting would be to tell me that free drugs would be provided afterwards. Rachel and I had fortified ourselves with a quick drink first and when we entered the crèche, the only room apart from the gym itself large enough to accommodate all of us, there were already quite a few people in the room, shifting around nervously in their chairs like children under Linda's basilisk gaze. Exercise instructors aren't much good at sitting still at meetings.

Linda had strategically positioned a table at the far end of the room and was seated behind it, pad of paper and glass of water neatly aligned in front of her. All she needed was a gavel. She wore a black catsuit; her hair was in a tight ponytail and her mouth in an equally tight line. Watching me sit down, she said, in a typical display of generosity and tolerance: 'Sam, you do understand that you don't have voting or speaking rights at this meeting?'

'Hey, Linda, relax!' Derek waved his hand at me. 'Sam's been here for years, right, Sam?' He was reclining in the window embrasure, rolling a joint. In his chinos and a loose white sweater, he looked like a Gap advertisement.

'As the chair of this meeting I just want to ensure that everyone is aware of their position from the start,' Linda said, though with a slight tenderness in her voice as she looked at Derek.

'Her position'll be hanging from the gantry with a trapeze twisted round her neck if she doesn't watch out,' I murmured to

Rachel, who snorted with laughter. For a moment it was like being at school: bad girls sitting in the back row and dissing the teacher.

The meeting had been called for eight and Linda made sure it started bang on time. Anyone who straggled in after that was met with a hard stare and a pointed glance at the clock on the wall. Plastic toys in primary colours were propped against the yellow-painted walls, lending a note of frivolity to the proceedings. A frieze of crayoned drawings whose subjects appeared chiefly to be My House, My Mum and Dad (various permutations of that one – this was Camden, after all) and the already-dated My Ninja Turtle/Tasmanian Dust Devil/Little Pony ran round the walls in a display of cheerfulness which was soon dulled by clouds of cigarette smoke and rising tempers.

To give Linda her due, she wasn't a coward. She didn't try to fudge the proposal she was putting to the meeting, except insofar as she suggested that everyone would be better off in every conceivable way if it were passed, without deigning to explain exactly how these advantages would manifest themselves. The bare bones were much as Jeff had sketched them. While still ultimately under council control, the gym was to 'float free', as she put it, becoming 'profit-oriented', raising the membership fee and providing more services with the increased income.

'By services you mean Jacuzzis and steam baths, don't you?' Jeff broke in, his voice already cracking with emotion: Robespierre making his last speech in front of the guillotine. 'Luxuries for the well-off while ordinary people can't afford the prices!'

'Actually, I was thinking more of a new coat of paint for the gym and fixing the showers,' Linda snapped back. Fifteen-love to her.

'Why can't we fix the showers now?' Lesley asked, smiling winsomely in Derek's direction. Everyone ignored her apart from Derek, who smiled back.

Lou was sitting a few chairs down from me. You couldn't miss her; she was wearing a turquoise dress, matching turban, and about seventeen gold chains draped over her impressive bosom. 'I don't like the sound of this one bit,' she said firmly. 'Don't try tellin' me you're still goin' to keep this crèche on as a free service, for one thing. It ain't in that plan you got there, is it?'

'We would be making a charge for crèche facilities, yes,' Linda admitted, looking shifty. 'But let's put this in perspective—'

Most of the women in the room erupted. The voice that penetrated the uproar belonged to Fliss, who cultivated her mannish image to the extent of speaking in tones even deeper than Lou's rich contralto. Fliss looked short and stumpy when dressed, which was partly because of the clothes she wore. She dressed in second-hand men's suits or butch checked shirts with jeans; they did her no favours, making her seem squarer and bulkier than she was. To see her working out in the gym in singlet and shorts, however, was an education. Then she was a powerhouse to whom everyone deferred respectfully. She had forgotten more about bodybuilding than I had ever learnt. Her hair was cut extremely short in a barber's crop and her jaw was as pugnacious as a bulldog's. She protested now in her usual clipped, telegrammatic style, which always made me think of an officer giving orders to the troops: 'Can't charge for the crèche. Not if you're raising the membership fee. Completely unfair.'

'We are discussing raising prices in line with market rates,' Linda said, rattled, 'not actually making ourselves competitive with other privately run gyms—'

'But this is just the slippery slope!' Jeff broke in.

Don't say the thin end of the wedge, I prayed.

'It's the first step towards privatisation, isn't it? That's what you'd like to see happen. And your friends in their comfy seats on the council would use this place as a flagship to demonstrate their moderate credentials while poor people and single mothers in the borough can't afford the entrance fee! It's the thin end of the wedge!'

I cringed. Jeff was even waving his fist in the air in a *Citoyens, à la lanterne!* sort of way. But he had made his point: several heads were nodding. Linda was glaring at him as if she'd be only too willing to guillotine him with a rusty blade, spike his head on a pole and stick it outside the gym as a warning against committing *lèse-majesté*. Raising her voice over the babble, she said in reply: 'I don't think anyone who has worked here for a while can deny that the place needs reorganising. And yes, we do need to review the membership fee. It's hardly gone up in years and at the moment it's ludicrously low for all we provide.'

This was true, too. Linda looked around the room to make sure this had sunk in. Beside me, Rachel said reasonably: 'But are the alternatives really so all-or-nothing? Why can't we put up the membership fee, in line with inflation, say, and use the money to fix the showers and so on without radically changing the policy of the gym? I agree that certain things do need looking at, but isn't this proposal exaggerated?'

I turned my head to look at her. She seemed as calm and collected as always; even when Rachel was laughing she was somehow in control of herself. It was characteristic that she should be the only person here able to step back and look at the problem with perspective.

'Yeah, it's like throwing the baby out with the bathwater, innit?' said someone I didn't know; he should get together with Jeff, form an advertising company and peddle clichés for a living. Even more heads were nodding now.

'Actually, I think Linda's proposal sounds pretty interesting,' piped up Simon Wise. He was the sort of person who at school had sat in the front row, opposite the teacher, looked keen and nodded his head whenever she spoke. I could tell because this was exactly what he was doing now with Linda. Little squit. Bet he had a rough time of it in the playground and that was why he had taken up weight-lifting. 'I think we should think about it seriously,' he added.

'If you're thinking your salary will go up when the gym "floats free", Simon, you'd better get assurances beforehand in writing or you'll find yourself marooned,' I said. There was laughter and, from Linda, a one-more-remark-of-that-sort-and-I-throw-you-out-young-lady glare.

'It's not just about money,' chipped in someone else. 'I like the idea of making the gym pay for itself a bit more. We've got so slack here just scraping along and relying on the council to bail us out. It would be good for us to be more self-sufficient.'

The murmurs of agreement were broken by Lou's rich voice demanding: 'But how's everyone – not just *some* people – goin' to be able to afford to come to the gym if we do that? If we're more self-sufficient we got to price some people out of here. To my mind that's not what a council gym's about.'

'I agree with Lou,' Brian's voice boomed out from the back of the room. Silence fell. Brian was the strong silent type who never usually opened his mouth; he worked nights as a bouncer for warehouse parties, standing by the door, a black satin bomber jacket straining over his massive shoulders. Would-be ravers held up their hands voluntarily and muttered: 'No problem, man, let's keep things cool, yeah?' while he was frisking them. Brian never replied, apart from grunting ambiguously, which of course freaked them out still further, as they weren't to know that he hardly ever said anything apart from an ambiguous grunt. I had once made him a cup of tea and been driven to near distraction as I tried to work out from his responses whether he took milk and sugar.

So, coming from him, this brief statement had the weight of an oracular pronouncement. It was as if the Sphinx had unexpectedly volunteered the solution to her riddle in a deep bass rumble. Everyone turned their heads to stare at him. He was sitting back in his chair with his arms folded across his colossal chest in the classic bouncer's pose. It seemed that he had said all he was going to say.

Jeff, deciding to catch the pendulum while it was swinging in his direction, said eagerly: 'Right! Let's take a vote and throw out this neo-capitalist proposal!' I half expected him to add:'Next stop the Bastille!' but he restrained himself nobly.

Fliss, being a radical feminist and thus well accustomed to the strategy of formal meetings, said gruffly: 'I propose we take two votes. One on the original proposal. One on Rachel's suggestion – explore other ways of sourcing income. Like a small increase in the membership subscription.'

She looked round the room for approval and found universal agreement for this sensible suggestion. Her jean-clad legs were planted well apart and she had propped one hand on her thigh, elbow thrust out. I sometimes suspected her of copying attitudes from men's magazines. Apart from Linda, the only dissenter was Jeff, who had been hoping for a complete dismissal of the proposal and looked distinctly disappointed. Fliss counted the raised hands.

Linda's proposal gathered a few votes but the resounding majority went for Rachel's suggestion. This surprised no one. Linda gathered up her papers, her jaw set in anger.

'I will, of course, carry out the mandate of the meeting,' she said furiously. 'But I want to point out that certain councillors who were very interested by the original proposal will be extremely disappointed by this. I wouldn't be surprised if they didn't cut our budget. Which would mean corresponding job cuts. I hope some of you bleeding-hearts have taken that into consideration.'

There was a stir of protest at the bleeding-hearts crack, but Linda paid this no attention. She looked as if she were mentally drawing up a list of people who could expect their UB40s any day now. Her gaze passed from one offender to another. I was disappointed; I didn't seem to have been counted on the roll of iniquity. I must try harder next time. Then she looked over in Derek's direction. No one had expected him to speak during the course of the meeting; this kind of sedentary event wasn't his style at all and I doubted if he'd have shown his face if Linda hadn't insisted.

But if that was the case she must have regretted it now. In the rush of conversation after the result of the vote, Lesley had left her seat. Her yellow-Lycra-clad bottom was propped at a suggestive angle against the windowsill occupied by Derek, and she was smiling up at him, stretching out her hand for the joint. Derek had leant forward to pass it over and, in a pretence of steadying himself, his hand was lingering appreciatively on the tightly outlined curve of her buttocks.

His timing was terrible. We all saw it. Linda withered Lesley with a stare that would have torched a field of corn and stalked out of the room. Derek removed the offending hand and followed hastily. In the dead silence that immediately succeeded Derek and Lesley's impromptu tableau, we heard the door to Linda's office slam and then bounce back on its hinges. Linda was shouting something; I couldn't hear the words but the general tenor was unmistakable. A moment later the office door flew open again, bumping against the outer wall, and Linda yelled: 'Well, go then, if you're going! And don't bother to come back!'

'I bloody won't,' Derek said between clenched teeth, 'till

you've calmed down. All right?' We could hear him striding across the reception area. The main doors of the gym slammed behind him. Linda had better make a note to replace several sets of hinges in the next budget.

I looked back at Lesley. She was still leaning against the windowsill, the joint which had served as an excuse for her to approach Derek smouldering forgotten between her fingers. Her face was as smooth and smug as a cat that's just eaten the cream.

A cat that hasn't yet seen the Doberman coming up on its blind side, slavering from its jaws in anticipation.

5

A couple of days later I had finished my sketch for Son of Thing, starting it up as best I could – I've never been much good at line drawing. Plucking up my courage, I called Lucy, the TV researcher, to see if she was still interested in giving me and my sculptures a massive two minutes' exposure on her programme. It wasn't a success. Either she was having a bad day struggling with the inexperienced managers of up-and-coming bands who were too busy polishing up their image to write any songs, or she would simply have preferred not to have heard from me.

'Oh, look, Sam, I've been really busy,' she said curtly. 'I still am, actually.'

'You don't have time at the moment to come round—'

'No, sorry.' She sounded about as apologetic as Margaret Thatcher discussing the sinking of the *Belgrano*. 'And we've got that slot booked up for a while to come now. But keep in touch, yeah? See you round.'

She practically hung up on me. Had I stepped on her toes in some way that evening at the club? Or maybe she was pissed off with me because Tom had ranted on at her about Jim Morrison.

This reminded me that I hadn't seen Tom since that night. On impulse, I rang his number. He answered the phone almost at once; this probably meant that he was writing, it wasn't going well and he craved distraction. He was currently flat-sitting for a friend of a friend, an analyst who had gone abroad for six months, having been only too eager to leave his room at the squalid co-op house where he had previously been living – if you could call it that – for the opportunity to reside in luxury in a Belsize Park basement.

'It's me,' I said.

'Sammy! How's it going?' He sounded quite cheerful. Maybe the poem was working out after all.

'OK. Been working on a sketch for a new mobile.'

'Thing II?'

'Son of Thing, actually.'

'Did that TV girl come through?'

'Doesn't look like it. I've just rung her and she virtually told me to go and bury myself in a hole for fifty years and let my nails grow long.'

'It's a scummy little excuse for a programme anyway,' Tom said loyally. 'Anything else on the horizon, or are you sunk in despair?'

'No, something else came up last week. I forgot to tell you at the club. You know that art gallery I used to work for? Well, someone there gave my name to this woman who works as an art consultant for corporate clients.'

'You what?' Tom sounded baffled.

'Oh, you know, she wears Chanel suits and power earrings and convinces banks that if they put a giant copper statue of a nude woman with disproportionately large tits in their entrance hall people will take them seriously as a market leader.'

'Nifty,' said Tom approvingly. 'They get to show their compassionate art-loving side and have a pair of big bosoms on public display.'

'And they write it all off against taxes anyway.'

'Sounds like a good wheeze! Are you going to put a pair of tits on Son of Thing? Or a willy? Brings a whole new meaning to the idea of a hung sculpture.'

'Don't be silly, Tom. Banks are run by men. They certainly wouldn't buy a sculpture with an outsized thingy dangling from it.'

'You could make it small.'

'What would be the point of that?' I said, unanswerably. 'Anyway, hung sculptures seem to be popular at the moment. As soon as the word "mobile" was mentioned in conversation her interest level rose sharply. So she's supposed to be coming round to see the Thing whenever she can shoehorn a gap into her busy art-consulting schedule.'

'You'd better clear up there a bit.'

'I would not dream of depriving her of a cheap Bohemian thrill,' I said austerely. 'Are you doing anything later on, or do you want to come out for a Chinese?'

*   *   *

Down the road from Tom's palatial basement flat, we had recently discovered a *soi disant* Dumpling and Noodle Bar which served a dizzying array of the above-named foods at competitive prices. This time we ordered Pan-Fried Vegetable Dumplings to start and then Tom had his usual bowl of Chicken and Sweetcorn Noodles; comfort food at its best, swimming in broth. It was my theory that this was the Chinese equivalent of a Jewish mother's chicken soup – it even had the dumplings. I struck out for something new and had Hot and Sour Seafood Noodles. Both our main courses came in bowls big enough to contain the daily nutritional requirements of a German shepherd and were completely delicious. We slurped away happily.

'How's life at the gym?' Tom said, finishing his Ginseng Beer – whose label announced that, among other fringe benefits, it aided potency – with one mighty swig. He signalled the waitress to bring another one, perhaps feeling that the promised results needed constant topping up to prove effective.

'It's a nightmare.' I ordered another beer myself. 'Ever since that meeting – I told you about that, didn't I? – we've been as jumpy as frogs in the mating season.'

'Have the bimbo and Mr Throbbing Gristle shagged yet?' Tom enquired elegantly. Despite his infelicitous turn of phrase, Tom is a world-class gossip – an advantage unusual in a heterosexual man – and can be relied on to remember the last instalment of your narrative.

'I don't think so. Lesley's a verbal diarrhoetic in matters sexual – when it finally happens she'll spill it all out to us five minutes later. As it were. My God, what's this?'

I had found something in my noodles that looked like a Made-in-Hong-Kong vibrator attachment that promised more ridges for extra sensation. It was white and rubbery. I held it up.

'Looks like a vibrator attachment,' Tom commented. Pygmy minds think alike. 'See if it's got that little Made in Hong Kong sticker on the back.'

'You're disgusting.' I put it in my mouth. It tasted rather like squid.

'What about the Dragon Lady? She can't be very happy about the bimbo and Mr Gristle.'

Tom disapproved of Linda on the grounds that she was thin, blonde and attractive but lacked the necessary frail vulnerability which he looked for in a woman of that type. He's more Old Man than New Man.

'She's spitting blood from her fangs, what do you expect? Derek's tried to make up a couple of times but she's not having any. Yesterday she tore him to pieces in front of everyone who happened to be in the hall at the time she decided to throw a wobbly. And rumour has it that she's trying to convince a couple of councillors to force through her original proposal, even though it was voted out.'

'You mean the one to privatise the gym, pay herself a hefty salary and install a Jacuzzi in her office, staffed by an oiled team of Nubian slaves in loincloths?'

'Roughly, yes.'

'Can she do that?'

'God knows. But you can imagine that even if she can't, the rumour isn't helping to relax everyone at the moment. She made some threats to sack people that I don't think she can back up, but the mere idea's enough to make people tense.'

Tom had finished his noodles. He shot a glance round the restaurant to see if anyone was looking. They were. Deciding the hell with it, he tipped the bowl up to his mouth, drank down the remaining broth, and sat back looking replete. He had added a couple of extra stains to his once-white Aran sweater in the process, but the waitress didn't seem disgusted; on the contrary, when she came over to clear the table she directed a beaming smile at him.

'She's pretty, Tom,' I observed helpfully. 'And she thinks you've got a healthy appetite. Order a toffee banana, that'll really get you in good with her.'

'Wrong hair colour,' Tom said regretfully.

'You're so narrow-minded. Oh, that reminds me: how does a blonde spell her hair colour?'

'Dunno.'

'B – L – O – oh gee, I don't know!'

Tom burst out laughing. That's why I like him. He's easy to please.

*   *   *

The man with the grey suit and briefcase stood out in the gym like a smackhead at a speed freaks' convention. He had just come through the double doors and paused there, watching the class, his face as expressionless as Helena Bonham Carter trying to convey some complex emotion. Naturally I assumed he was from the council. And by that time it was too late, even if I had known who he really was. He'd already seen what he came to see.

I was spotting for Lesley's lunchtime aerobics class. There were about fifty people that day and the sheer numbers made it impossible for Lesley to check that all of them were doing the exercises safely. My task was to wander round and keep an eye out, making sure no one was ripping their ligaments. I didn't enjoy the job. No one likes being corrected in front of others, and the few people who did need a little help gave me hostile stares for ever after, no matter how nice I tried to be.

Lunchtimes were always popular, and Lesley's style of teaching was infectious; she bounced around with lots of whoops and cheers, her clothes the colour of sunshine and springtime, making everything look magically easy. In the short time she'd been here, she had already built up a large following. Probably this was why she felt confident enough to challenge Linda for Derek; she knew how good a teacher she was. Linda wouldn't want to sack her, and even if she did, Lesley should be able to walk into another job without difficulty.

The man in the suit put down his briefcase, opened it and took out a file. He placed this on top of the case, flipped it open, and started to make notes, which I assumed were on the condition of the gym. Suddenly all the peeling paint and cracks in the walls magnified themselves before my eyes. I resisted the impulse to obscure the worst crack by standing nonchalantly in front of it.

Few others had noticed him besides me, despite his incongruous appearance; they all had their eyes fixed on Lesley's platform, where she was gyrating away. And Lesley herself was happily oblivious to anything but the rows of flushed faces looking up at her and the encouraging cries she was giving them.

She clapped her hands now.

'Whoah there! Everyone get a mat!' she shouted. A stampede ensued which reminded me of my schooldays, when there were never enough mats to go round and if you weren't quick you had to share with someone or sit on the cold wooden floor. One thing the Chalk Farm Gym did possess was enough mats, even if some of them were rather ratty at the edges. The man from the council was scribbling again. Maybe fraying mats were a health hazard. Lesley took the class through twenty minutes of floor exercises, tightened their stomachs, tautened their buttocks, stretched them out again and sent them off happy, her enthusiasm never flagging. I had to give her credit; her style didn't suit me – it was too cheerful for my taste – but she was damn good.

A few people crowded round her at the end of the class to thank her or ask advice. The man with the briefcase picked it up, tucking the file under his arm, and stood waiting to speak to her. It was then that I felt the first pricklings of apprehension, though I didn't know why; it was possible, after all, that if he was doing a survey of the gym he might want to talk to an instructor or two. Why not? But there was something too determined about his manner, as if he were targeted on Lesley in particular . . .

The door of the gym opened and Lou's cheerfully turbaned head poked through. She looked distinctly worried. Catching my eye, she waved at me. I went over to her. She was staring at Lesley and the man in the suit, who had his file open, and was asking her something. Everyone else was leaving, hurrying back to their jobs or small children. We were in the way. Lou moved back into the reception area and I followed her out of the doorway.

'What is it, Lou?'

'He says he's from Music Performance Rights. Does that mean anythin' to you? He didn't make a good impression on me.'

'Shit,' I said. 'There but for the grace of God go all of us.'

'What do you mean?' Lou said impatiently.

I sighed. 'If you're taking a class to music, legally you're supposed to pay a royalty to them, the Music Performance Whatsits. Or you order a tape from a company which produces them and pre-pays the royalties.'

'I never heard of that.' I could see this was not what Lou had been expecting; she looked baffled. 'You mean every time you play a tape you send them a fee?'

'No, of course not. Nobody bothers. And nobody buys the compilation tapes because they're usually bog standard and very expensive, about thirty pounds each. Most people make their own. Derek's got his own mixing desk; he takes it really seriously.'

'What happens if they catch you out?'

As if our heads were being pulled around, we both turned to stare at the doors of the gym behind which this precise circumstance was happening to Lesley.

'If you don't have the proper form to show you've paid up,' I said reluctantly, 'they can fine you.'

'How much?'

I grimaced. 'Lots. I've heard as much as a grand. But the chance of being caught is so slight that everyone just runs the risk and crosses their fingers. I've never heard of anyone being nobbled before. Poor Lesley, what bad luck. She's only just started here.'

It hadn't dawned on me yet. Lou was shaking her head.

'Luck's got nothin' to do with this, Sam. More like messin' round with Linda's boyfriend.'

I stared at her.

'Man came right in here and asked for Miss Lesley Porter. Wasn't no random check. Someone gave them her name. And you tell me who else that'd have been besides Madam in there?'

Lou jerked her thumb at Linda's office door. We had been speaking in quiet voices; Linda couldn't have heard anything, but we both jumped like guilty schoolgirls when it opened. Fliss came out, looking preoccupied. We let out the breath we'd been holding.

'What's with you two?' she said. 'Plotting insurrection?' Shoving her hands in her trouser pockets, she rocked back on her heels. She was wearing a grey flannel suit over a white T-shirt. The trousers were held up with braces that looked as if they'd come from the same second-hand shop where she'd bought the suit – old-fashioned, button-on braces. Somehow Fliss got away with this sort of thing without looking too self-conscious; I had even seen her lighting a match on the zip of her fly. I'd met her boyfriend Andy a couple of times. He went with her look; he was a pretty little slip of a thing with fair curls and a soft voice.

Lou sighed. 'We're so jumpy nowadays,' she said, going back into the reception cubicle. 'These are *not* what I call good workin' conditions.'

Fliss looked at me with her eyebrows raised.

'Lesley's in there with a man from Music Performance Rights,' I said. 'Lou says he asked for her by name.'

Fliss's eyebrows went higher. 'Linda?' she said at once. 'Can't say I'm surprised. Shit's about to hit the fan, then.'

At that moment the gym door swung open and the shit himself appeared. We knew he was just doing his job but somehow it didn't seem much of an excuse; we stared at him hard enough to burn holes in his jacket as he crossed reception, knocked on the office door and went in. I caught a faint smell of singed viscose as the door closed behind him.

'Making his report,' said Fliss.

'Has it ever happened to you?'

She shook her head.

'How much do they fine you?'

She shrugged. 'Depends on how they feel.'

Lesley came through from the gym, carrying her tape box; her eyes were rather red, but her mouth was set in a hard line. She walked straight past us and down the stairs to the basement, her hips in their lime-green leggings wiggling much less than usual.

'Going to find Derek and spill her heart out,' Fliss said unsympathetically. 'Linda might find she's bitten off more than she can chew.'

'Well, she's out of luck if that's who she's after,' Lou said from her cubicle. 'Derek left half an hour ago.'

*   *   *

I found Lesley in the women's changing room, which was quiet now after the lunchtime rush. She was curled up on a bench and had obviously been crying. The yellow of her leotard and the green of her leggings, so striking when she was in good spirits, now drained her face. Even her eyes looked a paler blue than usual in their red, puffy sockets.

I got her an ersatz tea from the ersatz drink machine, pressing the 'Extra Sweetener' button twice. For people in emotional distress I prescribe tea during daylight hours and vodka the rest of the time. It seemed to help. She was silent for a while, drinking her tea, and I was wondering whether I should leave her in peace when she put down the cup and said: 'It was Linda, wasn't it? That guy had my name, everything. He even knew when I started at the gym.'

'We don't know for sure.'

'It was her.' She drank some more tea. 'That bitch!'

'Do you know what the fine's going to be?'

She shook her head. 'He said he was going to go through the books and check what I'd earned here first.'

'Well, that can't be much yet,' I said encouragingly. 'You should get off lightly.'

Lesley's thoughts were running along quite different lines.

'Jealous bitch!' she said. 'It's pathetic if you ask me. Just because she's getting on a bit—'

'She's *thirty-two*, Lesley,' I said, meaning to bring her down to earth. Instead she pouted and said: 'Exactly!' Her expression resembled one of those dolls with scrunched-up plastic faces who cry on demand when you bend their arms behind their backs. More of her comments on people's ages and I was going to try this manoeuvre on her myself.

'She does have a right to be jealous,' I pointed out. 'You've been making a massive play for Derek.'

'So what? He's not her property! Even Rachel told me to go for it. I don't know why you're being so moral all of a sudden.'

'Rachel told you *what*?'

Lesley shrugged. 'Like I said before, if Linda can't hang on to him she should let him go.' Her eyes narrowed. 'Wait till I tell him what's happened!'

She stood up and started stripping off her clothes.

'Wait till I tell him!' she repeated to herself. I stood up too and left the changing room. Lesley obviously didn't need any consolation I could provide. Behind me I heard the shower being turned on. I wondered if Fliss was right. Had Linda bitten off more than she could chew?

6

There was a message on the machine from the art consultant when I got home. Her name was Felice Borsch – or Borsh, or Bortshe – she had a slight American accent and she wanted to come and see me on Friday at 1 p.m. Presumably she added the p.m. in case I thought she was an insomniac who would be popping round at one in the morning for a chat about the current art market. I looked around the studio dubiously. Maybe Tom had had a point about the clearing up.

My studio is a thirty-foot-high warehouse extension in a non-residential zone in a rather dirty part of North London. It came cheap. Still, I didn't have enough money left over from the purchase to start installing fitted kitchens or toilets with heated seat covers and matching bidets. In one corner of the ground floor is my kitchen area, comprising (a) gas stove and (b) fridge, divided off from the rest of the room by a profoundly ugly Formica-topped table. A wooden ladder leads up to a sleeping platform built halfway up the wall, and beneath the platform – supposedly because the ceiling's lower and I lose less heat, though it never feels that way to me – are the living room (ancient sofa and TV) and bathroom.

The rest of the studio is my work area. Felice Bortshe wouldn't have to be a Rhodes scholar to work that one out from the pieces of scrap metal, wire, tubing, assorted welding tools and plastic crates full of more of the above which were scattered about the floor, combining to give the room that chic junkyard emphasis which is all the rage this year.

I wouldn't even know where to start tidying up. Felice must

be used to this kind of thing, surely. They say that artists are all yuppies these days, but those are just the ones featured in *Vogue*; I've never met one whose studio wasn't a squalid pit – apart from the anal retentives, and their art tends to be a little wrapped up in itself. Perhaps I should get in a good bottle of wine so I could offer her a drink. No, if she were American she would think I was an alcoholic for drinking in the afternoon.

What should I wear? This, of course, was the crucial question. I climbed the ladder to my boudoir. At the foot of my futon with its piles of duvets and blankets was a big painted screen done by a friend from art school in the style of Keith Haring. The colours were rather too bright, especially in the mornings, but they gave me a burst of energy with which to start the day. Something had to. Behind the screen were a big industrial free-standing clothes rail and several cardboard boxes containing underwear and my extensive collection of boots.

I rifled thoughtfully through the hangers on the rail, pondering my dilemma, which ran as follows: from the available options, should I try to look smart, thus indicating that I would be presentable enough to attend cocktail parties at which I could discuss my work and charm potential clients? I paused for a moment at a little blue linen suit I had bought from Jigsaw on sale; I had never actually worn both parts of it together. Perhaps this was the moment. Or I could go for scruffy, which would mean that I was serious and uncompromising. Scruffy was easy: I could do endless permutations of that. But which to choose? God, it was so difficult being creative.

On consideration, I doubted that Felice's and my idea of smart would coincide. Maybe I should simply go full out for shock value and wear my rubber dress with tartan tights and my leather boots with lots of zips on them . . .

I lay down on the bed to calm down. If I went on like this I would give myself a headache.

* * *

Rachel said I should on no account go for smart.

'These people love their image of what an artist is, you know? Try to look sort of sexy and tough, but serious.'

'Which, translated into clothing terms, would mean?'

She pursed her lips.

'You could wear your leggings with the skulls on them.'

'But I was going to wear my boots with all the zips, and if I wear them and the leggings as well she'll think I'm a rabid humourless feminist. You know what these women are like. They think feminism's something you catch, like cystitis.'

'Well, the boots and a short skirt, then.'

We were sitting in Rachel's flat, a small, pretty place in a Camden backstreet, which bore as much resemblance to my home in terms of appearance as Princess Di does to Camilla Parker Bowles. It was in a sixties council development, with an open-slatted wooden staircase and floor-to-ceiling windows in the front room. Like Rachel herself, it was simple and elegant, the sofas covered in red material, the fitted carpets cream, the yucca plants healthy. Its surfaces shone and there were no visible stains. In sum, it represented a level of maturity that I could only dream of attaining.

'Rachel,' I said, suddenly remembering something that had puzzled me, 'I was talking to Lesley after that man from Music Performance Bollocks came round, and she said that you had told her to go after Derek for all she was worth.'

Rachel lit a cigarette.

'I don't know if she's stupid or just won't listen to what she doesn't want to hear,' she said, exasperated. 'We went out for a drink last week and she kept telling me how much Derek obviously fancied her. I couldn't see Derek taking her seriously for more than a one-night stand – she's too silly and immature. I thought he'd give Lesley a warning beforehand about not taking him too seriously and when she realised he meant it, that would be that.'

'So you did encourage her?'

'I thought she might as well be disillusioned sooner than later. And she would have gone for it anyway, Sam, no matter what I said.'

'You're probably right.'

'It seems pretty certain that it was Linda who gave Lesley's name to them, right?' she said, changing tack.

'There's no proof. But everyone thinks so. Who else would it have been?'

Rachel shrugged. 'Exactly, who else?' She blew out some smoke, narrowing her lovely eyes. 'Lesley must be gunning for Linda's blood. Apparently she was screaming at her – Linda, I mean – in the office yesterday.'

'Lou says Linda kept her cool – denied it all and told Lesley please not to get more hysterical than was humanly possible.'

'What about Derek?'

'Keeping his head low, I'd say. I haven't seen him around for days. Have you?'

'A couple of times.'

'If Linda meant to get Lesley to resign, she's missed her guess,' I said. 'She's going to stay and battle it out.'

'Derek's not going to enjoy that very much,' Rachel commented. 'He's all for the quiet life – he hates scenes. He's pissed off enough with Linda as it is for the tantrums she's been throwing.'

She stubbed out her cigarette and stood up, stretching out her arms. In her black leggings and cut-off sweater she looked lithe as a panther.

'Do you want a cup of tea?' she said prosaically.

'Please.'

She went into the little fitted kitchen and put the kettle on.

'I quite envy you,' she said over the rise of the steam, 'being able to come and go as you want. From the gym, I mean. Because we're there most of the time, we get sucked into this incestuous little world . . . things take on an importance perhaps greater than they really have . . . Linda drives you round the bend over the most minor little thing . . .' Her voice trailed off.

'You could always leave,' I suggested. 'You're highly employable.'

'And let Linda win?' Rachel said incredulously. 'No way.'

She filled the teapot and carried the tray back through to the living room.

'So what *are* you going to wear for this art consultant, then?' she said.

* * *

Originally, that afternoon had been branded on my mind as the day I found out that Marks and Spencer had discontinued the

Margaritas in their Cocktail-in-a-Tin line. I was very upset.

'Why?' I wailed pathetically at the sales assistant.

'It's been discontinued,' she repeated dully.

'But they were popular! They often sold out. Sometimes I came in to buy them and they were all gone already!'

She scratched her nose, unmoved by my distress.

'Sometimes,' she said, as if imparting a piece of wisdom from on high, 'sometimes they just – discontinue things, y'know? Don't matter if they sell out or not.'

'Do you have any Gin Fizzes left, then?'

'Nah. They're discontinued too. Only what's on the shelf.'

It was almost too much to bear. Those cocktails had represented the way I would live one day when I was a successful artist and could afford to stock my freezer with nothing but Margarita and Gin Fizz tins. To have them gone was like slipping down the slope again into squalor and deprivation.

I poked morosely at the Pina Coladas and Harvey Wallbangers that were left, wondering why shops deliberately discontinue the items you actually like and buy repeatedly – Next's Red Velvet lipstick, Holland and Barrett's Aduki Bean Burgers . . . I could go on and on. Bitterly I stalked out, chilling the store detective with a look of contempt, and walked down to the gym instead of catching a bus. I needed to do something with my frustration.

It was very quiet at the gym. On Tuesday afternoon we're never exactly squeezing them in through the doors, but still it seemed unusually deserted. Perhaps the general malaise among the staff had communicated itself to the members.

'Peaceful today, eh, Lou?' I observed originally.

Lou grimaced. 'Bad atmosphere,' she said weightily. 'I wasn't expectin' you in yet, Sam. Your class isn't till five-thirty.'

I looked up at the clock. It was only half-past three; I hadn't realised it was so early. 'I meant to do some shopping in Camden but I couldn't be bothered in the end,' I explained, not wanting to burden her with my cocktail trauma.

'You goin' to work out?' Lou said disparagingly.

Lou's attitude towards exercise was profoundly contradictory. She had been working at the gym for more than ten years, first as a crèche attendant, then promoted to crèche supervisor and finally scaling the dizzy heights of receptionist/administrator.

Thus she had never been directly involved with the nuts and bolts of exercising and, while appreciating that her job revolved around promoting the need for people to work out, she saw absolutely no point in it herself. Most of the time she behaved like a tolerant mother watching her teenage children experiment with some trend that she knows from experience will prove ephemeral.

This contradiction led to a split in her personality. One day she might reprove you strictly for your lack of commitment to your fitness levels; the next would find her pronouncing the words 'work out' as fastidiously as a *Spectator* columnist forced to utter the phrase 'all-night rave party'. This was clearly one of the latter days.

I shook my head. 'I hate working out before a class,' I explained. 'It makes me feel all relaxed and happy and I can't motivate myself to boss them around with the proper authority.'

'Whatever you say. So what you goin' to do with yourself? You want a cup of tea?'

'Love one. Sure I'm not disturbing you?'

Lou extended a perfectly manicured hand, waved it slowly over her desk to indicate that she had nothing urgent pressing, and, rising up majestically, went over to the filing cabinet in the corner and switched on the kettle that stood on top of it. She wasn't wearing a turban today; her bob was sprayed smooth and rolled under at the ends, Oprah-style, shiny and black. Her earrings were fake rubies set in gold and she wore a cardigan the colour of mandarins over a red blouse and skirt. Both cardigan and blouse were heavily shoulder-padded, which made her presence even more imposing.

'You don't have any biscuits, do you?' I asked hopefully. I had made the mistake of buying a low-calorie sandwich for lunch – cheese and plum pickle: very nice, but the psychological effects of knowing I had consumed a mere 67 calories or so were beginning to tell on me.

'Sorry, no. I'd offer you a cigarette if smokin' weren't considered the eleventh deadly sin nowadays.'

Lou brought the mugs of tea over to her desk. I pulled up another chair and we sat sipping for a while in peace. Lou was one of those people who don't open their mouths unless they have something particular to say, and the effect was very restful.

The office took up about a quarter of the floor space in the reception area. The doors to the outside world opened directly by Lou's desk; all classes and the use of the gym were paid for on arrival and no one could come in without showing their membership card. Opposite her were the stairs going down to the basement and the noticeboard, and to her left were the doors to the crèche area, the main gym, and the upstairs toilets. Mistress of all she surveyed.

'You have a great view here,' I observed. 'See all the comings and goings.'

'Not much of that right now,' Lou said. 'This is a dead time of the afternoon. I might have a cigarette. I shouldn't have mentioned it 'cause now I've got the urge.'

She stood up, picking up her bag, and headed towards Linda's office.

'Won't be long.'

I stared at her incredulously. 'Won't Linda hit the roof if she finds you smoking in her office?'

Lou tapped the side of her nose with one finger. 'Let's just say Miss Gestapo's got some vices of her own. This is one we share. I don't tell on her and she don't tell on me.'

She shut the door carefully behind her so no smoke could filter out. I couldn't help grinning at the thought of Linda surreptitiously puffing away in private. It's always nice to know that your enemy has a weakness. Flicking through the timetable I saw that the next class was Rachel's, at four o'clock. 'Pregnant Mums Yoga Stretching.' Who wrote this crap? One wasn't necessarily pregnant and a mum at the same time. Still, it avoided the ghastly phrase 'mums-to-be'. There's always a silver lining.

Lou emerged from the office looking slightly guilty but content, fanning the air behind her discreetly. As she seated herself, the main doors swung open and a very obviously pregnant woman lumbered her way through.

'No need to ask what you're here for,' Lou said, smiling at her and tearing off a ticket.

The woman smiled back.

'Bloody obvious, ain't it? Not long to go now and I can tell you

I can't wait to get the little bugger out,' she said, pushing some money over the counter. 'Am I the first, then?'

'That's right. Go straight through. There's chairs in there if you want to sit down.'

She crossed reception and went through into the crèche. Over the next ten minutes several more of them appeared, all, despite their relative sizes, walking in the same slow careful way, as if they might shake the babies loose if they broke into a trot. Lou said something friendly to all of them and to a woman they all smiled back at her; she had the knack of hitting the right tone, neither patronising nor sentimental. They went through into the crèche, from where a low hum of voices could be heard, punctuated by the occasional laugh. Lou looked up at the clock. It was five to four.

'Nearly time to start,' she said.

'They're probably swopping delivery horror stories in there,' I said flippantly. 'Why rush them?'

Lou, mother of four, looked at me disapprovingly. Just then Rachel came quickly up the stairs from the basement and turned for a look at the clock.

'You got a few minutes yet,' Lou said.

'Oh, I thought I was running late. Well, I might as well start, since I'm here. If anyone else turns up just send them in.'

She went into the gym, emerging a minute later with a pile of mats for her students to sit on. I jumped up to hold the crèche door open for her, laden down as she was. As it closed behind her the voices went silent. I could hear Rachel saying something but couldn't make out the words.

Gathering up my rucksack and jacket from the floor of the office, I said to Lou: 'Thanks for the tea. I might as well head down now and put my stuff in the locker. I can spend the time thinking up new fiendishly difficult exercises for my next victims.'

'Any time,' Lou said. 'Pop up here again if you get bored.'

At the top of the stairs I nearly cannoned into Naomi, on her way up. She looked furious, her face set into a scowl even sulkier that usual, and she barged past me without apologies, slamming out of the main doors. A histrionic friend of mine has a way of drawling 'How *rude*' to any major discourtesy, which always succeeds in putting the culprit firmly in their place. I wished I had the knack myself.

Descending the stairs, I could see Jeff in the office. He was sitting at the table, papers spread out in front of him, head bent, writing something. Hearing me clatter down the stairs, he looked up for a second to see who it was and then dropped his head back to his task.

The staff lockers were opposite the office. I hung up my jacket and hoisted in my rucksack, taking a handful of hairgrips from a side pocket. Like most teachers, I usually came to the gym in what I wore for teaching class, with a change of clothes and toilet bag in the rucksack for afterwards. It was too much bother to change twice. I was in my usual get-up: leggings, short-sleeved T-shirt and a zip-up top with long sleeves that I would tie round my waist as I warmed up. All had once been black and now were a faded charcoal grey, thin with use. The T-shirt was printed on the front with a woman's hand holding a gun and on the back with several bullet exit holes. It had been put out by a band I liked years ago and I had worn it to death ever since.

I turned the key in the locker. It was attached to a rubber band and I pulled this round my ankle, burying it in a fold of sock. I can't bear things dangling off my wrists. The only thing left was to put my hair up. Hairgrips in my hand, I strolled down the corridor, casting a glance at the posters tacked up on the walls, advertising all-day aerobics events, raves, macrobiotic restaurants, the usual collection.

On my left were the two gyms, the women's and the men's, and music blared out through each closed door as I went by, which meant they were both in use. Linda was very strict about saving electricity and checked regularly to make sure no one forgot to turn off the stereo if they were last out of the gym. To my right were the men's changing rooms and toilets, the women's changing rooms and finally the women's loos. Beyond was nothing but more tatty linoleum leading to the end of the corridor and the fire door with its lurid green notices informing you how to use the fire extinguisher without panicking. The central one said: 'This Door Is Alarmed.' Under it some would-be joker had scrawled: 'Well, I'm petrified!'

I pushed open the door to the women's toilets. It swung shut behind me. Someone was in there already; one of the cubicle doors was closed. I dropped my hairgrips on to the handy ledge in front of the mirror and started pinning my hair into a tidy arrangement which after half an hour, as I knew from experience, would settle into a loose mess of curls sticking out at odd angles. Once finished, I decided – as one does – that I might as well go to the toilet while I was here. It was only while sitting on the loo that it occurred to me that the woman in the next-door cubicle hadn't made a sound for a good five minutes, which struck me on reflection as rather odd. Of course, it often happened that people were too embarrassed to let themselves go when they knew there were others present, but surely five minutes should have been long enough for her inhibitions to break down. At least she should have made some noise – ripping off loo paper, say, or adjusting her clothes.

I flushed the toilet and came out of the cubicle. There was still no sound from my neighbour. Torn between feeling intrusive and wanting to help if anything was wrong, I bent down cautiously and squinted underneath the door, wondering if she would see me and take offence.

As soon as I saw the foot wedged at a strange angle against the wall, I knew I didn't have to be preoccupied about her seeing me. From its position it looked as if her head must be over the lavatory bowl. If I hadn't known that none of Rachel's yoga class had come downstairs I would have thought it was one of them having a quick bout of prepartum nausea. But there was something not quite right about the foot, torqued round on the ankle like that . . . Besides, why hadn't I even heard any retching? And how long could someone crouch over the toilet in such an uncomfortable position?

The lock on the door was turned to red and said 'Occupied' as well, just in case you had any doubts about its status. I knocked politely. There was no response. Wondering if I would have to pry the lock round with a hairpin, I pushed the door tentatively. It gave. I pushed it a little harder. It swung about halfway open and then stopped short with a dull thud, having bumped against something that sounded very much like an unconscious body.

I had absolutely no wish to look inside. My heart was beating very fast and the nape of my neck felt a sudden chill which had nothing to do with the fact that all my hair was pinned up, leaving it bare. But by now I had come this far . . .

No sensible thoughts about fingerprints or obliterating traces entered my mind for a second. I edged in as far as I could through the door. From there, I was able to look down at the person who was lying there, sprawled as if she had fallen over the toilet, limbs dangling uncomfortably to the ground. Now I could see why she had been silent. It's not that easy to make a noise when part of your face has been smashed in.

7

'And then what did you do, Miss Jones?'

'I went to the office to tell Jeff, who was in there, to go upstairs and tell Lou to ring the police. Then I went back to the toilets to make sure no one else could get in. And it's Ms, by the way,' I added for good measure.

'Are you sure that no one else could have had access to the toilets while you were away?'

'Quite sure. I was watching in case anyone came out of one of the gyms, or the men's changing rooms. I didn't go into the office; I stood in the doorway talking to Jeff and kept my head turned so I could look down the corridor. No one went in. Apart from Jeff, who followed me back for a look. I think he couldn't quite believe me. But he just did what I'd done – stuck his head round the corner of the door to see. He didn't touch anything.'

'Did you see anyone at all, apart from Mr Roberts?'

'Who's Mr Roberts?' I said blankly.

The policeman said patiently: 'Mr Jeff Roberts.'

'Oh, right. No, I didn't. No one at all.'

'And before that, you didn't see anyone in the corridor either?'

'No. But I was putting my jacket in the locker and then I had to get something out of my rucksack, so it's conceivable that in that time someone could have come out of one door and gone into another. They'd have to have been pretty fast, though, and quiet.'

I looked over at the other policeman, seated discreetly in a corner, notebook on lap. If he was going to be a secretary he should do it properly – cross his legs elegantly and perch the book on his grey-trousered knee. His pen was skimming over his note-book, hardly seeming to touch the surface; he didn't seem to be fazed by how fast I was talking. I told myself to take breaths, at least between sentences. It would calm me down.

'Let me just recap the earlier part of the afternoon,' the inspector said. He had introduced himself earlier, but I've never been great with names, and finding a dead body tends to take your mind off more mundane details. We were sitting in Linda's office, which they had commandeered for the purposes of inter-viewing us. Everyone who had been present at the gym had been herded with cursory politeness into the crèche, where they were being supervised by a police officer to make sure they didn't cook up deals to alibi each other.

The pregnant mothers, fortunately for them, were out of the loop, since both Lou and I could say with certainty that none of them had gone downstairs. They had left their names and gone, one hand pressed to the small of the back, the other working the air like distance walkers to get outside as fast as possible. We were lucky none of them had started having contractions out of shock.

'You arrived here at about three-thirty p.m., is that correct?'

'More or less.'

'And how did you know the time?'

'We both – Lou and me – looked up at the clock on the wall outside.'

I heard the secretary policeman scribbling. The other one was staring hard at me. He was exactly what you expect a policeman to look like: big and nondescript, with dull grey skin caused by the poor nutritional values of the station canteen, endless ciga-rettes and little exposure to natural light. His tie and suit were a perfunctory nod to convention and his shirt was a nasty shade of beige. He observed me as I assumed scientists did laboratory animals, with a detached interest limited to his strictly defined field of investigation, and he gave the impression of seeing most of what there was to see.

I knew why he wasn't taking his eyes off me, and it wasn't because my hair was starting to fall down. We had reached the crucial part now. Time to check out my alibi.

'And you didn't go straight downstairs when you arrived?' he said casually. 'Why was that?'

'I was two hours early for my class,' I explained. 'I had meant to do some shopping but Sainsbury's looked crowded and I couldn't be bothered.' I was damned if I was going to confide in him about M&S discontinuing their Margaritas-in-a-Tin. 'Lou offered me a cup of tea and I sat up here with her in the cubicle in the hall until Rachel's stretch class started.'

'That would be at four o'clock,' he said, looking at a sheet of photocopied paper in front of him which I recognised as the timetable of classes.

'Yes. It started a few minutes early, but it must have been four before I went down.'

'Mm. Who did you see downstairs, Ms Jones?'

I gave him points for courtesy. 'Jeff – Jeff Roberts – was in the office writing something. Oh yes, and at the top of the stairs I bumped into a girl called Naomi. She's a member here. I don't know her last name.'

'Did Mr Roberts see you come downstairs?' he asked.

I looked at him hard. He had already talked to Jeff and he knew perfectly well that Jeff had seen me.

'You couldn't help it if you were sitting where he was,' I said. 'There's a view of nearly the whole staircase, and each stair has metal edges; he would have heard anyone coming downstairs. He looked up at me for a moment and then went back to what he was working on.'

We had come full circle: they already knew what I had done next. But the inspector took me over it again, presumably to see if I would contradict myself. He was particularly keen to know whether I had touched the body. I said 'no' three times in different ways. I hadn't needed to touch her: that she was dead had been beyond any doubt. Then he asked me if either Jeff or Naomi had looked different in any way and reluctantly I admitted that Naomi had been in a hurry and seemed preoccupied. I know that sometimes it's necessary, but I have a primitive prejudice against telling the police things they don't already know.

We went through the procedure of reading back my statement, and then I signed it. The secretary policeman had a surprisingly attractive voice. He wasn't bad-looking, either. I reproved myself firmly for having the bad taste to think something like that, particularly as he was dressed so badly. His grey trousers looked like the kind with permanently pressed front creases that are advertised in the back pages of the nastier Sunday colour supplements.

While the inspector lit up a cigarette with the air of someone who had been promising himself this treat for the last half-hour and now was luxuriating in the moment, the secretary policeman took my fingerprints as carefully as a new recruit but about three times as fast.

Then he ushered me out of Linda's office and went to fetch the next questionee from the crèche. It was Lou. She looked very tired, her face drawn, and I remembered with a start that she was fifty. Usually she looked so much younger. I stood for a moment in the reception area, not knowing what to do. The secretary policeman was just disappearing back into the office.

'Excuse me,' I said, 'but is it OK if I go downstairs and get my rucksack and jacket? They're still in my locker.'

He thought for a moment.

'I don't see why not,' he said. 'Hang on a moment.'

He went into the office, said something to the inspector and emerged again.

'It's OK,' he said. 'I'll just cast a glance over the contents, if you don't mind. Otherwise we couldn't let you take it off the premises.'

'Fair enough. I'll just wash my hands first.'

He looked dubious. I said: 'D'you want to watch? I give good nail-brush.' He shook his head.

'Go on, then. Just be quick.'

I nipped into the upstairs toilets to scrub as much of the finger-print ink as possible off my hands. Though managing to remove enough to avoid staining everything I touched, the result was still dismal; this kind of ink seems to work itself into your pores. Also it reminded me of the last time my fingerprints were taken, which had not been the happiest of occasions. I had decided to let them find out about that in their own sweet time. There was no sense in rushing things now; they'd have been questioning me all day if they already knew about it. I was calculating that when it did come to light it would be tempered by the fact that a contact of mine would put in a good word for me.

We went downstairs and I opened the locker in front of him.

He flicked through the pockets of my jacket and the contents of the rucksack. The weapon with which she had been killed had been by her side, so he couldn't have been checking for that; bloodstained clothing, maybe? It hadn't looked as if that wound would have splattered much blood, but even a drop or two would be enough for their purposes. I shivered.

He was going over my jacket. Violet suède; that would show any marks. In my rucksack were the clothes I had been meaning to change into: dark green sweater and velvet leggings. He stared at them thoughtfully.

'Could I ask you to change into these, Ms Jones?' he said. 'Then you could leave the clothes you're currently wearing with us.'

My heart sank. This was my favourite T-shirt. I'd never get it back once they filed it away as evidence.

'If I had killed her, which I didn't,' I pointed out coldly, 'I wouldn't have been so stupid as to say I hadn't touched the body – I'd have said I tried to pick her up or turn her over, to account for any bloodstains. Anyway, I didn't have time. She'd been dead for a while when I got there; the blood wasn't flowing any more. I told you that.'

He looked abashed but unyielding. 'Sorry,' he said. 'Nothing I can do.'

I changed quickly and gave him the clothes I had been wearing. 'I want them back,' I said firmly. 'That's my favourite T-shirt. What's your name?'

'Detective Sergeant Hawkins,' he said, rather formally. His eyes were a nice shade of blue and his shoulders were wide under the identikit grey jacket. He looked in reasonably good shape, though you never knew; the awful suit might be hiding a multitude of figure flaws.

'I'll remember,' I said, pulling on my jacket.

'I like the colour,' he said unexpectedly. 'The jacket, I mean.'

'Oh. Thank you.' I looked him up and down. 'Well, on that subject, navy would be better for you than grey. It'd bring out your eyes.'

I shouldered my rucksack and left the building. It was seven o'clock and the sky had been dark for some time; the haloed streetlamps seemed very orange, over-bright, as if I had never really noticed them before. For a moment I stood still, looking around me. The only indication of anything out of the ordinary was the police cars parked outside; otherwise the street was as quiet as ever. When someone has been murdered the real shock is that the rest of life continues as normal. It's like losing your virginity. You want the whole world to recognise what's happened, but how can they when you look just the same as before?

Before my eyes I saw Linda's body again, slumped over the toilet, head skewed round against the cistern, her eyes staring blankly up at the ceiling. Blood had drained out of the wound which obscured the side of her head, clotting in her fair hair, leaving her face so pale that the strokes of blusher stood out vividly on either cheek. There were a few drops of blood on the floor and great smears of it behind her on the toilet seat. One arm was flung out below her head and that too was thick with blood, though on her black catsuit the stains were hardly visible, just slightly darker patches that would be moist to the touch.

Beside her on the floor was a silver hand weight, placed neatly on one end the way one was supposed to do, so that it couldn't roll away. I wondered now if that meant the murderer had been someone used to gym equipment; anyone who worked out in the gym would automatically have put the weight down that way. The end that faced upwards had been sticky with blood. A gym frequenter, then, and a tidy one, if their instinct had been to put down the weight stained side up, to avoid dirtying the floor.

There was a noise behind me and I started, swinging round. It was just an empty beer can clattering along the pavement. I realised with embarrassment that I had raised my fists as if to defend myself, and felt ridiculous. Suddenly I was aware of how much I needed a drink.

*   *   *

I had left my minivan up towards Camden Town, so I started walking up the high street, still in a daze. Unusually large quantities of traffic seemed to be rushing along the road, but maybe it was my disoriented state which magnified every swish of a car, every tread of a passer-by. Nothing seemed quite solid, but it was making a colossal amount of noise all the same. The lights of the cars, the red neon sign of the kebab shop, were blinding. I turned my head away from the street to avoid them and found myself looking into a pub. Through the big window I saw a familiar head, bent over a pint of beer. He was alone at the table. The measure of my need to talk over with someone, anyone, what had just happened could be gauged by the fact that I deliberately chose to have a drink with Jeff.

I pushed the door open and went across to his table, finding myself sinking down gratefully into the chair opposite him. My legs were wobbly.

'Hi, Jeff. Have the police questioned you already?' As an opening sentence it beat a comment on the weather.

Jeff's face looked drawn. There were hollows sunk in his cheeks I'd never noticed before, and he seemed huddled into his big donkey jacket as if for comfort. The fluorescent orange plastic on the shoulders caught the light of the green-shaded lamp that hung directly over our table.

'Fascist pigs,' he said automatically. The first thing they taught you when you joined the Living Socialists was to give this response as a reflex every time the word 'police' was mentioned. I imagined it could become somewhat wearing when a large group of them were gathered together. Still, it hadn't come out with much conviction; Jeff had other things on his mind. I remembered that I still needed a drink.

'Do you want another pint?' I asked. 'Bitter, right?'

He shook his head. 'No, thanks.'

It was very odd for Jeff to refuse a free drink. He must still be in shock. Jesus, I thought pettishly, I was the one that had found her, after all. I ordered a neat tequila and found to my surprise that in the interval between handing over some money and getting change I had drunk it all, so I asked for another. The barman gave me a look that said if I'd wanted a double why didn't I just bloody order one in the first place.

I sat down at the table again. I couldn't drink anything beyond the second tequila, because I was driving, so I did my best to sip it very slowly.

'No wonder they interviewed you first,' I said. 'You were in the perfect place to see everyone coming and going.'

Jeff shrugged. 'Bloody bastards. I should've refused to tell them anything.'

'Come on, Jeff,' I said, even more impatiently, because I recognised traces of his attitude in myself. 'This isn't policemen beating up demonstrators on anti-National Front marches. Someone's been murdered. They've got a right to ask questions. And you can take that from me. You know I'm not exactly a rabid Tory.'

Jeff was already aware that his politics weren't that far removed from mine, though this doesn't necessarily count for the Living Socialists; to the majority of them, if you're not a paid-up member you're automatically suspect. They loathe other fringe left groups with the same virulence they reserved for Margaret Thatcher.

Still, he relaxed slightly, becoming less combative.

'There wasn't much to see anyway,' he said. He hadn't touched his pint yet. Something was definitely wrong.

'Doesn't matter. You saw who went up and down those stairs, and that's the important thing.'

He focused on me. 'You're OK,' he said unexpectedly. 'You wouldn't have had the time.'

I had started to think this one through already. 'I might have done,' I said slowly, 'as long as I had the weight with me. I could have popped into the women's gym to pick one up, but whoever was in there would have seen me. No, I'd have to have had the weight in advance. But then how would I have known how to find Linda in the toilets?'

'You couldn't have done all that in five minutes from start to finish. Besides, she was already dead when you found her.'

'How do you know that?' It came out too sharply. Jeff smiled humourlessly.

'The blood wasn't flowing, was it? We all read detective stories now, you know. It was clotting. If you'd just killed her it would still have been dripping on the floor.'

I had to thank my lucky stars that Jeff had followed me back to the toilet to see Linda's body for himself. Otherwise, by the time the police arrived, a very important corroboration of my alibi might have been lost.

'Who was down there, Jeff?' I said directly. Once the news had got round, a group of people had collected by the door of the toilets, unable to believe what they had heard and wanting a look, not so much out of ghoulishness as sheer incredulity. In my effort to hold them all back I had felt like Horatius keeping the bridge. But I hadn't seen which ones had just come downstairs or who had been in the basement all along.

'Derek, Fliss, Brian. That girl Naomi. And me, of course.'

'What about Rachel? She came upstairs earlier.' I didn't for a moment think it had been Rachel, but it was as well to make sure we weren't missing anyone out.

Jeff shook his head. 'After Rachel went upstairs I saw Linda going down the corridor. And Rachel didn't come back down again. She's off the hook.'

'You're sure about that?'

'Of course I'm sure!' Jeff snapped. 'Don't you think I know how important it is?'

'Sorry!' I had obviously hit a nerve. Jeff didn't like his word being doubted. He had probably stormed out of many a Living Socialist meeting because a fellow comrade had challenged his interpretation of Engels's definition of hegemony.

He calmed down. 'I remember particularly,' he explained, 'because I thought it was Lesley from the back. You know, they're about the same height, blonde . . . and then Linda turned to look at one of the posters on the wall and I saw her face. It was her, no question about it.'

I stared at him. Until this moment the question of who had done it hadn't been at the front of my mind. But now it stood out a mile that the person with by far the strongest motive was Lesley herself.

'There's no way it could have been Lesley?' I asked cravenly. I didn't want it to have been anyone, but since Linda clearly hadn't chosen that way to kill herself—

'Definitely not. I didn't see her at all. Besides, even if Lesley had come downstairs without me seeing her – which she couldn't – there's no way she could have gone back up again. I was in that office all the time, and you and Lou were upstairs, right? You'd have clocked her even if I didn't.'

I nodded slowly, my brain racing over the names Jeff had mentioned. Fliss, Brian, Naomi, Jeff, Derek. It was a very small roster of suspects indeed . . .

8

'No one,' Lou said firmly, 'is goin' to tell me that Derek smashed that woman's face in.'

'Who do you think it was, Lou?' I leaned forward.

'That's not the point,' Rachel broke in impatiently. 'What we're concerned about is that the police already think it was Derek. It's a foregone conclusion for them – he's a black man with a white girlfriend. They'll decide that Derek and Linda were quarrelling and he hit out at her.'

'Derek wouldn't have needed to hit Linda in the face with a weight if he'd wanted to do her some damage,' I observed. 'He could knock most people out with one punch. If he used the weight it would mean he wanted to kill her, I should think.'

'But we don't think it *was* Derek, Sam,' Lou said.

'I've known him a long time,' Rachel said, her beautiful eyes troubled. 'We grew up in the same place. There's no way he'd ever do something like this.'

I tried to imagine big, easy-going, trouble-avoiding Derek angry enough with Linda to pick up a hand weight and hit her in the face. It was impossible. Derek was non-combative; his instinct was to leave a situation as soon as it jarred on him. If Linda had started in on him I thought he would simply have picked up his things, walked out of the gym and left her to stew, as he had done after the meeting when she'd caught him copping a feel of Lesley's bottom.

'We're worried,' Rachel continued, 'that the police will have made their minds up it was Derek and not look any further than him.'

I stared at her. 'What evidence do they actually have? Enough to arrest him?'

'They know that Derek and Linda hadn't been getting on well.'

'Do they know why?'

'I think so. We'll have to hope they don't question that idiot of a Lesley, or she'll make it sound even worse than it was to build up her own importance.'

'They'll talk to everyone,' Lou said. 'They're not fools.'

'Still, that's not enough of a motive,' I argued. Rachel looked at me pityingly.

'It's never that hard to convince some white people that black men can't control their urges, Sam. They'll say it was a quarrel and he snapped.'

'Jesus.' I sat back, thinking hard. The three of us were gathered in Rachel's flat for a mini council-of-war. Outside it was a beautiful day; sun streamed in through the huge windows behind me, casting a golden glow over the coffee table, lighting up the red sofa. Only a few dust mites were visible within its beam, testimony to Rachel's good housekeeping. Lou and Rachel were smoking and even I was becoming tempted to cadge a cigarette. You could tell we were all under stress.

Rachel's words had struck home; when she had rung and asked me to come round I thought she and Lou were being unnecessarily dramatic. But for the first time I understood why they were taking this situation so seriously. It was easy to imagine some prosecution lawyer putting Derek in the witness box and trying to wind him up, letting the jury see how tall he was, how strong, and then reading out Linda's height and weight. And skin colour. Rachel was right.

'Who are we looking at?' I said finally. 'Brian and Fliss don't seem that likely to me, unless one of them killed Linda to make sure that her plans for the gym didn't get passed by the council, and that strikes me as rather flimsy as far as motive goes. That leaves Jeff and Naomi, as far as I can see—'

Rachel moved impatiently in her chair, as if uninterested in speculating on who might actually have killed Linda. I looked at her. She was definitely strung out. Her hair was pulled tightly back off her head and she was dressed with less than her usual fastidious care.

'Rachel,' I said, 'unless we know who actually did it and can tell the police, how else are we going to help Derek? As far as I can see there's no other way to prove him innocent.'

Lou poured herself some more tea.

'That girl Naomi was in a nasty temper,' she said. 'Not that I'm wantin' to stir shit . . .'

'She fancied Derek,' I said, suddenly remembering that scrap of conversation I had caught in the changing room. 'She was talking about it to a friend of hers a few days before; I heard her. It must have been Derek she meant. What was she doing down there when Linda was killed, Lou? Naomi's not accredited yet to use the gym – she hasn't done enough induction classes. I should know. I'm the one trying to whip her into shape. Why d'you let her go down?'

'Said she'd left somethin' in a locker. But she was gone way too long for that.'

'I can't see her being so filled with desire to lift weights that she scammed her way in under false pretences,' I said drily. 'She must have been looking for Derek.'

'What I thought.'

'So she probably found him. Brian and Fliss say they were working out and didn't see anything, right?'

Both of those two were seriously addicted to pumping iron, out to build as much muscle as they could. I could quite believe that they could stay in their respective gyms for hours on end and notice little of what was happening around them.

'Fliss says she saw Linda come in a couple of times,' Rachel said. 'She was taking an inventory and making notes on the state of everything, apparently. Probably to demonstrate how much work the gym needed and why we needed to raise the membership price more than we voted to do.'

'What about Brian?'

'Same thing,' said Lou, lighting another cigarette from the stub of the last one. 'He says Linda came in and out a couple of times. And Derek was there when Brian came in, but he finished his workout after about half an hour and went to have a shower.'

'Neither of them saw Naomi, then,' I said, continuing my train of thought. 'Suppose she was looking for Derek and Linda caught her at it. Linda has a very sharp eye for girls chasing after Derek;

she'd know already that Naomi was making eyes at him and when she found her wandering round the basement it wouldn't be hard to guess what she was up to. They quarrel, Naomi hits her – no, it had to happen in the women's loos. Linda wasn't carried there – no one would have taken the risk of dragging a dead body down the corridor with Jeff sitting there in the office.'

'Unless it was Jeff who did it,' Rachel said immediately, leaning forward.

I pondered this. 'He kills her in the office – very public, isn't it, with those transparent walls? Anyone could have seen in. Maybe somewhere else; think about that later . . . He looks around, the coast is clear, he picks her up and takes her down the corridor. Why not just put her in the women's changing rooms, though, which are nearer? Let's say Naomi's in there, so he can't. Dumps her in the cubicle, shuts the door, makes his escape. But why would he want to kill her in the first place? If we don't think Brian and Fliss would've murdered Linda to make sure the gym didn't get privatised, why would Jeff have done it, more than them?'

'Maybe he found out that she was making a deal with the council behind our backs?' Rachel suggested rather half-heartedly. We thought about this one.

'You didn't hear anything of that sort, did you, Lou?' I asked.

She shook her head. 'It's possible, though. We all know what a bitch she was – pardon my frankness. Lovely day, ain't it?' She slipped the cardigan off her shoulders to let the sum warm them.

'Can I have a cigarette?' I said, finally cracking. I don't even enjoy smoking much. Call it silent peer pressure. 'I like Naomi for it,' I continued. 'And not just because she's bloody rude. She had a motive, the opportunity – let's face it, it's much more likely to have been a woman, considering that it happened in the women's loos.'

'Not if she was carried there,' Rachel pointed out.

'That's less likely. It would have been such a risk. And what about the weight? That's what interests me. It suggests that the murder was planned. Unless it was Jeff, because there are some spare hand weights in the office, and I expect he could have snatched one up in a fury and whacked her with it. Then, of course, he'd have left it by the body to avoid betraying where it had come from. Or, if it was Fliss or Brian, they would probably have killed her in the gym and then needed to move the body to avoid incriminating themselves. But then we get back to the same objections: in Jeff's case, the office is so public for a murder. And either Fliss or Brian would have been at terrible risk of being seen by Jeff – in Brian's case he'd have to avoid being seen coming out of the women's toilets, too, in case Jeff noticed and thought it was odd.'

'It could have happened in a fit of temper, without being planned,' Rachel suggested, 'and then whoever did it just had to make the best of it. Get rid of the body.'

'All this talk about motive,' Lou said heavily. 'I don't think it was the plans for the gym. I'd bet Linda said something with that sharp tongue of hers that got under someone else's skin, badly, and they saw red.'

She looked at us.

'She could really needle a person, you know? She'd know their weak spots and she'd go for them every time. I'd swear that's what happened here. She got someone so angry they hit out at her to stop her mouth. They just . . . saw red.'

*   *   *

Driving back home, the faces of the five people who had been downstairs in that gym floated one by one before my eyes. I agreed with Lou and Rachel. I couldn't believe it had been Derek. I couldn't see him hitting anyone, let alone a woman half his size; and I certainly couldn't see him doing it with a weight in his hand, aware as he would be of the damage that would cause.

Derek wasn't a friend of mine; I couldn't claim a deep knowledge of his character. But in all the time I'd been at the gym I had hardly heard him raise his voice, let alone show the slightest sign of a violent temper. Of course, some people school themselves so well that you have no idea of their potential for violence until they finally snap; but Derek gave no indication that there was anything he even needed to keep under control.

What about Fliss? Again, it seemed unlikely. I had a lot of respect for Fliss; she lived her life on her own terms and took no shit from anyone. Resolutely independent, she ran a stall in Camden Market on the weekends and the odd weekday, selling bric-à-brac. I had walked past it a couple of times and she seemed to be doing pretty well. Try as I might, I could think of no plausible reason why she should have wanted to kill Linda. Although I knew that she felt strongly about the gym redevelopment, I could hardly see her committing murder to preserve the Chalk Farm Gym and Leisure Centre in its current virginal state, unstained by the corrupting touch of the free market. Even if she had found out that Linda had been plotting with a couple of councillors to force her original plan through regardless, Fliss would have been much more likely to organise a protest campaign than to bash Linda's head in. She was eminently sensible.

And I couldn't see Lou's suggestion of intolerable provocation applying to Fliss either. Of all the people who had been downstairs at the time Linda was killed, Fliss struck me as the least easily rattled. If Linda had tried to wind her up, Fliss would surely just have told her to fuck off and gone on pumping iron.

Jeff made a much more credible murderer on both of these two counts. Though it was hard to see Linda's plans for the gym as a motive for murder, it was undeniable that he seemed to be the person who felt most strongly about it. I could easily imagine him and Linda arguing furiously; Linda had certainly blamed Jeff for having done all he could to thwart her proposal, and I didn't doubt she felt strongly enough about it to throw some pretty nasty personal comments his way. Jeff would have been susceptible to that. He was very sensitive and it didn't take much to wind him up. Besides, there had been some weights in the office, conveniently close to hand if he happened to snap.

What did strike me as odd, if it had happened that way, was that he should have bothered to tell the truth, giving me and Rachel our alibis. He would have done better not to clear anyone, in order to keep the field of suspects as wide as possible. I had always thought he had a yen for Rachel, but why help me out too? That pointed to his being innocent, which was a conclusion I was reluctant to draw. He was one of the strongest possibilities.

And to Lou and Rachel, the only person more likely than Jeff was Naomi. But then where would Naomi have got the weight? Fliss would have noticed her coming into the gym to take one. And besides, you would have to be even more stupid than Naomi was – though maybe I was giving her too much credit – to plan to kill someone in a basement to which there was only one means of access, at such a quiet time of day that anyone would notice you coming and going. Even if Jeff hadn't been sitting in the office, there was still Lou upstairs, who didn't miss a thing.

I parked the van – a rather dented red Ford Escort to which, despite its neglected appearance, I was very attached – outside the studio and got out slowly, my brain still ticking over ideas and possibilities. It was very convenient that today was Thursday. Tomorrow Camden Market would be a hive of activity; an excellent opportunity for carrying out one plan I had in mind.

9

It was hard when I woke up in the morning to tell what the weather was like outside. As previously explained, daylight reached me only after having been filtered through the thickly crusted layers of decades' worth of industrial grime and pigeon shit clinging tenaciously to the skylights. There were a couple of windows, but they were fifteen feet off the ground and equally dirty. I made another mental note to ring my friend Janey about the pigeon problem.

One of the skylights was directly above my head as I lay in bed. That was why I had built the sleeping platform here and put the futon where it was: I liked to lie in bed and look up at the sky – not that I could see much of it now, due to the thickly crusted layers, etc. But I loved to be in bed at night when it was raining, the drops pounding on to the glass above while I was tucked up snug and warm under a pile of duvets. The disadvantage to the arrangement was that on waking, the sound of rain pattering down directly over my head was often depressing enough to make me pull the covers up and go back to sleep again.

Today at least it wasn't raining yet. Early spring in London offers a wide selection of weather possibilities, usually changing every half an hour; working out what to wear in the morning was therefore an attempt to anticipate all eventualities. My plans for that day involved dressing as warmly as possible, so I put on a long-sleeved body and then my leather jeans, with a pair of tights – too ripped to wear alone, but not quite ripped enough to throw away – underneath for extra insulation. I added a big hooded sweater, a padded jerkin, two pairs of socks and my Doc

Marten hiking boots. By this time I was bearing a strong resemblance to the Michelin Man and could hardly climb back down the ladder to the main studio. I took this as a good sign. Then I needed to go to the loo and had to unzip and unpop everything again.

By the time I reached Camden Market it was eleven-thirty. I parked the van in a backstreet where it would be safe from marauding packs of traffic wardens – I believe the council is now having them raised by wolves to ensure their ferocity – and strolled down towards the part of the market clustered round Camden Lock. For some reason known only to themselves, the shops along the high street had decided to specialise in the selling of boots. Practically all those on offer were black with silver buckles, but it was easy to distinguish between the pointy heels and toes favoured by Goths and the clumpy ones preferred by punks and indie kids. There were also some in bright green or red patent leather, presumably intended for circus clowns and pop stars.

I wandered into the shop where I had bought my little silver hoop earrings. Even at this comparatively early hour it was full of Goths with black-dyed hair and green fingernails flicking their way through racks of PVC frocks split down the back with laces that were meant to gape open over sections of white, putrid-looking flesh. Some of them – the dresses, that is – were rather nice. I looked at some rings but there was such a wide selection that any choice was impossible. A sales assistant in a calf-length kilt and Cure T-shirt was hovering behind me, but I didn't want to ask him for help. He had one of those rings in his nose which goes through the skin between the nostrils and hangs down over the upper lip; I liked to think I was broad-minded enough, but the last time I had been in here he had offered to show me all the other places he was pierced and it had been very hard to decline without seeming prudish.

The interior was kept as dark as a cavern to placate its more vampiric customers, and I found myself blinking when I emerged into daylight. Next door was the shop where they had a giant lava lamp in the shape of a rocket, blue with red bubbles, which I had always coveted, so I walked straight past to avoid temptation and made my way slowly along the pavement past the various racks of boots, sunglasses, and T-shirts which jutted out from the shopfronts like little promontories. I missed the second-hand clothes shops which had recently been driven out by the higher rents paid by the boot emporia. But Camden wasn't what it used to be, not since they tore down most of the old buildings round the lock and built a whole new inside market with green-painted wrought-iron staircases, a Victorian fantasy. Doubtless the tourists preferred it that way, which is the worst criticism you can level at any new development.

I crossed the road and stood at the top of the bridge, looking down over the canal. The water was brackish and oil-green as always. In the summer people bought drinks from the pub and walked along the arms of the lock to sit in the sun with the water lapping mossily around them and watch street performers juggling or fire-eating rather amateurishly on the towpath. Inevitably some of the spectators would get drunk and fall in. I didn't think that anyone had ever drowned, but you could probably catch more diseases than exist in the entire Indian sub-continent just from being immersed in that water for five minutes.

An old mooring for canal boats was in the centre of this part of the market, and the stalls ran around it in a U-shape. There was a strong hippy emphasis to this section; heavy hand-made mugs painted with stars and smiley faces, jingly wind-chimes that would drive you mad after a couple of hours, every item of clothing tie-dyed or batiked or both. Lots of inlaid turquoise earrings and nasty woolly sweaters the colour of industrial sludge. I walked on fast. I'm allergic to hippies. At the centre of the U was a hat stall I've already spent too much money at and another one, selling huge clunky silver watches, which I've only been prevented from spending too much money at because I've never been able to make up my mind which watch I wanted. Beyond the stall was an archway, and through the archway on the right-hand side, in a nice sheltered position, was the stall I had been looking for.

Fliss had arranged her stock very well. The larger items extended in two wings around the stall itself, so that once you stopped to look at something that had caught your eye you found yourself encircled by dozens of tempting objects. One of the wings was a carefully positioned pile of old leather suitcases, stacked in a domino effect, the one closest to me covered with ancient luggage labels. It might have come straight out of a black and white film. Above it were a couple of Bakelite radios in beautiful condition.

Fliss was leaning against the stone wall behind her, sipping from one of the polystyrene cups that most stall-holders seem to have surgically attached to their gloves.

'Hi, Sam,' she said laconically, showing no surprise at seeing me. Fliss never displayed much emotion. I supposed it wasn't macho.

'I love your stuff,' I said, momentarily distracted by a silver hand mirror with elaborately chased initials on the back. 'Where does it all come from?'

Fliss shrugged. 'I go to the dealers' markets – Bermondsey, Greenwich. They're getting more expensive, though. I drive around looking in junk shops, second-hand places, charity shops. You'd be surprised how much I find in places like that.'

'Does Andy come with you?'

'When he can. He's at work most of the time, though.'

I picked up a little carved box. 'This is nice, too. I bet your home is a real treasure chest.'

Unexpectedly, Fliss smiled. I had hardly ever seen her smile; it made her look much younger and prettier. 'It's OK,' she said gruffly. 'Hard sometimes to give things up, you know? I put things on display and hope they won't sell. Stupid, really.'

'Oh no, I understand.' I put down the box reluctantly. 'I was just going to get a bun,' I said casually. 'Do you want one?'

'All right. Thanks.'

At the nearest hippy food stall I bought two slices of carrot cake with raisins and took them back, wrapped in paper napkins. I handed a slice to Fliss and bit into the other myself. It was on the heavy side. Too much organic flour.

'Have some coffee if you want.' Fliss indicated her thermos.

'Thanks.' I poured myself a cup. A smartly dressed couple had stopped by the stall and were examining the leather suitcases. 'Did the police keep you late last night?' I kept my voice down so the couple wouldn't think Fliss was a receiver of stolen goods and try to haggle.

She shrugged, sipping at the coffee. I noticed that her cup had a plastic lid in which she had torn a small hole she could drink through, a device to keep the coffee as hot as possible. Every little helped when you were standing outside in the cold for eight hours at a stretch. Glad as I was of my protective layers, I had already lost any feeling in my nose and ears.

'It wasn't too bad,' she said. 'Couldn't tell them much. I was in the gym the whole time. Only came out when I heard the commotion. Couldn't remember the last time Linda came in. I don't look at the clock when I'm working out. No point. So I wasn't much help.'

'Was Jeff already in the office when you came down?'

She nodded. 'Drafting some petition about the gym. Thought it was premature myself. That kind of thing can backfire if you do it too early.'

'Did you tell him that?'

Fliss nodded again. She didn't believe in wasting words. 'Wasn't any use, though. He and Linda have never got on. Couldn't wait to put a spoke in her wheel. Bad tactics, though.'

'Excuse me,' said the male of the couple, 'would you mind telling me the price of this suitcase?'

I cursed him inwardly.

'Prices are on the handles,' said Fliss.

'Oh, right. Thanks.'

She turned back to me.

'You were saying—' I began.

'And what if we took two? You know, to make a pair,' he added, in case she wasn't quite sure what he meant by two. He was wearing an old tweed jacket and his chin was negligible. 'I mean, would there be some sort of discount?'

Fliss shook her head. 'Not on two. Three, maybe.'

They went into a little huddle and emerged with an offer on two medium suitcases and a vanity case. Fliss agreed to give them five pounds off.

'They're heavy,' she said. 'Best-quality leather. Not much good for flying.'

I gave her full marks for conscientiousness.

'Oh, they're not really for *travelling*,' the female said, speaking for the first time in a cut-glass voice. Her hair was held back with a velvet band, the kind that schoolgirls wear. Another blonde. I wished I knew how to curl my lip. 'We thought they'd be perfect for weekends in the country. In the summer, you know, with the roof of the car down. They'll look super on the back seat.'

Fliss shrugged and counted out their change. The young man stacked the vanity case inside one of the suitcases; then he picked the suitcases up, one in each hand, and staggered slightly. The woman put a hand on his arm; I thought she was going to offer to carry one.

'Perhaps not all at once, Julian,' she said. 'Think of your back.'

'I'll take them for you,' Fliss offered. She took the suitcases out of his hands as easily as if they were a pair of handbags. The man looked impressed, the woman disapproving. 'Keep an eye on the stall, Sam?'

'Sure.'

She shouldered her way through the crowd, followed by her customers. I would have rifled through her bag in her absence for anything vaguely incriminating, but of course, being Fliss, she didn't have one, only a money pouch which was attached marsupially to her body. I was hoping to sell something and thus endear myself to her, but nobody even stopped at the stall in the few minutes she was away.

'Pair of morons,' she said dismissively on her return. She pulled a small comb out of her jeans pocket and combed back her hair, which was already greased smooth. It seemed to be an automatic reflex, one she must have picked up from fifties films.

I had thought it would be hard to wrench the conversation back to the interesting point we had reached before, but to my surprise Fliss seemed happy to engage in what with anyone else I would have called a gossip. Perhaps having just taken over a hundred pounds in cash had helped to relax her. It would have had that effect on me.

'I felt sorry for Linda,' she said unexpectedly. Her hands were shoved in her pockets, one foot propped against the wall behind her. 'Very insecure. Ambitious, though. Desperate to be the gym manager, but when she got the job she panicked. Of course, she knew what she was doing – good at her job and all that. But she had a chip on her shoulder about not having been to college –

left school young. Never done office work, either. Thought people would look down on her.'

I raised my eyebrows. 'I'd never have guessed. She seemed so confident, like she'd been managing the gym all her life.'

Fliss shook her head. 'Just a year or so. Only came here a couple of years before that. Fast learner. Bossed everyone around so she could look tough. But there she was slaving away at work and Derek messing her around as well. Should have dumped him.'

'He's quite a catch,' I objected.

'Should have thrown him back, then. Exhausted herself fighting little girls off him the whole time. Wasn't worth the aggro.'

She poured us more coffee. 'That's why she and Jeff were always locking horns. She hated people challenging her. I understood that – keep the peace. But Jeff was always suggesting changes. She thought it was personal. Didn't understand that Jeff would've done it to anyone in authority. I tried to explain it to her but she wouldn't listen. So she did everything she could to get back at him. Undermine him, point out that Derek's classes were more popular. Ask him if he was still drinking those milk shakes. You know, extra protein. Load of nonsense. At least it wasn't steroids. Enough of those around already.'

I nodded. 'But that wouldn't be enough to make him kill her, though, would it?'

Fliss stared at me, taken aback. 'What?'

'Well, someone killed her, Fliss. It wasn't me and I'm sure it wasn't you.'

Fliss didn't seem to give a damn about this last assertion. 'Well, it wasn't Derek. Known him for donkey's years. Wouldn't hurt a fly.'

'That only leaves Brian, Jeff and Naomi.'

'That girl shouldn't be in a gym at all,' Fliss said, frowning. 'Complete waste of her time and ours.'

'But do you think—'

'Don't think anything at all,' Fliss said flatly. 'Not my job.' She stared at me hard. She could look very imposing when she wanted to. 'And not yours either, Sam. I'd be careful if I were you.'

I opened my mouth but she forestalled me.

'Prices are underneath,' she said to a girl looking at the Bakelite radios. 'They're all originals. Turn it on if you want.'

She walked over to the girl. It wasn't difficult to deduce that she had nothing more to say to me.

* * *

I strolled back towards Camden Town, feeling reasonably satisfied with what Fliss had told me. It didn't prove much, but then if she had had anything more concrete to tell, the police would already know about it. I hadn't been expecting to catch her off guard; she was that rare kind of person who thought about what she was going to say in advance, and only then opened her mouth. The case against Jeff was strengthening. I was gratified that Fliss was sure Derek was innocent. I enjoyed playing detective, but it was nice to feel that I was fulfilling a public duty rather than simply jumping at any opportunity to poke my nose into other people's affairs.

I wandered into the covered market to look at the second-hand clothes stalls, though there would have been more of them if it had been the weekend. Here everyone hung their stock on the long lines of rails that ran like a grid across the market, turning it into a maze. Part of the pleasure was winding your way through the racks, never knowing what treasures might be hanging in your face as you turned a bend.

The guy from whom I had bought my fake leopardskin coat didn't seem to be around today. It was just as well; I didn't have much money to spend. A Pearl Jam song blared from two giant speakers roped up to a stall selling pirate versions of unreleased albums and illegally recorded live concerts, all in lurid fluorescent cases. From the food stall on the corner the smell of frying samosas and veggieburgers, without which Camden's atmosphere would be incomplete, wafted temptingly in my direction. I rifled through the contents of several stalls and surrendered to the charms of a silver miniskirt which looked as if it would fall apart after I'd worn it a few times: fair enough for six pounds fifty.

There were sheepskin coats everywhere. They must have been the latest fashion. I wove my way past several rails that gave the place the look and odour of a traditional Afghan bazaar at the poorer end of Kabul, trying not to brush against them to avoid contamination. Emerging unexpectedly on to the street, I found myself face to face with a girl who was fingering the lapel of a particularly noxious full-length fleecy number. She looked up at me with a start of recollection.

'Oh, hiya,' she said.

I knew her at once. She was Naomi's cellulite-afflicted friend.

10

I don't mean to mock people who have cellulite; I'm not immune to its ravages myself. But since the only time I had seen her she was stark naked in the showers loofahing her bottom, its attendant pockmarks were the main characteristic for which I remembered her.

She showed no signs of embarrassment. Perhaps she had forgotten the occasion.

'I've seen you around the gym.' she said. 'You must be Sam. You teach weights, right?'

'Yes.'

'I'm Cath. My mate Nayo – Naomi – did one of your classes. Said afterwards she couldn't move for a week.'

'It's always hard at first—'

'Oh, don't worry. She's always exaggerating, that one. I should know, she's my best mate. It was me got her to come to the gym in the first place.'

Cath had a thin pointed face with a bump in the nose. She wore no make-up and her eyelashes and eyebrows were faint light brown shadows against her colourless skin. Her hair was parted in the centre and done in two plaits tied with ribbon at the ends – the little-girl look was big this year. It seemed rather too plausible on her, though; she looked barely twenty and was small and narrow enough to be pre-pubertal. She was lightly clad in a shrunken little T-shirt that made her breasts look as if the same adjectives could have been applied to them, baggy jeans and a skimpy cut-off cardigan. Perhaps she was one of those people who didn't feel the cold.

'Awful about what happened to that Linda, innit?' Cath went on. 'The police went round to Naomi's yesterday evening to ask her about it.'

'Oh really?'

'Yeah. There were two of them. Apparently Naomi was downstairs when she was killed, right?'

Her eyes were sparkling: she seemed distinctly excited at having a friend who was involved in a murder investigation. I decided to impress her with my own gory claim to fame.

'I was the one who found the body,' I said.

Her mouth dropped open gratifyingly. 'You never!' she said. 'What was it like? They wouldn't tell Naomi much.'

'The side of her face was smashed in,' I said, pandering shamelessly.

'Was there much blood?' She said eagerly. 'My boyfriend gets all the true-crime magazines. He'll be dead impressed when I tell him about this.'

'It hadn't bled much.' She looked disappointed. 'It was already clotting by the time I found her, you see.'

'Oh right! That means she'd been dead a while. Wait till I tell Darren.'

'I hope the police didn't give Naomi too bad a time,' I said, fishing. I felt I deserved some information in return.

'What d'you mean?'

A couple of Kurt Cobain lookalikes were hovering behind us, wanting access to the sheepskin coats. We moved aside to let them past. They didn't seem like people who would be fazed by a little eau de sheep. I was worried that the interruption might have distracted Cath from the subject under discussion, but no, she was still looking at me expectantly. Every enquiree should have a boyfriend who collects true-crime stories.

'Well, she's a suspect,' I pointed out. Cath's eyes widened still further. 'Technically at least.' I bent the truth slightly. 'So am I, in fact.'

'But why would Nayo have wanted to kill Linda . . .' Her voice tailed off. After a pause she said: 'But it's the 1990s, innit? You don't kill someone just 'cause you fancy her boyfriend. That'd be really st-*you*-pid,' she finished dismissively.

'You mean Derek?'

She looked at me slyly. 'Well, Nayo's not the only one to fancy him, is she? I'd give him one myself. And everyone knows he messes around. Linda must have known it too.'

'She didn't like it much.'

'Well, that's her problem, right?'

'It's bad luck for Naomi she was downstairs that afternoon.' I allowed a puzzled note to enter my voice. 'What was she doing down there anyway? She hasn't done enough weights classes to use the gym by herself.'

Cath made a tutting sound. 'Stupid cow was chasing after Derek, wasn't she? Don't take much to tell you that.'

'I hope she didn't tell that to the police.'

'Nah, don't worry. I mean, she's not a total prat, is she? Said she'd left something down there and was looking for it. Lucky they didn't ask her to explain why she thought she'd find it in the men's changing rooms!' She giggled. 'Wanted to catch him with his knickers down. I bet *that's* something to see.'

I couldn't help grinning. 'Did she get a chance to see it?'

'I dunno. *Something* happened, I know that much. But she was a bit off about it. Wouldn't tell me nothing.'

'I saw her coming upstairs,' I added. 'She looked pretty pissed off.'

'Yeah, well.' Cath shrugged. 'I think, you know, they maybe didn't *do* it – be a bit *Fatal Attraction* shagging up against the wall in the men's changing rooms with his girlfriend wandering round, wouldn't it? But you know, they must've done *something*.' She sighed in a worldly sort of way. 'Naomi can be pretty stupid about that kind of thing.' She drew the 'stupid' out as she had done before, till it became three syllables dripping with contempt. 'I mean, someone like Derek, you know the rules, don't you? He's got a girlfriend already, and she just happens to be the manager of the gym. He isn't going to want to make any waves, is he? If he's offered it on a plate, he's not going to say no. But it don't mean nothing if he says yes, either. Nayo's thick about men. She thinks it means something if they shag you. Well, lots of times it don't. I keep trying to tell her—'

She looked at her watch. 'Shit. I've got to go. I'm on late lunch this week, but there's late and then there's late.'

'Where do you work?' I asked, strolling along beside her in the direction of the tube station. Despite the lateness, she showed no inclination to hurry.

'Satins, on the high street. I'm a hairdresser.'

'Oh really? Can I ask you something?'

She shrugged. 'Yeah, what?'

'Do you think I should bleach my hair?'

She stopped to look at me. 'Yeah, why not?' she said. 'You'd have to cut it, though.'

'That's OK.'

'I could do it for you. Takes a while. Then you could just pop in when you wanted your roots done. Mind you, lots of people like the roots showing nowadays. I could do you a nice short cut.'

'I'll come in then, when I make up my mind to do it.'

'You can just have a cut if you like, to be going on with,' she offered. 'I wouldn't mind doing something with your hair.'

'Thanks.'

'See you around, then.'

She waved at me and crossed the road. At a distance she looked tiny inside her clothes, but not remotely vulnerable or any of the other adjectives usually applied to small, thin girls. She was as tough as whipcord.

Wondering vaguely what time it was, I looked at my watch. Twelve-forty. Well, that wasn't so bad. Then with horror I remembered that it was Friday.

Which meant I had an appointment with Felice Bortshe at my studio in precisely twenty minutes.

*　　　*　　　*

At least my mad rush to get home resolved the debate about what I should wear. I barely had time to slap on some red lipstick and eyeliner before the doorbell rang. One o'clock on the dot. I thought you should never be on time for an appointment – or was that dinner parties? Putting on my silver hoop earrings I crossed the studio, making the mistake of taking a last glance around. At least there weren't any dirty, festering plates in the sink. Or were there? I resisted the impulse to dash over and check.

'Hi!' said Felice Bortshe as I swung open the heavy door. In her royal blue suit with gold buttons and short skirt, high heels, and one of those power haircuts that's blown and streaked and moussed to within an inch of its life, she looked like an extra from *Dynasty* who had successfully carved out a new career for herself when the show finished its run. Her face was comprehensively made up and her smile was bright. The contrast between her appearance and my own, let alone the mess awaiting us inside, was almost too much for me to bear. A wave of panic hit me. I wanted to shut the door in her face, run upstairs and lie sobbing on my bed.

'You must be Sam!' she continued.

'Yeah, um, that's right, won't you come in?' I managed, with a concentrated effort, not to apologise for the condition of the studio; somehow I felt that once I started I wouldn't stop.

'Some place you've got here!' she observed, looking round her with unashamed curiosity. Felice Bortshe seemed to speak in exclamation marks.

She held out her hand to me. I was reluctant to touch it, feeling rather dirty by contrast with her obviously spotless hygiene. Besides, I might pull off one of her fingernails by accident. They were surely too perfect to be real. Gingerly I extended my hand. She shook it so firmly I saw stars. The nails had to be genuine. Nothing else could have survived that grip.

'Um, er, would you like a cup of tea?' I said.

She laughed, revealing eerily perfect teeth. 'I love it! So English! No, ta very much. Is that right? I mean, is that what I'm supposed to say?'

'Yeah, um, well, sort of . . .'

'Is that where you sleep?' she observed, pointing up to the high platform across the room. 'Up that little ladder? I'd be terrified!'

She seemed friendly enough, though I couldn't for the life of me understand why. What are you *doing* here, I thought, why bother to be polite? Why don't you be honest and just say: 'Gee, this place is the pits!' and leave me to stew in the filth of my own making? She was wandering around now. I resisted the impulse to chase after her and stand in front of everything that looked as if it wasn't up to her standards of cleanliness. It would mean spreading myself over an impossibly wide surface area.

'And this must be the mobile!'

'Um, well, yes,' I muttered. What else could it have been – the boiler? I wondered why some people think it good manners to ceaselessly restate the obvious.

Her head was tilted back appraisingly. She circled slowly beneath the Thing like a well-groomed shark. I shoved some welding tools out of her path. If she took a fall from those four-inch heels I couldn't answer for the consequences.

'What do you call it?'

'Um. Well, it hasn't really – I haven't really—'

'Undiscovered Planet!' she proclaimed triumphantly, swinging round to look at me. 'I love it!'

'You *do*?'

'Mobiles are big now,' she said with the preternatural solemnity with which those in the know refer to the latest fashion. 'Very big.'

She looked round the studio again. Her sweeping gaze, like a moving spotlight, crossed the huddle of tools, wire, metal and general debris on the floor; for a moment I saw each wretched item picked out and illuminated in its full glory. *Please* don't look at those, I whined silently. I was meaning to clear them up. Honestly.

'And this is so authentic,' she said approvingly. 'Really! You should meet my son Jake. He'd love this. The English have a real knack for the Bohemian, don't you think?'

I was warming to her. That was the nicest way of saying 'squalid' I'd ever heard.

'Well, um, I—'

'Do you have representation?'

I was learning by now. Instead of saying anything, I shook my head.

'Well, that's OK. You must meet my friend Duggie Sutton. What are you doing next Monday? I think it's Monday – hang on, let me check.' She dived into her shiny padded handbag and emerged with an electronic gadget. With the tip of one fingernail she poked at various keys and looked up triumphantly. 'Yes, it is! Do come along. He's having a drinks party at his flat. Let me write down the address for you—'

She put back the gadget and produced a Filofax; flicking through the pages she found a blank one, scribbled something on it, tore it out and handed it to me. I took it automatically. It was grey marbled paper and looked expensive.

'And I'll give you one of my cards—'

She replaced the Filofax, and produced a gold cardholder. Flicking one card loose with an expert manoeuvre involving the nail of her index finger, she put it into my hand.

'Do you have any work in progress?'

'Yes, I do actually, over here . . .' I waved at the kitchen table. She clicked over on her heels, deftly sidestepping a welding mask, two beaten-up pairs of work gloves and a spanner, and examined my designs for Son of Thing with flattering interest.

'Mm, yes, very contemporary,' she said. 'How big would this be? I mean, would it be *big*? You know, *big*?'

I stared at her blankly, not knowing what she wanted to hear. Hedging my bets, I said cautiously: 'Well, it could be . . .'

'I mean—' She flung her arms wide. 'You know, *this* big?'

By this time I had clocked on to the fact that mobiles were big this year in all senses of the word.

'Absolutely,' I said devoutly, 'very big. *Huge*, in fact. I would say we're talking very, very large indeed . . .'

'Excellent!' She blinded me with a smile. 'Well, it all sounds very promising! I'll see you on Monday, then? I can't wait for you to meet Duggie!'

I walked her to the door. She paused for a moment on the steps, looking me up and down, a comprehensive survey that started at the hooded sweater and finished with the hiking boots.

'Oh, and Sam,' she said, 'the clients I represent – they *love* Bohemian, of course, but you can only go so far with that, don't you think? You're a pretty girl! Why hide your figure? Go out and buy yourself a nice little dress for Monday. Think of it as an investment!'

She smiled at me in what was almost a motherly way. 'You do remind me of my son Jake,' she said. 'I know you young people have your own ideas! But trust me – I know my market. Red, perhaps?'

She shook my hand again and was gone. I reeled back from the door in shock. Now I knew why hurricane survivors were so disoriented. As if in a trance I looked down at the two pieces of paper I held in my hands. One bore the name of Duggie

Sutton, an address in Holland Park and the note 'six to nine-ish'; the other was Felice Bortshe's card, which was thick and white and said merely: 'Felice Bortshe, Art Consultant', followed by a New York address. I shoved both into the pocket of my jeans.

Still dazed, I looked up at the Thing. I supposed I would now have to learn to call it Undiscovered Planet. What would I name Son of Thing, though, if a client of Felice's ever commissioned me to make it?

There was a ring on the doorbell. I cowered back. Please don't let it be Felice again. I wasn't feeling strong enough yet; I needed a few days lying down somewhere in absolute quiet to recover. I would have to start training for Monday right away.

I went to look through the spyhole I had recently installed. As soon as I saw who it was I relaxed.

'Coming!' I practically yodelled in relief.

It was the secretary policeman in a phenomenally nasty brown blouson leather jacket. I sighed in pity at the waste of such good raw material. His eyes were as blue as ever.

'DS Hawkins,' he said rather formally. 'I wonder if you'd mind coming down to the station to answer some further questions, Ms Jones?'

'No, not at all,' I said cheerfully. 'Want me to come right now?'

'If you don't mind . . .' He looked rather taken aback. People probably didn't usually behave this exuberantly when confronted by a police officer who wanted to haul them off for questioning.

'Fine, no problem.' I gave him a beaming smile.

He was staring over my shoulder; I followed his gaze up to the mobile.

'Do you like it?'

He looked at me thoughtfully. 'Did you make it?'

I gestured around me at the tools lying on the floor. Now Felice had gone the place looked relatively normal again.

'As you see.'

He nodded. 'It's very good. Very powerful.'

'Well, thank you!' I was feeling practically back to my usual self now. Nothing like a spot of light art criticism with a policeman to raise the self-confidence. 'I'll just get the keys to my van.'

'Oh, don't worry,' he said rather too casually. 'I can drop you back here afterwards.'

I raised my eyebrows. Either he didn't have much to do, which seemed unlikely, or he was hoping to pump me for information on the drive back and forth, or he wanted the chance of another look at the Thing, or . . . well, the possibilities were endless.

I was glad I had my lipstick on. I find the knowledge that I'm wearing make-up very important in any kind of formal interview.

I closed and locked the door behind us.

'I'm thinking of calling it Undiscovered Planet,' I said, trotting down the steps. 'What do you think?'

11

Police interview rooms are always ugly and this one was no exception. Only the secretary policeman, or DS Hawkins as I supposed I ought to call him, raised the aesthetic tone, having mercifully removed his horrible jacket upon entering. What could have impelled him to buy it? Even the word 'blouson' was naff.

Detective Inspector Monroe, the one with the poor nutritional values, chainsmoked away. They had offered me a cup of tea, which probably meant that they were softening me up for the bastinado later. I had refused, not to maintain my psychological superiority, but because I had drunk so much tea over the past few days that my blood must be fifty per cent tannin by now.

DI Monroe made me recount one more time the events of Tuesday afternoon, but I could tell he had something else on his mind. I answered pretty automatically. It was nice not to have to tell any lies for a change.

'Why didn't you tell us on Tuesday that this isn't the first violent death in which you've been involved, Ms Jones?' he said suddenly, obviously hoping to startle me.

I knew this would come up sooner or later. That's the downside of centralised computers.

'I wouldn't say I was involved in this one, apart from finding the body,' I pointed out.

'It must be becoming quite a habit for you,' he said sarcastically. 'Finding bodies.'

'I hope not,' I snapped. 'DS Hawkins has still got my favourite

T-shirt, among other things. If I make a habit of it, soon I won't have any clothes left that I like.'

He lit another cigarette from the stub of the old one and surveyed me with a stare that was not devoid of intelligence. Obviously realising that the sarcastic approach wasn't yielding high dividends, he changed tack.

'Still, you must admit that it is a coincidence,' he said politely.

'Certainly.'

'You have of course not been tried or convicted of anything, Ms Jones. The jury at the inquest gave a verdict of death by misadventure.' He looked at me hard. 'Which was rather stretching the point, don't you think?'

'It was self-defence,' I said firmly, and pushed all my memories back to the farthest corner of my mind. I wouldn't think of that now, not with Monroe watching my every movement. 'Why don't you try talking to Detective Inspector Fincham? He used to work out of this station. I don't know if he still does. He'll probably tell you I'm not the kind of homicidal maniac that gets my kicks out of smashing someone's head in on a regular basis. Not that he'll phrase it quite that directly.'

'We have already,' he said unexpectedly. 'He vouched for you.'

'That's nice.'

'He also said he hadn't believed much of the story you told at the inquest.'

I regarded him with a limpid gaze. 'That saddens me,' I said. 'It really does. Or are you just saying that because you're jealous of our friendship?'

Monroe stubbed out his cigarette impatiently. 'Is there anything you haven't told us about the death of Linda Fillman that you feel like sharing with us?' He lit another cigarette at once. 'Who do you think did it, for a start?'

'I'll tell you who I don't think did it,' I said. 'Derek. Her boyfriend.'

He raised his eyebrows. 'You're not the first person to say that.'

'I wish I hadn't now. I hate being unoriginal.'

'Why don't you think Mr Brewster killed her?'

'You mean Derek, I take it?'

He stared at me in astonishment. 'Don't any of you people know each other's surnames?' he asked.

'We all went to public school,' I explained. 'It puts you off that kind of thing for life. Derek was called "Brewster Minor" for years at prep school. Can you imagine the psychological damage that caused? The mental scars never really fade, you know.'

Hawkins, to my right, was grinning. Monroe cast me a look in which scepticism was mingled with profound disapproval.

'But, getting back to the fundamentals, you want to know why I don't think he killed Linda. That's Ms Fillman,' I said helpfully. 'I know that one. Do I get a gold star? Anyway, the answer's simple. Derek wouldn't hurt a fly. It's not in his nature. If he wasn't getting along with Linda, he'd just leave her. Why not? He's already left a girlfriend who he had a kid with.'

'You can't deny that he is the most likely suspect by a long way, Ms Jones. He would have been able to go into the men's gym and remove a weight without Mr . . .' He was about to say Brian's surname but cut himself short. '. . . Without being noticed. The only other person who was observed entering either one of the gyms was the victim, and we're not exactly entertaining the theory that she committed suicide.'

I love police sarcasm; it's so blunt. Like being hit over the head with a piece of wood.

'There were some weights in the office,' I pointed out.

'Mr . . . Jeff Roberts says that no one removed any of them. And since no one knows how many there were in the first place, we have no way of checking that out.'

'There were about two or three,' I said. 'And – without prejudice – if Jeff did it himself that's only what you'd expect him to say.'

'Oh, so that's what you think?' he said quickly.

I shook my head. 'Just indicating the obvious.'

'What about Naomi Fisher? You say in your statement – hold on a moment – that she "was in a hurry and seemed preoccupied". Do you want to add anything to that?'

This was coming at me thick and fast.

'She looked,' I said slowly, 'angry about something. Worked up.'

'And what might she have been angry about?'

'I couldn't say. I don't know her.'

113

'But you know Derek Brewster, enough to testify as to his character.'

'Yes.'

'He has the reputation for being a ladies' man, isn't that so, Ms Jones? The resident stud at the gym?'

He looked at me so sharply I wondered if he thought that I myself had had a fling with Derek.

'Derek and the girls have a mutual admiration society going,' I agreed, leaning back in my chair. There was no point denying it.

'And was Naomi Fisher one of his conquests?'

'I really don't know.'

'Because she's given us to understand that she spent the best part of half an hour downstairs searching for an earring she thought she had lost. Since – um – Felicity Brady says Fisher definitely did not enter the ladies' gym, that seems a very long time to spend looking for an earring, wouldn't you say?'

'Particularly,' Hawkins added, 'as when asked she was completely unable to describe what the earring looked like.'

'That must be why she spent so long looking for it,' I said flippantly. 'No, OK. Sorry. Well, what do you two think she was doing all that time? Murdering Linda? With what motive? And with what, come to think of it? Where would she get the weight from?'

'We think,' said Inspector Monroe, fixing me with a look, 'that she was pursuing Derek Brewster. Or that she had arranged to meet him.'

'You can rule that last one out. I don't think Derek's exhibitionistic enough to relish the thought of being caught by his girlfriend in the middle of a romantic assignation with Naomi in the men's changing rooms.'

'Why the men's changing rooms?' said Hawkins, picking up on that one fast.

I turned to look at him with wide eyes. 'Where else?' I said, recrossing my legs. The leather of my jeans squeaked. I made a note to watch my step with Hawkins; he didn't miss a trick. Monroe ripped open the plastic on a new pack of cigarettes.

'Detective Inspector Fincham,' he said in measured tones, 'gave me to understand that the first time he met you was shortly after a friend of yours had died and you were convinced that there was more to it than met the eye. A few weeks later you were . . . let's say *involved* . . . in another death. Inspector Fincham thinks that the deaths were connected in some way. In other words, that the second death was a sort of revenge, you might say if you were speaking melodramatically, for the first.'

'He should stop watching *Poirot Investigates* on TV. All those little grey cells. It's making him over-imaginative.'

'Maybe.' DI Monroe stared hard at me, the regulation hard police stare they all copy from American TV programmes. It lasted quite a while. Then he said: 'You can go now, Ms Jones.'

'Roger.' I saluted. Then I hoped that didn't happen to be his first name. I wouldn't want him to think I was being familiar. I turned to Hawkins. 'Do I get my lift home now, then?'

* * *

It was the first time I had ever sat in the front of a police car. I fiddled with all the buttons in an attempt to annoy Sergeant Hawkins but he pretended not to notice, and finally I gave up. We drove back to the studio in relative silence which, out of boredom, I broke myself.

'I thought you offered to drive me so you could take me off guard and pick my brains,' I said. 'Or are you applying for a chauffeur's licence and getting in some practice on the side?'

He didn't take his eyes off the road. 'The former,' he said.

'Well, hadn't you better get on with lulling me into a false sense of security? We're nearly there.'

He grinned. 'You realise your alibi depends to a large part on the testimony of Jeff Roberts?' he said unexpectedly.

I shrugged. 'So what? I know I didn't do it and I think you do too. What was my motive?'

'Jealousy on Derek Brewster's account? It seems the most popular one at the moment for the female suspects,' he suggested.

'You guys may have a slightly exaggerated idea of Derek's horizontal capacities,' I said drily.

'Are you speaking from personal experience, Ms Jones?'

'It's Sam, and don't be vulgar.'

We had pulled up outside my studio. Hawkins slid the gear

lever into neutral and put on the handbrake without turning off the engine. He turned to face me, clearly about to say something.

'Yes, I've been waiting for this moment,' I said cordially. 'Don't think I don't realise that detective inspectors aren't usually that matey with their suspects. Let me guess the procedure: you turn up unexpectedly and ask me in for questioning, hoping to give me a scare. But Monroe goes surprisingly easy on me, to soften me up, and then you drive me home in order to volunteer some friendly advice about not keeping back information from the police, because it could be dangerous for me. In the hope, of course, that I'll go all feminine and helpless and tell you everything I know. Right?'

Hawkins's expression didn't change. I gave him points for cool. 'Inspector Fincham,' he said, 'told Inspector Monroe that if a mysterious death happened in your vicinity, it would be impossible to stop you sticking your nose into it. If you hadn't caused it yourself, of course. He said you were as tenacious as a bulldog.'

'*What* an attractive image. A bulldog with a big nose.'

'And that if we got your back up you would go out of your way to be unhelpful. So, yes, you could say this is the softly-softly approach.' He looked me straight in the eye. 'You're not complaining about that, I assume? Would you really have preferred us to have given you a hard time?' He had turned that round rather nicely, I noted. Not that I was going to let him get away with it.

'So if I turn up any information,' I suggested in dulcet tones, 'I should come running to you with it shoved in my mouth and my tail wagging happily?'

Hawkins gave me a look. 'Sounds interesting. Particularly the latter part.'

'Oh, *please*.' I unfastened my seat belt. 'Is that it, innuendos apart? Hadn't you planned a subtle cross-examination while I was off my guard?'

'It's not a game. Someone killed Linda Fillman,' he said, ignoring this, his blue eyes serious. He had a nice mouth too, I noticed, a straight line that looked as if it could soften when it wanted to.

'I know that!' I snapped. 'I just hope that you're keeping your minds open as to who it was.'

'If you really are worried that we'll think it was Derek Brewster, you should give us any information you can which might help.'

'With my tail wagging. I'll keep it in mind.'

I got out of the car and shut the door behind me, expecting to hear the car move off. Instead his door slammed too. He moved fast; he was standing next to me almost before I had my keys out.

'Your clothes,' he said, handing me a plastic bag.

'Thanks,' I said ungraciously, taking it from him. He was standing so close the blouson jacket was nearly touching me. I looked up into his eyes.

'If you're trying to work out what perfume I'm wearing, it's Fidji.' I pushed my hair behind my shoulders and tilted my head to one side, offering him a stretch of bare neck, still keeping my eyes on his. I was hoping he would blush. He didn't.

'I *have* been carrying your clothes around for a couple of days,' he said. 'Sam.'

As an exit line, it wasn't bad.

* * *

The Chalk Farm Gym and Leisure Centre had now been allowed to reopen and I duly went along the next day. I couldn't say the atmosphere had improved markedly since the last time I had entered it. Distinctly subdued would have been an overstatement. I had wanted a word with Lou, who now bore the lofty title of acting manager, but she was in what till recently had been Linda's office and the door was closed.

'She's in there with a reporter from the local newspaper,' Lesley said, sitting in the reception cubicle. 'She asked me to cover for her.'

I turned to look at Lesley. She looked inappropriately perky: her short fair hair was moussed into a halo and her big blue eyes contributed to the misleadingly angelic effect. Her bright yellow catsuit and the tangerine cotton cardigan she was wearing over it, knotted at the waist, made me squint on reflex.

'Don't you have any darker clothes, Lesley?' I said fretfully.

She shook her head, the halo bouncing like a hairspray advertisement.

'Not since I had my colours done. I'm Spring to Summer.'

I eyed her rather wistfully. As DS Hawkins had pointed out so acutely, someone had killed Linda, and I would have loved the culprit to have been Lesley. But somehow I couldn't see her sneaking past Jeff and Lou, to say nothing of myself, without attracting even a passing glance – even if she had been wearing a less neon-bright outfit than usual. And that would argue premeditation. I wasn't sure if Lesley's brain was up to that.

'Lesley, where were you the afternoon that Linda was killed?' I asked her without preamble. Not much point beating around the bush with her.

She widened her eyes to celestial blue saucers. 'Shopping. And then I went home.'

'Were you with anyone?'

'No. Does it matter?'

I shrugged. 'The police will probably want to know where everyone was that afternoon. I mean, everyone who had a motive to kill Linda. Have they questioned you yet?'

Lesley nodded. 'They asked me all about that quarrel we had. You know, the man from Music Performance thingy who fined me, and it was Linda who gave them my name?'

'Yes, I remember, Lesley,' I said patiently.

'They went on and on about it.' She pouted. 'I had to ask the one who was asking the questions not to smoke. It was making me feel sick.'

'Did he stop?' I imagined the look Inspector Monroe must have given her.

'Yes, though he didn't look very happy about it. But I wasn't there when Linda was killed, so what can they do? They weren't very happy about that, either.'

'I take it they found out why Linda set the Music Performance people onto you.'

'What do you mean? Oh, I see. Yes. They asked me a lot of questions about Derek, like did any other girls in the gym like him. I said, yes, everyone! Then they said did he like anyone, and I said me. And they said they bet Linda didn't like that very much. So I said, well, that's her hard luck, isn't it? It's silly to say I would have killed her for that. I mean, he could always have left her.'

I leant against the door of the cubicle. 'He'd been with Linda for years, though. He left his last girlfriend and their baby for her.

Everyone knew he had plenty of flings, but to get him to leave Linda might have been another matter.'

I wasn't worried about the wisdom of asking Lesley so many direct questions. Her favourite occupation might be watching herself in the mirror while working out, but talking about herself ran a close second.

She didn't answer for a moment. Then she said, rather reluctantly: 'It was really silly, making such a fuss about it. I mean, it wasn't a matter of life and death, was it?'

'It was to someone.'

'Ugh.' She shuddered. 'Mum and Dad want me to leave here after what's happened. I said no way. I mean, there'll be more opportunities here now, won't there, with Linda gone? I've already filled in for a couple of her classes.'

I stared at her, lost for words.

'Rachel's doing the more advanced ones, though,' she added. 'She can have those as far as I'm concerned. The people who come are so serious. I like my classes to be fun.'

By now I had regained the power of speech. I never lose it for long. I asked: 'Did you tell Derek what Linda had done? Reporting you, I mean?'

'What?' She frowned.

'When we were talking downstairs in the changing rooms you said you were going to tell Derek.'

'Oh yes, I told him and he was really nice. I just said what had happened and he said not to worry about it, because he'd talk to her. So I didn't actually have to complain directly about Linda. I thought that was clever.'

'So did he talk to her?'

'Derek said he had. But she was just as snotty to me as ever the day after. He told me he'd got her to agree to keep out of my way, but she was bitching at me like she always did. So finally I told her where to get off. Frustrated old cow.'

'Yes, I heard you two had a quarrel in her office.'

'She was such a bitch! She just sat there and looked at me with her eyebrows raised! I said Derek had told her not to bother me any longer and I'd be grateful if she'd do what she'd agreed instead of making personal remarks to my face.'

'What did Linda say?'

'She said I should try using my brains for a change . . . Can you believe that! So I said I certainly hadn't agreed to keep out of *her* way, and as far as I was concerned if she tried something like that on me again, I'd know what to do about it.'

'What did you mean by that?'

Lesley didn't bat an eyelid. She said sweetly: 'Take Derek away from her. Show her up in front of everyone.'

'But you were going to do that anyway,' I pointed out. 'Surely you must have had something else in mind?'

She looked confused. At that moment, however, the office door opened and a bulky man in an ill-fitting grey suit emerged ponderously into the reception area. If I hadn't known already that he was a reporter I would have assumed he was a policeman. Lou stood in the doorway behind him.

'Off you go now,' she said, practically shooing him out of the door with flaps of her hands. 'You got what you came for.'

'Perhaps just a word with this lady here—' he said hopefully in my direction.

Lou cut him short. 'She don't know nothin'. Off you go.'

Reluctantly he made his way through the swing doors. Lou slapped her palms against each other in a gesture of dismissal.

'That was a pushy one,' she said. 'Give him an inch and he'd take a mile.'

She looked from Lesley to me. 'Hope I'm not interrupting.'

I shook my head. 'Just talking over the only topic of conversation round here at the moment.'

'I'm tryin' so hard not to think about it I'm givin' myself a headache,' Lou said.

'Do you want an aspirin?' Lesley asked brightly. We both turned to look at her for a moment in silence. Lou said to me suddenly: 'Come for a walk outside? I'll get my coat.'

She ducked into the office and emerged with a creation in dark brown fake fur which flared out from the padded shoulders and kept on going. It must have been metres wide by the time it reached the hem. On Lou it worked; on me it would have looked like a walking teepee.

The sun wasn't actually visible through the clouds, but it had lightened the sky to a pale blue-white, which was better than grey. Lou and I passed the tube station and crossed over to the railway bridge which led to Primrose Hill. There used to be a little branch station there but they closed it to make the line easier to privatise. Don't let anyone tell you the Tories have softened now that Thatcher's gone.

By the time we had reached the bridge, I'd given Lou a brief resumé of my conversations with Fliss and Cath.

'*Something* happened,' Lou said slowly, echoing what Cath had said to me about Derek and Naomi. 'And suppose Linda caught them at it? Calls Naomi all the nasty names she can think of till Naomi hits her to shut her up?'

The sun was out now. It didn't help much.

'There's still the problem of the weight to get round,' I pointed out. 'But Derek might have had it with him, taken it out of one of the gyms to repair or something. Then Naomi picked it up and hit Linda with it, and Derek didn't want to say anything because he felt responsible. Is that possible? Would he be that chivalrous? You know him better than I do.'

Lou was thinking it over. Reluctantly she said at last: 'He can be very protective of his girls. And he'd feel it was his fault if Linda had caught them at it. He'd probably keep his mouth shut and tell the police nothin' they didn't already know.'

'Someone should talk to him. Tell him that he shouldn't hide anything from the police. They questioned me again yesterday and I have to say they didn't seem particularly stupid. Or racist. Though you can never tell. But they'll know if someone's keeping information from them and if Derek is, that will make them as suspicious as hell.'

Two kids passed us on beaten-up old skateboards, going at full lick. I thought those were unfashionable now, but maybe they'd already made a comeback. Things seemed to be going faster and faster nowadays. Like the skateboards. The kids shot round the corner of the bridge and disappeared onto the road. No squeal of brakes or honking resulted. I was selfishly relieved; I'd seen enough corpses to last me a while.

I looked at Lou. She was hugging her coat around her.

'Could you tell him?' I said. 'Give him a kick up the arse? He'd listen to you.'

We were walking towards Primrose Hill. On my right was a wine merchant's called Bibendum, which I thought meant 'needing to be drunk'. I knew how it felt.

'Lou?' I said. She had stopped in her tracks. Then I saw where she was looking, straight ahead; Derek was walking down the street towards us.

'Talk of the devil,' she said.

12

For a few seconds Derek didn't recognise us, but as he was looking like the 'Before' part of an advertisement for stress relief ('Tense? Nervous? Under Pressure?'), that wasn't surprising. The sight of me and Lou did not seem to relieve his mood. He muttered a greeting and would have walked past us if Lou had let him. Which she didn't.

'I want a word with you,' she said. 'And now's as good a time as any. Come back here.'

She turned on her heel and walked over to the pub on the corner of the road, outside which were a few wooden tables with benches attached. No one was sitting outside with the weather this fitful; we had the place to ourselves. Lou arranged her coat carefully so that she sat on it rather than the bench. Derek hovered reluctantly a few paces away.

'You all right there, Sam?' he said to me as I propped myself on the edge of the table. 'The wood's a bit damp.'

'This ain't the moment for good manners,' Lou said impatiently. 'Sit yourself down and listen to what I've got to say.'

He had no choice. Lou was fixing him with a glare, her earrings jingling inside the fur collar of her coat. Inspector Monroe could have taken staring lessons from her. Derek didn't quail but he sat up straighter than I'd ever seen him and paid attention, neither of which, I was sure, he did for Monroe. I remembered that Lou had four sons. I bet they didn't stray off the straight and narrow too often.

'Have you told the police everythin' you know about what

went on down there when Linda was killed?' she said straight out.

'I—'

'Because if so, I've got nothin' more to say. But if you ain't, you could be in a lot of trouble. Did Linda catch you with that girl Naomi?'

Derek shot an uneasy glance in my direction.

'Don't you worry about Sam,' Lou said. 'You just tell me what I asked.'

Derek shifted on the bench. All his normal ease of manner was gone. Lou had turned him into a twelve-year-old who had just been caught by his mother smoking in his bedroom.

He shoved his hands in his pockets and looked down at his lap. A gust of wind scurried up the street, lifting my hair and putting it down again with unflattering alacrity. OK, so it needed a wash.

'I don't know what you're talking about,' Derek said unconvincingly.

'Don't get clever with me, Derek. We know you and Naomi weren't discussin' the weather.'

'OK.' He shrugged. 'We were getting friendly. So what? And Linda didn't see us.'

'Where were you? In the men's changing rooms?'

'Yeah.'

'How far did it go?'

Derek being the glossy colour of a coffee bean, it was impossible to tell whether he was blushing or not. He cleared his throat noisily. 'Come on, Lou, you're not my mum—'

'And lucky for you I'm not,' Lou snapped back. 'Far enough for Linda to take objection to, then?'

'I tell you, she never came in,' Derek insisted. 'I didn't see her.'

Lou eyed him suspiciously. 'So what happened then?'

A train rattled noisily under the bridge. I hoped it wouldn't distract them. Personally, I was so embarrassed at being present that I was keeping my mouth firmly shut and trying as far as possible to blend into the background. Since I was wearing my violet jacket, which was a touch conspicuous, it wasn't that easy, but I kept my face blank and my eyes directed at the pub frontage, hoping that when Derek glanced at me, as he did from time to time, he would think that I had lost interest in the conversation and was attempting to finish the *Guardian* crossword in my head.

'Nothing,' Derek said rather sullenly. I was seeing a whole new side to him. His cool self-possession was melting in the nuclear sun of Lou's stare. It's not easy being hauled in front of your parents, at whatever age. Mine are dead and I hardly remember them. That's why I'm so cocky: I know I'm safe.

I shot a glance at Lou, but she was already waving one finger at him in an admonishing gesture.

'Derek Brewster, don't you lie to me. That Naomi came tearin' upstairs in a temper and nearly knocked Sam down. Don't you tell me nothin' happened.'

'She was pissed off,' Derek admitted. 'But I didn't promise her anything. I never do.' He ran one hand over the top of his head, ruffling the short curls. 'I thought she understood! I mean, she knew I'm – I was – with Linda! What did she expect?'

'You mean she felt used?'

Derek sat up, folding his arms. 'Look,' he said, 'I don't use anyone. I show everyone respect. I don't call a girl names because she goes to bed with me, OK? The opposite, in fact. Still, I don't promise anything either. I thought Naomi knew the score. I'd have said something if I thought she didn't. Not that she gave me a chance.'

'You mean she came after you?' Lou said.

Derek directed a scathing glance at her.

'You really think I took her into the men's changing rooms for a quickie, knowing Linda was downstairs already? Give me some credit, Lou. I'm not boasting, OK? I don't like talking about this stuff – it's between me and the lady in question. Personal business. But give me credit for not being that stupid. She followed me in there. I'm not saying any more than that.'

'And what?' Lou wasn't giving up. 'You thanked her, told her nicely that it didn't mean nothin', and she took offence?'

'More or less.' Derek was looking uncomfortable again, but he wasn't going into further detail. 'She called me plenty of names and slammed the door behind her.'

'Which direction did she go in?' I said, unable to help asking.

'I didn't see.'

'The door's got a window in it.'

'Yeah, but it's not clear glass – it's got those little bubbles in it.

You can hardly see anything, not unless you press your face right up against the glass. Anyway, I wasn't looking after her. I went to have a shower. Again.'

'Do you think she killed Linda, Derek?' Lou asked, looking him straight in the eyes.

'Why would she do that?'

'Jealous about you. It's as good a motive as any.'

Derek looked deeply, profoundly embarrassed. He ducked his head and stared at his lap for a moment, perhaps in order to contemplate directly the cause of all the trouble, now somnolent in his sports briefs and feigning innocence. Two young men came out of the pub, arguing, and passed our table.

'How *can* you prefer Altman to Tarkovsky?' one of them was saying in impassioned tones.

'I didn't say that,' the other one said angrily. '*I* don't make that kind of facile judgement— '

Bloody students. The voices died away down the street. I glanced over at Lou. She was implacable.

'What's it to be?' she repeated.

Derek looked up finally. 'No. No, I don't think it was Naomi, OK?'

There was something in his voice that hit a false note. We both heard it.

'Then who do you think it was?'

'I don't know.'

He stood up, levering his legs away from the table.

'Have you told the police about what you and Naomi were doing?'

'You think I'm crazy?' Derek said incredulously. 'Something like that's exactly what they want to hear. They'd say I killed Linda myself because she caught me with another woman. They'd love to arrest me for it, don't you know that, Lou? Black guy and a white girl. Just the kind of thing the police go for.'

Lou looked worried. The balance of power had shifted for the first time. Now she was a mother who knew that her son was about to do something dangerous and didn't have the power to stop him.

'If you don't tell them, they'll know you're hidin' somethin'—'

'Let them. I didn't kill Linda and they can't say I did. All I have to do is keep my mouth shut. There's no proof against me.'

He gave Lou a long compassionate look.

'I know you're trying to help, Lou, and thanks. But believe me – I know what I'm doing.'

Derek glanced at me. Our eyes met and held for a moment. There was challenge in his stare, and something else I recognised. Then he was gone, walking swiftly away. I noticed he wasn't heading in the direction of the gym.

'Shit!' Lou said with such force that my eyes snapped back to her on reflex. Her face was furious. She swivelled off the bench and stood up in one swift angry gesture.

'Lou?' I said nervously.

'Damn that boy! I *know* there's somethin' he ain't saying! Shit, I should have slapped his face! That'd teach him to lie to me!' She stamped her foot. Her voice was raised; people on the other side of the road were looking over at her. 'If I get my hands on him, so help me God I will next time. Playing the innocent like that when there's a woman been killed, not that *she* was worth all this fuss. I'd talk to his mother but she ain't never been able to make Derek do something he don't want to do, more fool her. He needed a couple of good hidings when he was little. When my boys earned one, they got one, and it didn't do them any harm, I can tell you!'

'Lou?' I said again. 'Shouldn't we be getting back?'

She took a deep breath.

'I'm sorry, Sam. It just gets me so worked up when I see these boys messin' around with the police, like it's all a game to them—'

Lou and I started walking back the way we'd come. The wind had gathered force and was whipping across the bridge; we instinctively leaned in the same direction to balance ourselves. I didn't know what to say, having never seen Lou in this state before. It had taken me aback. I had always thought she was a monument of calm; it was as if a statue had just abandoned its pose to give a pigeon a good kicking.

In an attempt to distract her I said:

'Look, Lou, forget Derek for a bit. You should be worrying on your own account.'

'What are you talkin' about?'

I summoned up a grin. 'You're as happy as a pig in clover in the gym – it suits you down to the ground being the manager. You'd better watch out that no one accuses you of killing Linda so you could step into her shoes.'

Lou didn't say another word to me on the walk back. It was almost as if she hadn't found my suggestion particularly amusing.

* * *

I wanted to talk to Rachel, but she was teaching and her class didn't finish for another fifteen minutes, so I strolled downstairs to see if I could bump into Brian or Naomi accidentally on purpose. Naomi wasn't around, however, and when I wandered into the men's gym, Brian, though present in the physical sense, was performing bench presses with such total concentration that I could have lain down on the leg-curl bench and done a vigorous imitation of Madonna miming self-abuse while singing 'Like a Virgin' without even causing his eyelids to flicker in my direction.

I hung around for a while, having nothing else to do. No one minded people hanging out in the men's gym, whatever sex they might happen to be. Most of the men welcomed the attention, being terrible peacocks, and the few tail-free males wouldn't have the nerve to tell you in front of the preeners that your stare was putting them off their stride. It was the opposite in the women's gym, where the atmosphere was one of conviviality and mutual interest – unless your chromosomes were XY, in which case you would be badly scorched by hostile stares from several pairs of female eyes as soon as you crossed the threshold. Derek was the only man who dared to enter, and even he didn't hang around for long.

I amused myself for a while by awarding each of the bottoms present – pertly displayed in a variety of shiny shorts and leggings – marks on a scale of one to ten. Then I graded their owners in order of desirability. Mr Best Bum only came fourth, thus proving that rears are not enough. When I had exhausted the opportunities for spectator sport I left. Brian was still doing bench presses. He didn't seem to have stopped the whole time I was there.

I checked the clock in the downstairs corridor. Rachel's class should have finished ten minutes ago. I went upstairs, but as I approached the double doors to the gym, I couldn't help hearing Rachel, still inside, shouting at someone. I had never heard her even raise her voice before, but it was definitely Rachel and she was bawling out the unfortunate victim with conviction. I paused outside, wondering what to do; I couldn't make out what she was saying, and I was just about to go back downstairs when one of the doors swung open and Jeff slunk out, wearing a very sheepish expression. He started visibly on seeing me, as if I'd caught him out in some nameless crime.

'You OK, Jeff?' I said curiously.

'Oh, yeah, fine . . .' He was looking paler and skinnier than ever, sunk into his ubiquitous donkey jacket, shoulders hunched forward. His light brown hair looked as if it had been cut with a pair of nail scissors while wet and left to dry. The hollows under his cheeks were cavernous, and his skin in general was even spottier than usual. He clearly needed to eat more fresh vegetables. I had the vague idea that he was a vegan; he probably lived entirely on Vegemite sandwiches, made with soya margarine, and reconstituted beanburgers.

He looked as if he were about to speak; then, muttering something I couldn't catch, he brushed past me and out through the main door. I stared after him in surprise. People certainly were behaving oddly these past few days.

Rachel was by the pile of mats, stacking them up after her class. She had one in her hands, and from the expression on her face she would have hit Jeff over the head with it if it had been made of a sturdier material than plastic and padding.

'What's with Jeff?' I said. 'He just gave me the weirdest look and practically ran out of the gym.'

She looked tired; there were dark shadows under her almond-shaped eyes, though, being Rachel's, they didn't detract from her beauty but made her look perversely sexy instead. Still, her movements were slower, wearier than usual. This could be attributed to having just put thirty super-fit athletes through a punishing bout of circuit training. But Rachel could usually do that kind of thing on Mogadon.

'He's been boring me to death about his petition,' she said exhaustedly. 'I just haven't got the time to think about it at the moment. Finally I just lost my rag and told him to fuck off and stop pestering me. I shouldn't have done it, but he was *so* annoying . . .'

Her voice tailed off. She seemed to have forgotten that she was still holding the mat. I stared at her, surprised.

'But surely, now Linda's dead,' I pointed out, 'the whole issue can't be so important? I mean, she was the only one pushing for privatisation.'

Rachel shook her head. 'He's got some idea that he wants to safeguard the gym against the possibility of it ever happening again – he wants to get up a petition to confirm that it'll always be council run, or something like that. As if we all haven't got other things to think about.'

'You look pretty tired,' I observed.

For a moment she looked at me in silence. Then she let the last mat fall on to the pile with a dull smack. 'No, I'm fine. It's just stressful working such a busy schedule. I'm taking almost all Linda's classes as well as my own, and I'm giving Lou a hand with the management work. There are a lot of practical things she doesn't know about. I haven't had much time to myself recently.'

'It must be a bore, all the admin,' I said. 'I hate sitting behind a desk.'

'Oh no, I don't mind it. I used to work part-time as a secretary for a printing firm and I organised them all. It was fun. No, it's just everything together that's getting me down. I need a lot of sleep in a darkened room.'

'We just talked to Derek,' I offered. 'Or rather, Lou did. I just sat there and tried not to put her off.'

'What did he say?' she asked quickly.

I gave her a brief summary of the conversation, including our doubts at the end. She looked concerned.

'You mean you think he knows it was Naomi?'

'I don't know,' I said slowly. 'Perhaps. But there's definitely something he's not telling. And if we knew that, the police certainly will.'

'Shit.' She looked hard at me. 'Do you know what it is?'

'I haven't the faintest idea.'

She let out her breath. 'That doesn't help much,' she said finally. 'Sorry, Sam, didn't mean to criticise you.'

She put her arm around my shoulders and we walked towards the door.

'I want to talk to Brian,' I said, 'but I don't know how to go about it.'

Rachel laughed. 'Who does?'

'He's working out right now but there's no way I can distract him from his machines.'

'Mmm,' she said. 'No, I agree – in the gym's going to be difficult. What about outside? Catch him off guard?'

'Like where?'

Rachel snapped her fingers. 'Go to one of the raves where he works. That way you can make it look accidental.'

'Brilliant idea,' I said respectfully. 'Now all I have to do is go round all the warehouses in London till I find Brian standing outside one of them dressed as a penguin.'

'Prat.' She cuffed the back of my head lightly. 'He always puts the flyers up on the noticeboard. Let's go and have a look.'

'No one likes a smart-arse, you know, Rachel,' I said reprovingly. 'You'll get your head kicked in at lunch break.'

We wandered out into reception and over to the noticeboard. Sure enough, in one corner was pinned a flyer, printed with psychedelic swirls of orange and yellow, advertising a rave that evening. It was called 'Paradisiac' and was to be held at a club in Lambeth.

'Shit,' I said. 'South of the river.'

'Only barely,' Rachel pointed out. 'And you've got your van.'

'Which means I can hardly drink or take any drugs. Everyone else will be off their face. I hate being the odd one out.'

'You're not going just to indulge yourself,' Rachel said severely, 'but for investigative purposes.'

We were speaking quietly but I glanced around to make sure no one heard. Lesley was still sitting in the reception cubicle, but she was engrossed in a copy of *Hello!*, doubtless picking up life tips from Mandy Smith.

'Why don't you come too?' I suggested. 'It'll do you good. Go home now, pass out for a while, and I'll pick you up at eleven.'

I thought she was going to refuse. Then she shrugged. Behind us I heard the main door swinging open. 'Yes, why not? It'd get me out of the house.'

'How gracious,' I said sweetly.

Upraised voices made us both swing round to see what the trouble was. As soon as I saw that the person who'd just come in was Naomi, my ears pricked up. She was leaning forward into the cubicle, both hands pressed on the ledge in front of her, shouting at Lesley: 'Just tell me if he's around, OK? I don't need you to tell me my business.'

Lesley was standing up, hands on hips. 'He isn't, actually,' she said sharply. 'And don't talk to me like that.'

'You're lying!' Naomi said furiously. 'I bet you want him for yourself, you skinny bitch!'

Lesley looked down her nose. She was considerably taller than Naomi, which added to the effectiveness of the gesture. 'Anyone would look skinny next to *you*,' she said. I was impressed. I hadn't expected even an attempt at basic repartee from Lesley. But Naomi didn't look a whit abashed. 'You don't know the first thing about what men like, do ya?' she retorted. 'I'm glad my arse isn't as flat as a board!'

'I know they don't like sluts!' Lesley said, descending rapidly to vulgar abuse.

'You fucking bitch— '

'Cat fight!' I said to Rachel eagerly.

Naomi had sprung round the corner of the cubicle towards the door, presumably to drag Lesley out by the hair and give her a good pummelling. Unfortunately, at this moment the door of the office swung open and Lou appeared regally on the threshold, her full-length purple embroidered cardigan and turquoise turban giving her the air of an Eastern potentate. Her mere presence was enough to freeze both participants into momentary stillness. Lesley had picked up a file box from the desk, obviously meaning to hit Naomi over the head with it, and now stood with the box poised in her hands, looking rather silly.

'What the hell,' Lou demanded, 'is goin' on out here?'

'She started it!' Lesley said at once.

'Tattletale,' I muttered to Rachel.

'She asked where Derek was and when I said he wasn't here she started swearing at me— '

'You bloody liar,' said Naomi, confirming, at least partially, the truth of this statement. She pointed a stubby finger at Lesley in a distinctly menacing fashion. 'I won't forget this, you hear? I'll get you!'

Turning on her heel, she stamped out of the gym. I wasted no time. Swinging my rucksack over my shoulder I said to Rachel: 'See you at eleven, OK?', waved at Lou and was out of the door in a flash.

13

Naomi was stumping down the street towards the main road, shoulders hunched in anger. She was wearing a bulky silk parka, gathered in at the waist, baggy jeans and trainers: basic home girl wear this year. Her hair was pulled up on top of her head and held there by a large gold plastic clip. I caught up with her at the corner.

'I couldn't help hearing what you were saying back there,' I remarked ingratiatingly. 'Lesley can be a real bitch, can't she?'

She turned her head to look at me and said in a hostile tone: 'What do you know about it?'

I shrugged. 'She pisses me off too. She pisses everyone off.'

'Fuck her.' Naomi kept walking, looking straight ahead. I hoped this wasn't her last word on the subject.

'I met a friend of yours at the market the other day,' I said, trying another line of attack. 'Cath. She was really nice.'

Naomi slowed her pace slightly. 'Yeah, Cath's OK,' she said. Coming from Naomi this was probably high praise. 'She's a mate of mine, you know?'

Her voice sounded slightly more normal. While I was racking my brains for something to ask that she wouldn't consider too intrusive, she said: 'She's after him, isn't she? That bitch.'

'You mean Derek?' I said.

'Who the fuck do you think I mean?' Naomi wasn't yet recovered from her bout of ill-temper. I let it pass for the moment but I chalked it up against her.

'Yes, she is. I think she's hoping that with Linda dead she can step into her shoes.'

I was watching Naomi closely but she didn't flinch at the mention of Linda's name.

'Fuck her,' she said again, with her usual elegance of expression. 'She's got it coming.'

'Like Linda, you mean?' I said daringly. But we were walking down Camden High Street on Saturday afternoon, towards the busy part, and there were no hand weights in the vicinity. I thought I was comparatively safe. Naomi stopped dead and glared at me.

'I didn't have nothing to do with that, OK?'

'I heard she caught you and Derek in the men's changing rooms,' I said, thinking I had nothing left to lose. Her eyes narrowed into dark slits and she shoved her head forward aggressively. 'That's not true. And he's a bastard,' she added. 'I came in to give him a piece of my mind.'

The pavement wasn't as crowded as it would be further towards the market, where you had to weave your way slowly through the hordes of people. But pedestrians still pushed past us impatiently. Anyone catching Naomi's eye, however, was silenced at once. She looked as menacing as a premenstrual pit bull and rather less attractive.

'He can't treat me like that and get away with it,' she said.

'Like what?'

'Not showing me respect,' she said at once. 'Treating me like some cheap tart, like that Lesley. Stupid cow. I'll show her. If she thinks she can just have him like that, she can think again. You tell her so.'

She turned on her heel and walked off, looking neither to left nor right. People veered hastily out of the way of her rolling shoulders. I stared after her thoughtfully, wondering whether her rather direct manner of courtship might not be as successful as any with Derek.

Obviously, despite her complaints, she still wanted him. And although incurably promiscuous, Derek tended to let the girls make the running. I doubted that he'd ever chased anyone in his life; he didn't need to. From what I'd heard, Linda had taken him from his last girlfriend and kept him in the teeth of concerted attempts to entice him away. Maybe if Lesley and Naomi did battle it out, he'd go with the winner. The race is to the strong.

* * *

Rachel and I reached the club at about a quarter to midnight, early enough to make sure we could get in. It would go on till dawn, like all the clubs whose clientèle were on Ecstasy: having come up, they needed time to come down again safely before being expelled into the cold morning air. But these small one-off clubs like Paradisiac, whose names, circulated on the grapevine, were the height of fashion for a month or so, tended to fill up fast at the peak of their success; having gone so far as to cross the river, I didn't want to arrive only to find that we couldn't get in.

It was in a perfect location, under some railway arches just a couple of streets back from the Thames. I parked the van and stood for a moment leaning against it, savouring the night. Chains of orange lights were draped high along the embankment, glowing in the dark like the fluorescent jewellery people would be wearing in the club. The bridge over which we had come was lit up like a Christmas ornament; along it slid a constant stream of cars, whose engines, heard from a distance, murmured like the sound of moving water. At the entrance to the club someone laughed, the sound carrying in the near-silence, and if I listened carefully I could distinguish the regular reverberations of the bass line. It was a wonderful feeling to be out at midnight with the evening just beginning, knowing that most other people were already tucked up in bed or falling asleep in front of the television.

My head was as clear as the night air. At her flat, Rachel and I had done a line of speed apiece to perk us up; it would put us out of synch with everyone else, but we weren't here for the atmosphere. There was a line of people outside and we waited, stamping our feet to keep ourselves warm, as it moved up. It didn't take long, as this wasn't the kind of club with a door policy: tucked away in this location, it was for initiates only. They didn't have to worry about tourists or lager louts wandering by.

We saw Brian as we neared the head of the queue. I waved to him. He surprised me by raising a hand to us and saying: 'All right?' in quite a friendly way.

'We saw your flyer,' I said.

He nodded magisterially. 'It'll be a good one,' he said, or rather rumbled. 'Enjoy yourselves.'

I exchanged a brief look of amazement with Rachel. She had had the right idea about coming to find him here; he had already volunteered more words than I had ever heard him utter before. A couple of other bouncers were hanging around the door, trying to look menacing.

'Friends of yours?' one of them said to Brian. 'You're doing all right, aren't you?'

The other one sniggered. We had reached the door.

'Don't just stand about,' Brian said in bass tones to the sniggering one. 'Hold the door open for the ladies.'

Though large enough in his own right – he looked in fact as if he had been constructed of giant potatoes with an inexpertly peeled one for his head – the sniggerer obviously deferred to Brian. He dived for the handle immediately and swung open the door for us. We entered a small black-painted vestibule filled with another bouncer and a strung-out-looking boy in a tartan suit and cap who was pleading with him about something I couldn't catch.

'Friends of Brian,' called Potato-Head. A girl behind a glass panel took £7 off each of us. A sign saying '£10 Entrance, No Re-Admittance' was pasted over her head. I assumed that Friends of Brian got a discount. We passed through another black-painted door into the club itself. The bar was on the right and there were a couple of sofas and a few chairs grouped against the left wall in a desultory attempt at comfort. Most of the space was given over to the dance area; we had entered one of the railway arches and a door on our right gave on to another, with its own little bar and separate platform for the DJ. There were already a few exhibitionists dancing, but most people were saving their strength for later.

It had a Gothic atmosphere that made me feel at home at once. Everything was painted black, apart from the huge marble-effect pillars that flanked the way to the dance floor. Coloured lights played over the walls in a way that would be trippy if you were that way inclined, and most people were dressed in bright clothes that would reflect the lights and make their heads spin. Silver, gold and tartan were the favourites, though next to us at the bar was a group of girls with their hair in bunches, wearing cheap sequinned dresses. The most adventurous had on long white gloves and an ankle-length, halter-neck red sequinned number; her friends' legs were bare under their short A-line skirts, as was the fashion, but they were adorned with a coating of goose-pimples which I doubted was equally modish. The stone walls and floor were damp and unheated. As more people piled in the place would warm up, but until then the girls could have done with a pair of leg-warmers apiece.

Rachel ordered a couple of beers, each of which seemed to cost about as much as the entrance fee, and we hung out at the bar, watching the club fill up. There was no point trying to talk to Brian now: it was too early. People were still pouring in. We would have to give it a couple of hours or so, until both railway arches were full and all he had to do was stand around outside in case of trouble.

I had to admit that the music was more tuneful than usual. It's the repetition that normally kills me. If you're on E, the simplicity of the music and words seems terribly profound; but if you're on speed and want to throw yourself around and bounce off the walls, a song that consists entirely of some girl screaming 'Come With Me To Ecstasy' or 'I'm Coming Up On Love' hundreds of times – and always on the same notes – tends to set your teeth on edge. I consoled myself with the thought that I was broadening my horizons and keeping up with the latest trends.

The boy in the red and green tartan suit was next to us at the bar, ordering a bottle of orange juice. Turning his head he said to us: 'All right, girls. You sorted, or d'you need anything?'

We shook our heads in unison and he wandered off, swigging from his bottle, in search of other prospective customers. His cap was twisted round at a crazy angle and he had one of those bony, mobile, almost rubbery faces that look as if they're up to every trick in the book. Under his jacket his chest was bare; though goose-pimple-free, it was as thin and hairless as a piece of chewed string.

'Shall we go and dance?' said Rachel, putting down her empty glass. The girls with the bunches and sequins had placed them-selves in front of the main lights and were demonstrating how to dance to this kind of music, probably needing to warm up their bare flesh. Rays of light outlined their every movement; they were pretty good. And the atmosphere was, unlike any other club I'd ever been to, friendly with hardly a tinge of sexual charge. You didn't come here to pick someone up, but to go happily wild; these people weren't strangers but friends you didn't yet know. I was surprised how many people I had never seen before greeted me as I passed them. While finding this rather hippy-ish as a philosophy, I had to admit that it was nice to see people positively enjoying themselves. At the grungey clubs I preferred there seemed to be an unspoken requirement for the clubees to look, if not verging on the suicidal, at least clinically depressed.

Once I had started dancing I couldn't stop for some time, thanks to the speed; and Rachel, who actually liked this kind of music, was enjoying herself tremendously. A boy in a white shirt hanging open over silver trousers had caught her hands and was dancing with her, making patterns with their joined arms, and she was laughing with him. Sensing that I was looking at her, she turned her head and made a face at me, still laughing, her long black ponytail swinging from side to side, her movements smooth and supple.

Beside me was a podium, one of several scattered around the dance floor, on which the sequinned girls were dancing, making waving motions over the heads of the people below which looked particularly effective when performed by the girl in the white gloves. I made my way through the mêlée towards the exit and paused for a moment by one of the pillars, looking back at the dance floor. Rachel was still dancing with the boy in silver trousers and didn't seem to notice I had gone. I had no idea what time it was, but no new arrivals were coming through the doors. I bought a bottle of beer from the bar and strolled out into the vestibule, paying no attention to the sign that said 'No Re-Admittance'. I was a Friend of Brian, after all.

Brian and the bouncer who had been inside when we had first come in were standing at the far end of the entrance hall. The latter was saying: '. . . but he doesn't have to be so bleeding obvious about it, does he? Practically hung a sign round his neck saying "Get Your Drugs Here!" I mean, what's he expect?'

I assumed he was talking about the boy in the tartan suit.

'All right, Sam,' Brian said, catching sight of me. 'Having a good time?'

'Excellent.'

The other bouncer peeled off to go inside. With the opening of the door, a draught of cold air sliced through my T-shirt, but womanfully I ignored it. I offered Brian my bottle of beer.

'Want some?'

'No thanks. I don't drink.'

'Oh, right. Um.'

I hadn't thought out in advance what I was going to say to Brian, and now I was lost for words. Being talkative myself, I find strong, silent types a damn nuisance.

'I saw you working out today,' I offered at random.

Brian's only response was an ambiguous grunt. My heart sank. Another silence fell. I fidgeted with the bottle, consoling myself with the thought that although he might be bored – his face was so impassive it was impossible to tell – at least he was still standing here. His black bomber jacket was hanging open and his pectorals, which were roughly at my eye level, bulged out of it, a pair of hub caps snugly covered by a white T-shirt. Music was pounding constantly through the thin set of doors like the sea trying to break through a harbour wall.

'It's terrible, all this trouble at the gym, isn't it?' I said rather hopelessly.

Brian gave another grunt. I had made some progress, however; this one seemed to imply a positive response. If he could convey a 'no' as well, we were in business. I hadn't played Twenty Questions in years but I was ready to start. Then he said, as if making a tremendous effort: 'But it won't happen now.'

I didn't know what I had expected, but it wasn't this. 'What won't?' I said blankly.

He condescended to explain. 'I mean,' he said, 'now Linda's dead the gym won't go private.' His voice resounded up from the lowest recesses of his diaphragm in a manner that would have been applauded by any speech teacher.

'Oh, right. No, what I actually meant was about her being killed.'

Another grunt followed; this one was definitely dismissive. I waited for a moment but it seemed to be all Brian had to say on the matter.

'You were downstairs too, weren't you, when it happened? The police have already questioned me twice.' I put this in as a cunning ploy to show I was a suspect too.

'Yeah, I was working out. They took my clothes away for testing to see if there was any blood on them.'

'Oh yes? Mine too,' I said enthusiastically, hoping the experience would bond us together. 'Have you got yours back yet?'

'Yesterday. There wasn't anything on them. I told them so.'

'Mine neither. I mean, obviously.' I paused for a moment to contemplate the idiocy of this statement. 'Did the police give you a hard time?'

He raised his shoulders and let them fall again. His muscles were so heavy I could almost hear them clunk back into place. This seemed to be the only answer he considered necessary.

'I wonder who they think it was,' I said, trying to sound casual.

Brian rumbled up one word from his chest. 'Derek.'

'You mean they think it was Derek?' I said carefully.

He nodded.

'How do you know?'

'They asked me lots of times if he'd taken a weight from the gym. I said no but they didn't believe me.'

He seemed on the verge of saying something else, so I waited. A few moments passed and nothing emerged. Finally, just as I was about to open my mouth, he rumbled: 'But it wasn't him.'

I took a long slug of beer to calm myself down.

'How do you know?' I said nervously. I didn't really think Brian was going to confess to anything but I eyed up the distance between me and the door, just in case.

'Derek would never do that,' he said in such deep tones that they seemed loaded with significance.

'Oh, right. I mean, I agree.' I was sounding very insincere. I drank some more beer. For some reason this conversation was unnerving me and I didn't know why.

'Who do you think it was, Brian?' I blurted out.

He looked down at me. 'You,' he said. It took me a while to realise he had made a joke. The corners of his mouth were raised slightly.

'Oh, ha ha,' I said, 'very amusing.'

Brian was laughing soundlessly. I could tell because the hub caps were rising and falling faster than usual.

'Well,' I said, finishing off my beer, 'I'll go and have another dance. Nice talking to you.'

I meant to give this a sarcastic spin, but he seemed to take it seriously.

'Yeah. You too, Sam. See you around.'

I strolled back to the door leading to the bar. As I pushed it open I looked back for a moment. Then I wished I hadn't. Brian was staring after me with an unidentifiable expression on his face.

* * *

While I had been absent, the dance floor had transformed itself into a tightly-packed confusion of sweaty bodies. The boy in the silver trousers who had been dancing with Rachel was now gyrating on one of the podia. He had taken his shirt off and was displaying a nice set of stomach muscles. Behind him was the dealer in the tartan suit, now jacketless but still with his cap on; he had obviously ingested a good proportion of his own wares. The physical comparison with Silver Trousers did him no favours. Still, he was so out of it he was incapable of being embarrassed. I was surprised he could stand up, let alone balance on a waist-high block. He had a beatific expression on his face and his arms were raised above his head as if he were worshipping the sun.

I wended my way slowly through the heaving mass. The dancers were not only up but floating by this time, they were also undeniably sticky. When you take a large quantity of dancing people, give them drugs that make them perspire and put them down in a couple of damp stone railway arches, the resultant humidity is clearly visible in the air. As I passed a girl in a silver dress, she moved back and brushed my arm with her shoulder. The material was slippery and slimy, leaving a trail of moisture like a snail's in its wake.

Finally I gained the toilets, which were rather bacchanal in feel. Boys and girls were sitting over the sinks and through them – in one case even between their legs – others were pushing, trying to drink from the taps. I wondered if the club management had turned off the water in order to force their clientèle to buy overpriced mineral water at the bar. Besides being illegal, this was also dangerous; people dehydrated pretty easily in these conditions. From the vociferous complaints, I gathered that the management had compromised by turning off the cold water but leaving on the hot.

Three girls emerged from the toilet cubicle for which I was queuing. I went in, had another little line of speed to pick me up, and emerged refreshed. No one was staring at me, but I was conscious of standing out; here everyone was dressed in bright colours and the average age was eighteen. I gave myself a brief once-over in the mirror. Lipstick in place, hair not falling down yet, cross at front of choker still attached. Check, check, check. I *was* wearing too much black, I had to admit. It's a vice.

I found Rachel at the bar, drinking rum and coke.

'Hey, Sam!' she said, throwing her arm around my waist. 'Good to see you!' She was high on life, unless Silver Trousers had slipped her something while I was away.

'Do you want another drink?' I said.

'No. Oh, shit, go on, then, why not?'

'That's the spirit.'

We were practically shouting at one another, the music was so loud. I ordered our drinks. One more beer for me and that was my limit.

'Cheers!' we clinked glasses.

'You made a hit there,' I said, gesticulating to Silver Trousers, who was still up on the podium.

She giggled. 'He can't be more than eighteen.'

'Nice and corruptible.'

'I'd never get rid of him afterwards.'

This time we giggled together.

'Oh,' I said, suddenly remembering. 'I talked to Brian.'

Then I wished I hadn't said it. She came back down to earth with a bump. She was in one of those states where drunkenness is an attitude of mind, rather than a measure of intake, and it didn't take much to sober her up.

'What did he say?' she asked at once in a serious tone of voice.

'Nothing much. He doesn't think it was Derek either.'

She leant towards me to hear better. 'Who *does* he think it was?'

'He said me. It was a joke.'

She stared at me incredulously. 'Brian made a *joke*?'

I nodded.

'I don't believe it.'

'He was even laughing.'

'My God. Talk about letting his hair down.' She finished her drink and put it down on the bar. 'Shall we go?'

'I thought you'd want to stay on a bit.'

She shook her head. 'No, I'm fine. And it must be late.'

We collected our coats from the cloakroom and headed outside. Brian and his cohorts were grouped together just outside the door.

'Bye,' I said to Brian.

'Bye, Sam, Rachel,' he said, raising one enormous hand in a salute. If Brian had killed Linda it was hard to see why he had bothered to hit her with a weight; his own hands must be equally heavy. 'See you around.'

Rachel looked astounded. I mouthed 'Told you so' at her as I buttoned up my coat, shivering with the cold. This was a perfect recipe for catching the flu: coming out from the warm, damp, sweaty club into the chilly night air. But I was still so happy with my leopardskin coat that I didn't care about mundanities.

The clock in the van said it was two-thirty. Closing time at Silver, while Paradisiac was just getting into its stride. I navigated back across the river without too much difficulty. We were mostly silent on the drive home, which suited me. Driving through London late at night has a peacefulness, a sense of completion; the roads are nearly empty, the offices dark. We were out in the night sea and the occasional cars that passed by were other ships on other courses, each of us cocooned in our own dimly-lit space. I felt as if London belonged to me, and I was surveying my territory. The great, beautiful, floodlit buildings along the Thames looked like palaces, bathed in pale white light. My brain was ticking happily away. God, I'm poetical when I'm on drugs.

As we reached the outskirts of Camden, Rachel yawned, saying: 'Thanks for dragging me out tonight. I really enjoyed myself.'

'It was fun, wasn't it?' I said, turning my head for a moment to grin at her. 'The music was more your kind of thing than mine.'

'Next time we should do some E ourselves. Come prepared.'

'So when's the next time?'

'What about next weekend?' she suggested.

'Fine by me.' I turned into her road, slowing the van to a crawl; the council estate in which Rachel lived ran practically the whole length of the street and it was easy to overshoot the block in which she lived.

'It's this one,' she said as we approached it. 'Thanks'.

I parked the van outside the right entrance. She kissed me goodnight and got out, bending down to say through the window: 'Next Saturday.'

'It's a date.'

I watched her climb the stairs and turn into the walkway that led to her front door. She was wearing her black raincoat, belted tightly around her waist, her hair twisted into a top-knot. Rachel was so graceful she made the simple act of climbing a flight of stairs look like Odette's big solo from *Swan Lake*.

I've never been one of those people who has always had their own crew of friends, from school onwards, to hang out, squabble and mess around with; I'm solitary by nature. But Rachel and I suited each other. We were loners who could understand one another's need for space, and party animals enough to enjoy letting our hair down in company. I was pleased she'd enjoyed tonight as much as I had. The more I knew her, the more I liked her; how many people can you say that of? I have plenty of acquaintances, but I don't make friends easily. It looked as if I could add another to the short list.

The flats were well designed, for urban safety at least; all the front doors faced on to the street. I didn't pull away till I saw Rachel's door close behind her and the lights go on. A moment later they went off again. I yawned, stretched, put the van into gear and drove home.

14

When I woke up, my head was still buzzing and my body twitching with energy; nothing like a speed hangover to get you spring-cleaning. I spent about an hour tidying up my sleeping area, which in practice meant putting away the clothes and books that were strewn all over the floor. Then I actually made my bed, or rather futon, instead of just throwing the duvet and blankets at it and hoping they would stick. Going downstairs, I put on Depeche Mode – 'Songs of Faith And Devotion' – turned it up full blast and went to clean the bathroom. I even did the underside of the toilet seat, which in general I leave, on the principle that if men want it clean they can do it themselves: they're the only ones who ever see it. The lyrics were irredeemably gloomy and I knew them all by heart. Nothing like a bit of existential misery to help you get the chores done.

I yodelled away happily as I cleaned the soap dish with a sponge liberally coated with Jif, thinking that I infinitely preferred this kind of music to those happy-clappy numbers about eternal love put out by artificially skinny soul singers who can't stay married for longer than it takes to play one of their own songs. By this time I had half my arm down the toilet but I was still singing along. Whistle while you work.

When the music finished I called it a day, threw the sponge into the sink and flopped down on the sofa, virtue oozing from every pore. I rang my friend Janey, the one with the mutual pigeon problem, but her answering machine was on so I left a message explaining my predicament. Hanging up, I switched on the TV. *Eastenders* had just started and I plugged myself into the

TV for the duration. Halfway through Tom phoned but I snarled at him to ring back at three, when it would have finished, and slammed the phone down. He should know my Sunday schedule by now.

Tom called back at a quarter past three, while I was in the middle of a plate of beans on toast, and we arranged that I would go round to his flat later on to watch some videos and eat take-away pizza. The effects of the speed were fading fast but they lasted long enough to enable me to wash up the plate and saucepan. Then I got dressed and went out. There was someone I wanted to talk to.

I'd got her address from Lou yesterday. I didn't really know why I wanted to talk to her; thoroughness, perhaps. No, it was more than that. I had a kind of hunch that it might be interesting, even if it was just to know whether or not she thought Derek was innocent.

The address proved to be a large Victorian house opposite Parliament Hill, divided into flats. She must be doing pretty well; either to own or pay rent on a flat in this area would cost plenty. It faced on to the main road, but directly beyond that was the green woodland of Parliament Hill itself and behind that Hampstead Heath. Parking would be a problem, though; it was for me. Up and down both sides of the road were signs identifying this as a zone where if you parked for five minutes in order to collect your aged grandmother and take her to the doctor's, they would clamp your car, douse it with petrol and set fire to it with your granny still inside. How was I supposed to find a place to watch a house in these conditions? Town planners are so selfish.

By a stroke of luck, however, there was a bus stop a few doors down, on the same side of the road. I parked the van around the corner, settled myself into a seat at the bus shelter and unfolded the *Observer*, which I had prudently purchased to keep me entertained. If there was no sign of her in an hour or so I would either invent some excuse to ring the doorbell or go down to Camden for a drink. Probably the latter. My intellectual resources were at a low ebb.

I was reading a rather good article in the magazine when I saw someone coming out of the front gate and for a moment I was annoyed at being interrupted. Then I saw her face and forgot all about what I had been reading. I knew already this must be Janice, Derek's ex-girlfriend; Lou had described her to me, and how many slim elegant blondes – Derek running true to type here – could there be living in one house, especially when they were accessorised by a small boy who was the spitting image of Derek, reproduced several shades lighter? She had her back to me at first, latching the gate, but when she turned I recognised her at once.

She was the woman I had seen Derek with that night at Silver.

* * *

I buried my head in the magazine. Out of the corner of my eye I could see her walking down the street towards me, holding the boy's hand. They made a striking contrast: she was dressed all in black – not a scruffy, Camden, it-doesn't-show-the-stains-and-hides-my-fat-black, but a designer-label it-allows-me-to-express-my-elegant-simplicity sort of black. It was the kind of thing Rachel might have worn: jodhpurs, a polo-neck sweater and a belted jacket of very soft leather. Ankle boots with the latest square heel. The little boy next to her, however, was a riot of colour: bright yellow jacket, red baseball cap, stripy multicoloured sweater with a padded waistcoat over the top, green jeans. Trendy little bastard. He looked very excited about something and was so good-looking she could have made a fortune selling him to an advertising agency. I could just see his photograph on a box of soap powder, smiling happily in a spotlessly white sweater which set off his milk chocolate skin.

I was saved any debate about what to do next by the fact of them entering the bus shelter and sitting next to me. How considerate. I glanced at her briefly, as you do when someone sits down next to you, returned to my magazine and then looked back at her as if I had just thought of something.

'Excuse me, but didn't I see you down at Silver a while ago?' I said, trying to sound affable and outgoing, the kind of person who would strike up a conversation with a complete stranger. I smiled in the least mad-nutter way I could contrive.

She smiled back at me, relaxed and friendly. 'Is that the club below the Underworld? Yes, we went there. A couple of Saturdays ago.'

'That's right!' I said, letting it all come back. 'You were with Derek, weren't you? I work at the Chalk Farm Gym, that's how I know him.'

She nodded, but I could see that my mentioning Derek had caused her to lose a little of her bonhomie. I couldn't blame her. In her time I was sure that plenty of girls she didn't know must have mentioned Derek's name to her in equally enthusiastic tones.

'I was surprised to see him there,' I went on. 'I didn't know it was his kind of thing.'

She smiled despite herself. 'It isn't! He went there very much under protest. We were out for a meal and I got it into my head to go somewhere different afterwards.'

She had the kind of good looks you couldn't argue with, a calm, elegant beauty that reminded me of Grace Kelly. Hitchcock would have loved her. Clear blue eyes, smooth pale skin; her fair hair was gathered to the back of her head in a French plait, showing off her graceful neck. Not your typical Silver *habituée*. But I remembered that she had looked much more down-to-earth that night.

'Did you have a good time?'

'Oh yes, it was fun. But most things would have been fun that evening; I'd had a terrible week – I felt like a dish rag, frankly – and I just wanted to get out of the house. Derek got a friend to babysit Devon and took me out for a meal. It was just what I needed.'

'I'm Sam,' I offered. 'Sam Jones.'

'Janice King.' We smiled at each other. Soon my mouth was going to crack with all this cheer and goodwill.

'I've heard your name before,' I said, indicating the little boy, who was swinging his legs wildly on the seat. 'He must be Derek's, right? He's so like him.'

'Devon. Yes, he's Derek's. Just like his dad already.'

She put out a restraining hand, which Devon exuberantly ignored. Her nails were long and painted with clear, pink-tinted varnish.

'You must have heard about what's happened at the gym, then,' I said. 'That Linda's been killed.'

Janice was frowning. 'Derek told me.' She gave me an assessing glance and said frankly: 'I should be upset, but I can't be.'

On seeing that I wasn't backing away or making the sign of the cross, her forehead cleared. 'I always hated her,' she added simply. 'She took Derek away from me. I mean that literally.' She looked at me. 'I'm sorry. Was she a friend of yours?'

'Far from it,' I said firmly, seizing the opportunity for us to do some bonding. 'I couldn't stand her.'

Two women had come into the bus shelter by this time, one of them dragging along a little boy whom Devon recognised. He jumped up, ran up to him and cuffed him on the shoulder, shouting: 'All right, Tariq?'

Janice looked over at them. 'Hi, Sue,' she said to his mother. 'Taking the monster out?'

'Yeah, I give him some air every so often. Does him good, apparently.'

Sue leaned against the shelter and pulled out a packet of cigarettes, offering one to the other woman. They both lit up. Tariq and Devon were already pressing their faces against the glass behind her, making farting noises. A bus pulled up at the stop but Janice made no move to stand up, so I didn't either.

'She made my life a misery,' I continued, warming to my theme. 'Linda, I mean. If she hadn't been killed I would have left. I couldn't bear it any more.'

'Join the club.' Janice stretched her legs out in front of her; she cast a glance over her shoulder but Devon was on the other side of the glass, out of earshot. 'I'd always known that Derek screwed around. It was part of the deal. I didn't much like it, but . . .' Her voice tailed off for a moment. 'And I'd known for a while that he was having an affair with a woman from the gym. Ever since we met. But it was me he lived with. I told myself that most people have affairs, and at least I knew about it up front. I thought if I gave Derek enough room, he would always stay with me. He really loved me, you know. He still does. And he adores Devon.'

I didn't have to say anything, just let her spill it out. To her the wound of Derek's leaving was clearly still fresh, and she'd probably exhausted all her friends a long time ago with the subject. I suspected, however, that there was another reason for her talking this frankly to me, a girl she hardly knew; you might say that in her own subtle way she was warning me off any interest I might have in Derek by stressing how close the ties still were between him, Janice and their child.

'I was too proud in the end,' she was saying. 'Linda was like . . . I don't know, like a pit bull. She got hold of him and she wouldn't let go. I don't know what happened to make her so determined to take him away from me – after all, they'd already been having an affair for years and years. But she put him under incredible pressure. She rang up the whole time, she went on at him, she wouldn't give up.'

She looked at me. Her face was as calm and beautiful as ever, her blue eyes limpid. Perhaps she had told this story so many times by now that she could detach herself from it; or perhaps she always looked like that, even when strong emotions were raging in her head. Not a wisp of blonde hair had come loose from the French plait, despite the breeze that was blowing. She seemed to have most things under control.

'Derek's quite weak in some ways. He'll do anything for an easy life. Lou told me to fight for him, beat Linda away from the door. But I couldn't. My job's very stressful, there was Devon to look after – he's on the go non-stop from morning to night. I know Lou meant well, but I didn't have the energy or the inclination to go to war with Linda. I took the attitude that Derek must decide what he wanted to do, and of course for him that meant taking the line of least resistance.'

She stared ahead of her.

'I should have listened to Lou,' she said slowly. 'I wouldn't make the same mistake again.'

A C2 bus pulled up at the stop, its doors sliding open almost before it had come to a halt. This had to be Janice's bus; only two numbers stopped here. I stood up and she did too. Devon and Tariq piled up the stairs in front of the adults and ran shouting down to the far end, where they threw themselves on to the back seat, their legs dangling endearingly over the edge without touching the floor.

'How far are you going?' Janice asked me, showing her and Devon's pass to the driver.

'Regent Street,' I said, naming the end of the line.

'Oh? Me too. I'm taking Devon to the new Disney film and then to Planet Hollywood. *Big* treat. That's why he's so frenetic.'

She seemed to take it for granted that we would sit down next to each other, picking a seat in front of Devon and Tariq. 'Keep it down, you two,' she said over her shoulder.

'Mum,' Tariq said plaintively, 'Dev's going to Planet Hollywood. Why can't we?'

'Because we can't, OK?' Sue said firmly, and went back to talking to her friend.

'It's a very bad atmosphere at the gym right now,' I said to Janice, picking up the threads of the conversation. 'Derek's probably told you already.'

Her lips tightened. 'He said the police are giving him a pretty hard time,' she said, keeping her voice lowered so that Devon wouldn't hear.

The bus skidded to a halt outside Kentish Town station. It was one of those little red hopper buses, not much bigger than a small van, and the drivers were usually much less sedate than those in charge of the big two-storey jobs; this one expressed his individuality by opening the doors before he got to a stop and closing them after he'd pulled away. Two alcoholics got on, lurching and mumbling, cans of Tennent's Extra clutched tightly in their hands. I hoped they wouldn't fall out when the bus took off.

'Derek could be in some trouble,' I said. 'Did he explain about the circumstances?'

Janice smiled wryly. 'Oh, he said he'd been quarrelling with Linda because some girl was after him, and then there was another girl who followed him downstairs that afternoon. Typical Derek.'

'It was pretty frank of him to tell you that,' I said.

'Oh yes. He never felt he had to hide things from me. That's partly why we got on so well.' She paused. 'But that kind of thing is going to look terrible to the police. Here's this big black guy with lots of girls, and then his girlfriend gets killed, and she happens to be white, which won't help. Everyone knows that Derek wouldn't hurt a fly, but how can you prove that?'

We sat for a while in silence. For some reason the faces of Inspector Monroe and Sergeant Hawkins floated before my eyes. I lingered somewhat on the latter. How shameful. The alcoholics stumbled off at Camden and started shouting abuse at each other as the bus pulled away.

'How's Lou?' Janice said. 'I haven't seen her for ages. Derek says she's the manager now.'

'She's taken to it like a duck to water. That's the silver lining in the situation – she might never have been promoted otherwise, but of course she's perfect for it.'

'She was always so kind to me. Especially when Derek and I broke up. She was almost as upset as I was about it.'

'Lou's maternal instinct coming out again. She treats Derek like one of her sons.'

Janice smiled. 'I know what you mean.'

'You and Derek seem to be on very good terms, all things considered,' I said hesitantly.

'Oh yes.' Her voice softened and when I looked at her I saw that she was smiling, but not at me; at a picture of Derek in her own head. 'We still love each other. And of course there's Devon. Derek comes round a lot to see him.' There was an edge to her voice now. 'Linda didn't like that much, of course, but what could she do? You can't keep a man from seeing his own child. And when I'm feeling down I can always give him a call.'

'Like on Saturday night when you went to the club.'

'Exactly.'

The bus heaved itself up Delancey Street and round the outskirts of Regent's Park.

'You must have really disliked her. Linda.'

'Oh, I did, believe me! I've calmed down a lot now, though. It's been nearly two years.'

'Are you seeing anyone else?'

She turned her head to stare at me, looking completely surprised. 'No, of course not!' she said, as though it were the most obvious thing in the world. We were crossing into Great Portland Street. Nearly there. Sue and Tariq had got off at Camden Town and Devon was crouched on the back seat, staring out of the window. She cast a glance at him.

'We're meeting a friend of mine at the cinema,' she explained. 'She's got a little girl about Devon's age.'

'Mum!' Devon said indignantly. 'Julie's four and I'm nearly six!'

'Five and a half,' Janice said to me. Devon scowled.

The bus was passing the BBC building at the top of Upper Regent Street. Janice said suddenly: 'God, I've been so rude, blabbing on about myself like this. I'm so sorry – what must you think of me?'

'It's fine, honestly,' I reassured her. 'People often talk to me about themselves. I like listening.'

Tom would have given a massive horse-laugh at this and shouted: 'What a load of old cobblers!' Fortunately for me he wasn't present.

'Well, I've certainly done that!' Janice said. 'Thanks for listening. You're very good at it.'

I muttered something self-deprecatory, shuddering to think what Tom's response would have been. The bus was crossing Oxford Circus. Janice would be getting off at the last stop if she was going to see a film; all the cinemas were concentrated at the Piccadilly Circus end of Regent Street. I rang the bell and stood up, calculating that if I got off now I could double back and pick the bus up on its way back without her seeing me.

'Oh, are you off?' She looked rather disappointed. 'I hope we meet up again.'

'Me too. It's been nice talking to you.'

'I'm afraid I did most of that. Well, see you soon.' She looked as if she were about to say something else, like give me her telephone number, but the bus had come to a stop and the doors were already open. I was glad to get away; I liked her and I didn't want to be her friend under false pretences.

As I walked down the pavement I looked back at the bus and saw Devon's face pressed against the window. Janice was waving to me and I felt guilty. She had been so nice; I had led her on to talk and she had apologised to me for it.

I wished I had been able to think of a way of asking her where she was the afternoon Linda was killed.

15

'Saw your girlfriend today, Tom,' I said, tucking into a big slice of pizza. Being still on my eat-more-fresh-vegetables kick, I had ordered a Thin Crust Vegetarian. It was covered with sweetcorn, olives, onions and peppers. I don't know what the English would do without pizza. We were sitting on the carpet of the living room, backs against the sofa, pizza boxes on the floor in front of us. There was a six-pack of beer in the fridge and two videos waiting patiently beside the TV. Bliss.

'Which one?'

'The blonde from the club.'

'The one with the ponytail? Mr Stud-U-Like's hot date?'

'She turns out to be his ex-girlfriend and the mother of his child.'

'Lucky bastard! He actually impregnated her?'

'How elegantly you put it. Anyway, she looked great. She had her hair in one of those French plaits, tucked under at the nape. Sort of Grace Kelly for the nineties—'

'How can you taunt me like this?' Tom groaned. 'Don't you have any womanly sympathy?'

He folded a slice of Chicken Tikka pizza in half and jammed most of it into his mouth.

'It didn't get me very far, anyway,' I admitted. 'Apart from finding out that she's still in love with him.'

'Aren't they all?' Tom said bitterly, when he'd ingested the pizza.

'You have a point . . .'

'So who *did* kill the dragon lady?'

'I haven't the faintest idea.' I ate some more pizza gloomily. 'No, that isn't quite true. I can't believe it was Fliss or Derek, and I know it wasn't me. So that leaves Jeff, Brian and Naomi. I can't really see Brian killing Linda – he's so measured, he thinks about everything before he does it, even making a joke – and this seems to me like something that happened very much on impulse.'

'And this Jeff guy is supposed to have done it to stop Linda trying to privatise the gym?' Tom said. There was a note of scepticism in his voice.

'He's a Living Socialist,' I explained.

'Oh, *right*. Still—'

'I know what you're going to say. Everyone had voted out the proposal, why should he kill her when all we knew was that she had some nebulous idea of going over our heads to a couple of people on the council? It's too vague to be a motive, unless the plans were much farther advanced than we knew. I should check that out, I suppose.' I drank some beer. 'I bumped into him yesterday and he looked incredibly shamefaced. And surprised to see me. I mean, I work there, for God's sake! I think he must have heard that I'm asking questions, so he's got to have something on his conscience. Otherwise, why look at me that way?'

I ticked Jeff off on my fingers. 'Then there's Naomi. I think Derek knows more than he's saying. I wouldn't be surprised if Naomi did it and he's covering up for her. He wouldn't do that for anyone else who'd been down there. I mean, it was his girlfriend who got killed. The only reason for him not telling what happened is that he feels guilty about something, like it being his making out with Naomi that got Linda murdered.'

'You're taking all this very seriously,' Tom commented.

'After my last experience with finding someone dead,' I retorted, 'allow me to be slightly equivocal about police investigations.'

'So it's in the name of justice rather than for Mr Muscle's big brown eyes?' he said quizzically. 'Or should I say big—'

'Lewdness isn't wit, Tom. Remember that.' I finished the last slice of pizza. 'What films are we watching?'

'*Build My Gallows High* and *Gilda*.'

'Oh, wow.'

Tom is something of a film buff, with particular reference to forties *film noir*. He started educating me several years ago and now I even know the difference between Jane Greer and Greer Garson.

He put the first film in and turned on the TV. I switched off the lights and we settled back to watch the flickering screen. There's no point describing either of the films, apart from saying that if you haven't seen them your life is incomplete. Tom of course went soppy over Virginia Mayo. No prizes for guessing her hair colour.

'She'd bore you in a week,' I said, 'staring up at you with those big eyes, thinking you were wonderful and hanging on your every word—'

'Are you joking?' Tom said incredulously. 'That's my ideal woman!'

I looked at my watch. Nearly midnight.

'Bedtime for Sam,' I announced, standing up. I cast an eye over the pizza boxes and beer cans. 'Sure I can't help you with the washing up?'

'Ha, ha.' Tom stood up and we hugged goodnight. 'See you soon.'

I drove home, my head spinning with images of the films we'd seen. Jane Greer and Robert Mitchum on a beach in Mexico by moonlight, Rita Hayworth stripping off a long black satin glove . . . but, despite myself, my mind kept returning to Linda's murder.

For some reason it seemed just too neat, this business of five people down in the basement and no one else going in or out. The next time I went into the gym, I thought I might try out a possibility that had just occurred to me.

* * *

Felice Bortshe had written that the drinks party was from six to nine o'clock, so I aimed to get there at seven-thirty, playing safe. Red, she had said. I did actually have a red dress; it had short sleeves, a low, square neck and finished several inches above my knees. If I wore it with black opaque tights and my boots with all the zips and laces, it wouldn't look too girly. I wished I knew how smart it was going to be. Well, Holland Park wasn't exactly informal. I added a black plastic choker, put all my hair up and slapped on some red lipstick that was the same colour as the dress and didn't come off for days no matter what you did with your mouth.

Was I looking too tarty? I checked myself out in the mirror and decided that the boots saved it. I had polished them specially. The leopardskin coat, regretfully, would be too much with the red dress and choker. I put on my black leather jacket instead and sallied out. Then I sallied back in again and snorted up what remained of the gram of speed. It wasn't much, but it boosted my confidence enough to allow me to contemplate the thought of cocktail conversation without coming out in hives.

I drove to Holland Park. There wasn't much choice – taking public transport from point north-north-east in a south-westerly direction across London is only for those who like to spend their weekends getting lost in Hampton Court maze. The house was large, white and paralytically smart, located on one of those avenue-wide roads where very rich people live. Speed bumps were clustered thickly along the route to stop drunken aristocrats driving their BMWs too fast down it and crashing into one another. I sat outside in the van for five minutes trying not to bite my fingernails, saw a group of very Sloaney-looking people going in, finked out of joining them, sat in the van for ten minutes more and finally was only driven out of it by a twitchiness caused by the speed.

The front garden had been paved over, apart from a small square of earth in the centre in which there stood two waist-high trees clipped to look like lollipops. One was slightly smaller than the other. Next to the elaborate, keeping-up-with-the-Joneses displays in each of the next-door gardens, which screamed lavish expense and a full-time gardener and were lit up by searchlights so that you couldn't miss the point even if you wanted to, the two miniature trees were fastidiously restrained.

As soon as I entered Duggie Sutton's first-floor flat, however, I knew the trees hadn't been his choice. There were three tables in the hall alone, their surfaces lavish with trinkets and *objets d'art*. Gilt chairs clustered around the tables, the floors were thickly layered with rugs, and pictures lined the walls in strata right up to the dado rail, like they were once hung in Victorian art galleries. As far as I could tell the walls were painted pale green but they were so covered with oil paintings that I wouldn't have laid money on it.

The flat door had been opened by a small man in corduroy trousers, a mustard-coloured waistcoat and a tweed jacket. He had a fob chain strung across his waistcoat, a bow tie and bright little eyes like a woodland creature, reminding me of a mixture of characters from *Alice in Wonderland*. Duggie Sutton's name had been vaguely familiar to me when Felice had mentioned it, and since then I had rung the person who originally recommended me to Felice to get some information about him.

'Don't be fooled by appearances,' she had said. 'He's very sharp. And he's an odd mixture – deals in modern art but won't have it in the house. He's a partner in the Wellington Gallery, but when you see where he lives you won't believe it. If he takes you on you'll be doing very well, but don't let him get away with anything.'

The Wellington Gallery was one of those sleek white places that look like the inside of an ocean liner without the screwed-down furniture. Looking around me, I could see exactly what she had meant; a more striking contrast between his home and work-place was unimaginable. Meanwhile, Duggie Sutton seemed to have an inexhaustible line in patter.

'Well, aren't *you* fabulous?' he said, taking my coat. 'Love the frock. I'm Duggie, darling, who are you?'

'Sam Jones,' I said tentatively. 'Felice Bortshe invited me—'

'Oh, of course! You're Felice's new discovery. I've heard *all* about you.' He winked at me. I wished he hadn't. I hate it when people do that.

'I take it those trees in the front garden weren't your doing,' I said, looking around me.

Duggie clasped his hands theatrically. 'Darling, don't *talk* to me about them. Do you want me to have a heart attack? That old queen downstairs is into minimalism. So *repressed*! When it starts creeping into your private life you *know* you're in trouble. God knows I've pleaded with him, but it's no use. If you ask me, it's just because he's insecure.'

'Insecure?' I said, baffled.

He raised his eyes to heaven. 'About his *taste*, darling! That's what I call minimalism: insecurity. Or mental laziness. But I mustn't keep a lovely girl like you standing in the hall, must I? How greedy of me. Do come in and have a drink. Felice is here already.'

He led me through into a large sitting room which compassed the two front rooms of the house, knocked together and connected by a central arch that curved graciously under the high ceilings. I recognised the two big bow windows from my sojourn outside in the van, staring up at the house. It was a space made for entertaining. The room was as crammed with furniture as the hall had been: occasional tables, their tops groaning with more *objets*, scattered in every nook and cranny, the parquet floor thick with rugs, padded sofas and armchairs arranged in conversational groups, polished coffee tables between them, the walls as covered with paintings as the hall. At first sight it looked cluttered; only later did you appreciate with what care the various elements had been arranged.

The initial effect was heightened by the fact that the room was bursting to the gills with smartly dressed people who obscured a large part of the décor. Duggie guided me to a table covered with a white cloth, behind which stood a very handsome young man in a waiter's uniform.

'Stanford, sweetie, get this lovely girl something to drink, will you?' he said, and to me: 'Try the punch, darling, I made it myself. Felice is just over there.'

He disappeared into the crowd. I looked at Stanford. 'It's the punch, I expect,' I said. 'How strong is it?'

He sank a ladle into a gigantic silver tureen and poured me a glassful of some opaque red liquid. 'Uh, it's kinda lethal,' he said. 'Duggie just threw in everything without reading the labels first. It's good, though.'

He handed me the glass, accompanying it with one of those American smiles where they show you all their teeth so you can marvel at the dentistry involved, none of which seems to be available this side of the Atlantic. He looked like a male model – features so regular they cancelled each other out and a smile just like Barbie's boyfriend's.

'Sam! You made it!'

I swivelled to see Felice Bortshe bearing down on me. She

was wearing a white suit with black piping, and her hair-style was exactly the same as it had been last week. I swear. Down to the last auburn streak. Clearly she was the kind of person who could wear white without getting it dirty. I, on the other hand, need only put on a white sweater and sit motionless in an armchair for ten minutes to find on rising that various unidentifiable stains have formed all over the front.

Felice put out her hand. On it was a huge ring very similar to Princess Diana's diamond-and-sapphire engagement number, and just about as tasteful.

'Nice to see you!' Her conversation was as spattered with exclamation marks as ever. 'Isn't this a great place? I just love Duggie's style! Have you got something to drink?'

'I've got some punch—'

'Oh, wow! Go easy! Did you warn her, Stanford?'

'Uh-huh.'

'He's so cute, isn't he?' she said to me, leading me across the room. 'Not for us, though, honey! But I think Duggie has hopes!'

'This flat doesn't exactly go with a partnership in the Wellington Gallery,' I said.

She laughed. 'Duggie,' she said, 'is full of contradictions. Did you see the trees outside?'

'Yes, I—'

'The guy who lives downstairs is Duggie's partner. He's one of those minimalists who has two pieces of Le Corbusier furniture on bare floorboards, and everything stored away in floor-to-ceiling white cupboards. They fight all the time. Keeps them fit. Now, I want you to meet Jim and Betty Ashley. He's in oil, but she's the one that matters. If the wife doesn't like it—' She flashed a quick look at me. '*Love* the dress!' she added appraisingly. 'Good girl. And the boots are great. Real boho English!'

By this time we had manoeuvred our way right over to the other side of the room, to one of the big bow windows. Beside it was standing a woman of the height and shape Americans call petite, with hair so bouffant it resembled a puffball, and a dress to match. Under the dress she was skin and bone; her face was so taut it looked as if it would split if she opened her mouth.

Beside her was a large square man with steel-coloured hair and a mouth like a trap.

'Jim, Betty, I want you to meet Sam Jones!' Felice said enthusiastically. 'She's the sculptress I was telling you about, the one who makes those wonderful mobiles.'

Jim Ashley made some indecipherable grunt without moving his lips, and shook my hand. I wondered whether I should introduce him to Brian. They'd get on like a house on fire. Betty Ashley was more forthcoming.

'Delighted to meet you,' she gushed. I was relieved to see her skin was capable of stretching far enough to accommodate the big smile with which she accompanied the gush. 'Felice has told us *all* about you.'

What the hell had Felice been telling all these people? Or was it just a figure of speech?

'I hope not *everything*,' I said at random. Betty Ashley seemed to think this was as funny as something Oscar Wilde and Dorothy Parker might have concocted if they'd put their heads together and really concentrated. Felice, obviously deciding that I and the Ashleys were getting on like a house on fire already, disappeared, marooning me with them. I took a hefty slug of punch and then wished I hadn't.

Betty politely let me finish coughing. 'Felice warned us about the punch already,' she said. 'I guess you didn't know.'

'I forgot.' I wiped my eyes. 'Wow.'

'Packs a hell of a punch,' said Jim in a comradely way. Fortunately Betty didn't pick up on what I thought must have been an unintentional pun; she might have died laughing.

At least the experience seemed to have bonded us to some degree. Betty was a skilled conversationalist and steered me smoothly through my time at art school, my exhibitions to date (all two of them – that part didn't take long) and my theory of creativity. This was awful. I could tell I was supposed to spout some guff about the mystical unity of heaven and earth, as represented by my mobiles, and use the word 'philosophy' a lot. I racked my brains for as many long words as I could think of and lined them up one after the other. It seemed to go down reasonably well. Betty was nodding seriously and Jim grunted occasionally.

I was then allowed to ask a few questions, all of which I posed to them jointly and all of which were duly answered by Betty. I learnt that Jim had recently been sent to oversee the London office of Consolidated Drilling, which task they expected to last for a couple of years; that they had rented a lovely house just round the corner and were eating out a lot, and that it certainly was a change from California! (This was Betty's exclamation mark.) They were commenting on the weather to every English person they met, as they understood from other expat friends that this was practically obligatory. They loved London though they found the English rather inhospitable – a colleague of Jim's had warned him that English people hardly ever invited you to their homes to eat.

'That might be because they're embarrassed about their cooking,' I suggested.

Betty stared at me blankly. 'But you must have catering services over here!' she said.

'Samantha! Darling!' came a cry from behind me.

I recognised the voice at once; and if that hadn't been enough, she was the only person who called me Samantha. I completely hate being called Samantha – it makes me think of bimbos on TV with long blonde hair and vacant stares – and I suspected her of being well aware of this. Resignedly I turned round.

'Hello, Baby,' I said.

* * *

I was at art school with Baby Thompson, and I've never been able to shake her off since; she works in PR and is consequently as tenacious as a sexually transmitted disease. Tall and skinny as a rake, she made me feel like a dwarf with an excess of female hormones when I stood next to her. Naturally I tried to avoid the experience whenever possible.

There was no getting out of it now. She swooped down on me like a bird of prey, her aquiline nose heightening the resemblance, and pecked the air just above each of my cheeks in turn. If you ever want to know what the latest fashion is, just ring up Baby and ask her what she's wearing. At that precise moment in time it was obviously forties vamp. The last time I had seen Baby, her hair had been short and yellow. Now it was a dark brown, straggling to the nape of her neck, parted on one side and held with a diamanté barrette. Nothing casual about this: Baby's PR firm represented a glut of fashion designers and as a consequence she was fully informed on every new wave that was about to break. If she had done her hair straggly tonight, you could be sure that in two months *Vogue* would proclaim that Straggly Hair Was Right For Now and print lots of photos of Linda and Christy straggling away.

Baby wore heavy red lipstick and thick kohl round her eyes, a diamanté necklace, and a short-sleeved, skinny black sweater over a black pencil skirt. Her waist was cinched – as fashion magazines say – by a very narrow black belt; her tights were sheer and her heels were so high and strappy that they made her sway like a tree in a hurricane. I blinked. What most annoyed me about Baby was that she could – just about – get away with this kind of thing; if I dressed like that I'd get propositioned in the street by fat sleazy men. Also I resented the fact that plenty of boys at art school fancied her. I was still bitter about that one.

The Ashleys were staring at her in wonder.

'This is Baby Thompson,' I said to them. 'We were at art school together. Baby, Jim and Betty Ashley.'

'Lovely to meet you!' Baby cooed. 'I've known Sam for ever. What did you say you did?'

'I didn't,' said Jim Ashley sardonically. I was beginning to warm to him.

'Jim's a vice-president of Consolidated Drilling,' said Betty Ashley.

'Oh-how-interesting,' said Baby all in one breath. 'I work for Sophie Standing PR. You must give me a ring sometime. We're doing more and more corporate work.' She favoured Jim Ashley with a dazzling smile.

'So I hear Duggie Sutton's going to represent you!' she said to me. 'Congratulations!'

'He hasn't actually seen any of my stuff yet,' I said. I'm like Jim Ashley; confronted with someone like Baby I go as dry as a Martini that's barely acquainted with the vermouth bottle.

'Really? Well, I was talking to him and it seemed to be all sorted out,' Baby said. There's a line from Keats which goes:

My ear is open like a hungry shark
To catch the tunings of a voice divine.

You can tell it's from an early part of his oeuvre; I don't even
know whether sharks have ears. Anyway, Baby always reminds
me of the shark. Only it's the gossip grapevine she's listening
to.

I finished my punch. At least this time I was prepared.

'We're all going out to dinner later,' Baby said, waving a hand
in one of her expansive gestures. 'You must come too, Sam.' This,
I assumed, would be at some new restaurant so trendy it hadn't
even opened yet. Her eyes were flickering around the room
looking for important people she could network with, as was her
usual practice. However, I noticed that potentially being represented by Duggie Sutton had garnered me one whole minute of
exclusive attention. I had come up in the world.

'Oh, there's Gabby,' she exclaimed. 'Excuse me, won't you?'
She inserted herself into the throng, standing half a head above
almost everyone else. She looked like someone wading through
the sea, lots of effort but a slow progression; the pencil skirt and
heel combination only permitted her to take steps of about three
inches at a time. At least she wouldn't knock over any occasional
tables.

Felice was making her way towards us.

'I have to whisk Jim and Betty off now,' she said. 'The table's
booked for eight-thirty. Did you have a nice talk?'

'Oh yes, very interesting,' Betty said. 'Sam's been telling me all
about English manners. And then she introduced us to a friend
of hers who dresses exactly like my mother used to do.'

I wished Baby had still been around to hear that.

'I'll ring you, Sam,' Felice said to me. 'We must arrange for
Duggie to come round and see your sculptures!'

'I'd enjoy that too,' volunteered Jim Ashley to my surprise.
Felice shot me a look of approval.

'Absolutely!' she said. 'You'll love Sam's studio, it's so
Bohemian, just like a New York loft, only—'

'Dirtier,' I said. The punch must have gone to my head.

Felice burst out laughing. 'I love the English sense of humour!'
she said. 'Bye, sweetie.' She kissed me. I seemed to have passed
some test.

'Have a nice time with your friend,' Jim Ashley said to me without inflection.

'She's not my friend!' I retorted, goaded, and saw too late that there was a trace of a grin at each side of his mouth.

'I sort of gathered that,' he said. 'Well, good luck.'

I stood for a moment alone by the window, looking down at my empty glass. The air was full of laughter and upraised voices calling people 'darling'. What the hell. I made my way over to the drinks table and got Stanford to pour me some more punch.

16

I woke up the next morning and then wished I hadn't. Still, it was done now. Crawling out of bed, I scrabbled around on the floor till I found the packet of Solpadeine, ripping out a couple in a gesture so familiar I could do it with my eyes closed. The tablets were soluble and there was practically no water upstairs; I was in no state to negotiate that ladder and I wouldn't be for some time, so I had to drink them practically neat and they fizzed horribly at the back of my throat on the way down. I was maudlin enough to think this due punishment for having been so stupid as to spend the evening with Baby and her clique.

It was the first time I had been presented to her set as an up-and-coming sculptor rather than a friend of hers from art school, and while they hadn't exactly clasped me to their bosoms – that would have been uncomfortable, as they didn't have any and the underwiring of their Wonderbras would have cut into mine – they had deigned occasionally to notice my presence. My star was in the ascendant. We had gone first to a restaurant in some backstreet in Soho where, despite sitting in the bar area and eating salads that consisted, in my case, of a small circle of goat's cheese with two slices of grilled courgette wrapped round it and three different leaves arranged to one side, we had all spent an obscene amount of money.

Then we had gone to Bar Italia for coffee, where Baby had insisted on saying '*Ciao, bello*' to everyone who came in, those being the only words of Italian she knew, until it was time to go on to the club some people Baby knew had just started, which specialised in playing music at 60 beats per minute, which is very slow indeed. About three people were dancing superbly. No one else was even trying. They just stood around the edge of the dance floor gossiping aimlessly, or leaned uncomfortably on the concrete blocks that were the only available seats.

All in all it was an unremitting catalogue of horrors, and I wouldn't have stayed if Baby's cousin Tim hadn't joined us at the restaurant. He was a journalist on the *Sunday Herald* and had a sense of humour as dry as a duck's back. Nor could he help being related to Baby.

It was thanks to him that my van was parked outside instead of still being down a backstreet somewhere in Soho. Tim had offered earlier in the evening, on observing how much I was drinking, to stay sober enough to drive it and me home. This was by no means a small sacrifice for a journalist to make, yet I had exploited it ruthlessly by duly proceeding to consume so much alcohol that only someone much less gentlemanly than Tim, and certainly less fastidious, would have tried to take advantage of me afterwards. I couldn't have been a pretty sight; he had called a minicab without even trying to kiss me. Not that I remembered much about the later stages of the evening.

The Solpadeine was bubbling away weirdly in my stomach. There weren't many juices left down there for it to dissolve itself in and it was communicating its frustration powerfully. I felt sick. For the umpteenth time I wondered why I did this kind of thing to myself. Perhaps I was an unconscious masochist. At least, unlike the rest of Baby's unholy band, I didn't have to go to work this morning. Who was I kidding – they wouldn't go into work either. Nor would Tim. PR people and journalists never seemed to get into the office until midday.

It occurred to me suddenly and horribly that I had a weights class to teach at four. Well, that was still a long way away. Anything might happen before then. If someone else got themselves murdered, the gym would be closed. Maybe I should ring before leaving, just to check.

Thinking of the gym had not been a good move; my brain was ticking over with possibilities and in my current state this was excruciatingly painful. I curled up in a foetal position and tried to go to sleep again. It took some time.

* * *

I reached the gym at three with two further Solpadeine inside me and a slightly more stoic perspective on life.

Passing the main entrance, I walked round the side of the building, into the small alleyway which ran round it. Beyond the alleyway was a high wire fence, and beyond that was a neatly-kept housing estate. The only access to the gym from this side was a narrow flight of stone stairs, leading down to a door with a sign on it saying: 'Keep Clear – Emergency Exit'. This was the fire door at the end of the basement corridor. I went down the steps and leaned on the door. Then I gave it a good shove. It wouldn't budge.

I came up the stairs again and stood for a moment, looking around me. The wire fence was about six foot high and not easy to see through unless you were making a concerted effort. On its other side was the communal garden of the estate, comprising a children's play area in its own little enclosure and a stretch of scruffy grass with a few graffitied benches positioned on it here and there. There was not a soul in the whole garden. It wasn't the kind of weather to be standing out in the open.

Thoughtfully I walked round the building and entered the gym. Lesley was sitting in the reception cubicle reading a magazine. She wasn't actually following the words along with her index finger but I bet that was only because people might see. She had found her métier. Lesley was the perfect receptionist.

'Hi, Sam,' she said importantly. 'You're early.'

'Tick me off on the register. Is Lou around?'

'She's in the office.'

I knocked and entered. Lou was enthroned behind the desk tapping away at her computer. She looked up.

'You have an appointment, Ms Jones? If not, please make one with my secretary outside.'

'This new authority has gone to your head,' I said severely. 'You've become power-crazy.' I sat down on the corner of the desk. 'I want to ask you something about the alarm system.'

* * *

I had assumed that what I had to ask Lou would have cheered her up. Not a bit of it; her expression, when I explained what I was after, was more What Fresh Hell Is This? I expected that, now she was the manager, she had to take potential breaches of gym security more seriously than when she was a carefree receptionist who could snap her fingers at responsibility. Still, she had told me what I wanted to know.

I went into the crèche, which apart from me was deserted. It was only open for the duration of certain classes. They also ran some Saturday morning action-packed funfest guaranteed to exhaust even hyperactive kids for the rest of the weekend, but I had staunchly resisted all efforts made to involve me with that. I have about as much maternal instinct as a mother cuckoo.

In one corner, under the windowsill, were stacked toys too large to fit into the store cupboard: a giant teapot; what would have resembled a dismantled Native American tepee, if Native Americans made a habit of using red and yellow plastic sheeting as a construction material; and a blue trike with 'Speedy Boy' written down its side. Sun poured over them, streaks of light reflecting off the plastic as if it were a mirror, primary colours shining bright enough to blind you. One would almost think it was nice weather outside.

Inside a cupboard on the back wall was the electricity control box. Opening it, I ran my eye down the labels under every switch. It was so easy to find: one of the neat little labels simply said: 'Fire Door'. The switch above it was set to 'On'. I flicked it down to 'Off' and went downstairs. My timing was perfect; there was hardly anyone about. When I reached the fire door I took a deep breath, looked around, saw no one, braced myself for a possible clamour, leaned down on the bar and pushed the door open.

It was rather anticlimactic, like going to see a hyped-up film and realising after the first ten minutes that the only part of it one could take seriously was the publicity budget. In short, nothing happened, apart from the fact that I found myself looking out on to the same flight of stone steps I had previously descended. I nipped back down the corridor to the office, tore a piece of heavy cardboard off a box which contained spare paper cups for the water dispenser, and returned hastily to the fire door. Reopening it, I stuffed the cardboard against the lock, wedging it open, and closed the door again. Hopefully it would hold.

Then it was up the stairs and out through the main doors again. What a busy time I was having. I trotted back into the alley and down the stone stairs. This time when I pushed the door it opened, still in happy silence. Well, well, well. Pulling out the piece of cardboard, I shut the door once more. I couldn't go back into the gym this way; if I didn't re-enter through the main doors, even Lesley's little brain might start spinning. She was flicking through a photo spread on Michael Jackson's dream mansion when I came back in, and didn't even look up. Perhaps I had overestimated her capacity for observation. The clock in reception said that it was a quarter to four. I pushed open the door to Lou's office.

'Bad news,' I said. 'Or good, maybe. It's possible. Someone could have switched off the alarm, then used the fire door without ever coming through reception.'

Lou stared at me.

'Shit,' she said profoundly.

* * *

Lesley was absent from her desk when I went back into the hall, so naturally I nipped into the reception cubicle and started flicking through *Hello!*. I had reached Princess Di's tour of Japan – visit to war graves, pale blue bobbly suit with short skirt and matching hat – when Lesley emerged from the toilet. I snarled at her. I wasn't giving up *Hello!* till I saw what Di was wearing for the state banquet and dinner dance at the Imperial Palace. Navy-blue crêpe with a long skirt and side slit. I handed Lesley the magazine back reluctantly. It occurred to me that if I bought it myself I could put it in the loo for visitors after having read it and thus camouflage my interest; I don't read it myself, you understand, I buy it in case my guests are constipated.

Lesley looked at the clock pointedly, and then said when I didn't get the hint:

'Sam, it's ten past, and your class was supposed to start at four—'

'Bollocks.' I jumped up and went quickly downstairs, trying to look like someone who didn't care whether or not she read the feature on Princess Stephanie's new baby. Eight women were waiting patiently for their class downstairs in the women's gym. I apologised for my lateness. Josie, in the centre of the front row, gave me a forgiving smile that sent shivers down my spine. Her bob and her eyes were as shiny as ever. I put on my home-compiled Trashy Girls tape and my acolytes worked out to Dolly Parton, Madonna and Bananarama.

Josie came over to say something to me when the class had finished. A rush of panic swept over me and on instinct I placed myself strategically between her and the rack of free weights.

'I *love* that tape, Sam,' she trilled at me, smiling brightly. 'So much fun!'

She swung her bob and did a little dance step out through the door. Eek. I toyed briefly with a fantasy that involved Josie, in a fit of homicidal mania, sneaking surreptitiously into the women's loos and smashing Linda's head in, her lips fixed into a constant teeth-baring smile. I could believe Josie capable of a little advance planning. All the detective novels say homicidal maniacs are as cunning as a barrel of chipmunks. She could have brought the hand weight with her in her gym bag.

I strolled towards the downstairs office, having barely worked up enough of a sweat to justify a shower. The class had had it easy today. In the corridor I met Rachel, who was returning officewards with a kettle full of water.

'Teatime,' she said firmly. 'I've been dying for a cup all the way here. Only we're nearly out of teabags. You don't feel like going out to the shop, do you?'

'Can't we cadge some off Lou?'

'If she hasn't got so grand now that she's rationing them out.' Rachel said rather pointedly.

'I know – I was just telling her that this new power'll go to her head if she's not careful.'

Rachel put the kettle on while I popped upstairs to raid Lou's supplies. As I got to the top of the stairs I had a flash of déjà vu, for I could hear Lesley saying in unfriendly tones, just as she had done on Saturday: 'Derek's probably still teaching a class, I'm afraid. I don't know if it's worth your while to wait.'

However, this time her opponent wasn't Naomi, but Janice, looking as elegant as ever with her blonde hair in a top-knot and a black wool coat with the collar turned up: Alida Valli in *The Fifth Man*. Lesley wasn't in her league. By contrast she was some nameless bimbo from a beach movie.

'I know.' Janice gave Lesley a charming smile. 'I'm supposed to meet him when the class is finished, but I must be a little early. I'll wait in the crèche.'

'Derek didn't say anything to me about someone coming to meet him,' Lesley said, blue eyes narrowed.

Janice widened hers in response. 'Well, why should he?' she said sweetly. 'That's his private business, isn't it? Come along, Devon.'

It must have been the first time Lesley had looked closely at the little boy who was holding on to Janice's hand, because she shut up as tight as if someone had superglued her lips together. There was no mistaking Devon's paternity. Janice and Devon were heading across the hall towards the crèche when the gym doors opened and Derek appeared, a kit bag slung over one shoulder.

'Dad!' Devon let go of Janice's hand and hurled himself bodily on to Derek, who picked him up and swung him round.

'Hey!' Derek said, putting his son back down on his feet again. 'What are you, a cannonball?'

Devon wrapped both his arms tightly round his father's legs and wouldn't move.

'No, he's a leech,' Janice said, laughing. 'Let your father go, Devon.'

Devon didn't move. Janice crossed over to Derek and kissed him on the lips, in a show of strength. Derek threw one arm around her shoulders, towering over her. The effect was like a cover for a Mills and Boon romance, with Janice so fair and Derek so dark. Devon looked up at them with evident approval.

I stared at Derek's handsome face with its high cheekbones and full mouth, seeming as relaxed as ever; no sign of tension, let alone grief, to mar its contours. It had never occurred to me before to wonder what Derek really felt about Linda's murder – sorrow? remorse? even guilt? – but I realised in that moment that I would never know. Derek kept his real feelings in a place that perhaps even he rarely visited. For a moment a surge of anger on Linda's behalf washed over me: this was taking *laissez-faire* a few steps too far. If I hadn't needed to find out who killed Linda to satisfy my own inquisitiveness, I would have left Derek to sink or swim and let someone else throw him a lifebelt if they felt the urge.

'I wasn't expecting you two,' he said, but there was only affection in his voice, not reproof.

Janice smiled up at him. 'We thought we'd surprise you, didn't we, Devon? Take you back for dinner.'

'Yeah!' Devon yelled. 'Surprise, Dad!'

Lou had emerged from her office and was standing in the doorway, watching the scene with evident approval. Janice glanced over to her and for a second their eyes met, as if something had been confirmed. Or successfully achieved.

'Well, let's be off, then,' Derek was saying. 'No use hanging around, is there? Hope you got plenty of food in, Jan. Dev and I are starving.' He ruffled Devon's hair.

'Don't you need a shower?' Janice asked.

'No, I can do that at home.'

'Are you staying with us tonight?' Devon said eagerly.

'You just heard him say he was,' Janice reproved. 'Don't you ever listen?'

' 'Course he doesn't,' Derek said easily. 'Boys his age, what do you expect?'

The happy family group made their way through the swing doors and disappeared into the street, leaving something of a void in their wake. Lou retreated into her office, her smile as faint but unmistakable as the Mona Lisa's. Lesley, meanwhile, was pouting so hard she looked as if she were doing facial exercises. Appearing at the top of the stairs, Rachel said to me in the aggrieved tone of someone suffering tannin deprivation symptoms: 'So what happened to the bloody teabags, then?'

17

When Lou rang me the next morning with the bad news, that picture of a happy nuclear family was the first thing to enter my head. It was eleven, and I had only just got out of bed. I was still in my dressing-gown; I'd like to say it was a Japanese silk kimono, but I can't. I do have a couple of Japanese silk kimonos, but the temperature usually prevailing in my studio requires instead flannel pyjamas and a dressing-gown that looks and feels as if it's been made out of old blankets. Myrna Loy wouldn't dignify me with a glance.

'Derek's been *what*?' I said, holding the phone closer to my ear.

'You heard me,' Lou said. 'Arrested.'

'Jesus. But on what evidence?'

'How the hell would I know, Sam? They were waitin' for him outside with a warrant this mornin' and they took him off in the car as soon as he showed up. That's all I know.'

Lou sounded as if she had been crying.

'Who were they – the policemen, I mean?'

'Same ones as before, I think. Not the older one, the inspector. The other one, lookin' pretty serious. And well he should, arrestin' an innocent man like that. Had a couple of constables with him, in case Derek tried to run for it or somethin'.' Her voice was scornful. 'Ain't no tellin' *what* they expected.'

'I'll give him a ring, Lou. Sergeant Hawkins, I mean. I want to tell him what we found out yesterday.'

Lou sniffed. 'That won't be enough to make 'em let Derek go.'

'I know. But it might tie up with something they have. And I want to find out what they've got against him. They might have something else we don't know about.'

'They can't really think he did it, Sam!' Lou said. I could hear that she was fighting back the tears.

'I'll do my best,' I promised. 'I'll ring you as soon as I've talked to Hawkins. Oh, and there's something I wanted to ask you, about Janice. Because yesterday I noticed that she knew the best place to sit and wait for Derek would be the crèche. So was she once a member of the gym?'

Lou sounded puzzled. ' 'Course she was. That's how they met. And she used to bring Devon in sometimes for karate lessons. Didn't you ever see her around here before?'

'No,' I said slowly.

'You don't think—'

'I can't think of anything till I have a cup of coffee,' I said lightly, not wanting to worry Lou still further. 'I'll call Hawkins. I promise I'll ring you as soon as I've talked to him.'

I put the phone down, wondering whether to tell Hawkins that if we were looking for someone who had come into the gym through the fire door and left the same way, someone who had a small child and so might know the crèche cupboard well enough to have come across the switch for the alarm, and someone who was clever enough to work out what use it could be put to – then Janice would certainly come top of the list.

I didn't want to tell him. I couldn't help liking her.

* * *

It took some time to get through to Hawkins. I assumed he was still in an interview room, questioning Derek. I just kept insisting that it was urgent until someone cracked and hauled him out of the question-and-answer session.

His voice sounded resigned.

'They told me that there was some woman on the phone who wanted to speak to me and wouldn't be fobbed off. I assumed it was you.'

'You're doing yourself an injustice. It might have been Michelle Pfeiffer looking for a date.'

'If that's all you wanted to say—' he began haughtily. I cut him off.

'Look, I've heard you've arrested Derek.'

His tone was a little evasive. 'Not me personally. I mean, physically, yes—'

'Oh good. So you're dubious about it as well?'

'I didn't say that. And stop talking through me,' he said crossly. I wondered if I should tell him that I had read in the *Guardian* that in-depth studies had discovered that eighty per cent of conversational interruptions are caused by men talking through women, so I was only redressing the balance slightly. Then I decided that it might not be appropriate. Oh, the tact of the girl.

'Can we meet up? Like now?' I said hopefully. 'I've got something I want to tell you.'

'Go ahead. I'm listening.'

'No, it's too complicated to explain on the phone.' I didn't want to tell him that I wanted to pick his brains, which was always easier face to face. In his current state of grumpiness he might not have taken it too well.

'OK, but this had better be good,' he said, accepting the invitation with a marked lack of grace. 'And I can't manage now. Lunchtime, maybe. Come here at one.'

A police interview room was not exactly the atmosphere I had envisaged for our relaxed and frank exchange of confidences.

'No, that sounds very uncosy,' I said. 'What about a sandwich shop or something?'

I said sandwich shop because for all I knew police officers thought cafés weren't butch enough for their image. No police officer on TV would have been caught dead in a café.

'I can't say a specific time because I don't know when I'll be free,' he said, sounding harassed. I assumed by this he meant that he didn't know when he and Monroe would have finished attempting to persuade Derek that he had actually killed Linda in one of those momentary impulses of rage that we all have sometimes towards our girlfriends: we understand, my son, she started nagging you, did she? If you get the right judge he'll probably give you a suspended sentence. 'I'll come round to your place when I'm finished.'

'But I—' I began. He had put the phone down. How *rude*. I sulked for a while. Then I went upstairs and got dressed. I hadn't really ever envisaged myself as the kind of person who entertained police officers to lunch. Do come in, Sergeant, would you like a canapé? I would have to be careful not to tell anyone that I knew a policeman socially. Or I could just say that he had forced his way in, beaten me up and tried to plant drugs on me. The way things were in North London these days, anyone would believe that version.

Hawkins turned up at two o'clock. I hadn't wanted to leave the studio in case he showed while I was away, so I had read the *Guardian* cover to cover and finally been reduced to watching *Neighbours*, not the best procedure for someone who wants her brains in sharp condition. I had to do the crossword afterwards to regain some mental powers.

I was in jeans and a big black sweater. Nothing too terrifying. Still, to balance this, I had put on red lipstick, silver hoops through every hole in my ears and a fistful of rings, though I had left off my eye ring, which some people with weak stomachs don't like. By this time I was starving and was only saved from eating the rubber strip around the inside of the fridge door by his arrival with a couple of packets of sandwiches.

'Brilliant!' I said with enthusiasm.

'All vegetarian,' he said rather sourly. 'I thought perhaps you might be.'

He was wearing the blouson jacket but thank God he took it off straight away, though saying in a sarcastic tone: 'It's not that warm in here, is it?'

'My art consultant,' I said in a superior tone, 'says it's Bohemian.' I dug into an egg-and-cress sandwich with such vehemence that he looked surprised and handed me the other half.

'Haven't you eaten today?'

I shook my head. Bits of cress fell from between my teeth with the movement. I picked them up off my lap and ate them. He looked faintly revolted.

'I see you've taken my advice,' I said through a mouthful of sandwich, pointing at his navy sweater. 'You're wearing blue.' He looked down at himself.

'I didn't put it on especially. I mean, I had it anyway,' he said defensively.

'OK, to business,' I said, finishing the sandwich. 'What I

wanted to ask you was this: when you all came into the gym after Linda was killed, did anyone test the emergency door to see if the alarm was on?'

'The emergency door?'

'The fire door at the end of the basement corridor. Next to the toilets where she was found.'

'Yes, of course we did.'

'Oh. So it was set, then, the alarm?'

'If it hadn't been, don't you think we'd have been concentrating on the possibility that someone came in that way?' he said in an unnecessarily patronising tone of voice.

'Well, I don't know what you lot are concentrating on, do I?' I said pettishly. 'So that's ruled out, then.'

Damn, I thought. It had seemed such a good idea. I got up and went to make some coffee. He followed me across to the kitchen table. I filled up the bottom of the percolator with water, packed coffee into the middle section, screwed it all together and put it on the gas ring.

'Why don't you tell me,' I suggested, 'what evidence you have against Derek? You can't just have arrested him because statistically most people are killed by their husbands or boyfriends, or vice versa.'

Was I imagining things, or had his expression just become rather guarded?

'We talked to Naomi Fisher again,' he said. 'She told us that, instead of looking for an earring, as she had previously claimed, she was in fact in the men's changing rooms with Mr Brewster. You knew that already, didn't you?'

I stared at him guilelessly. 'I guessed it, of course. But you can't go to the police just with a guess, can you?'

He stared at me hard for a moment in the approved manner, and continued: 'And she apparently noticed that their activities were being observed by Ms Fillman through the window in the door.'

'How come she saw Linda and Derek didn't?'

To my delight, he blushed slightly. 'Um, apparently they were in such a position that . . . well—'

'In the *changing rooms*?' I said incredulously. 'They couldn't have been lying down, it would have been too uncomfortable –

unless he had his back to the door and she was . . . oh, I *see*. Lucky Derek.' I thought about it for a moment. 'He'd have to be at an angle to the door, actually. Linda must have made some noise and Naomi looked up and saw her. I expect Derek was too distracted to notice, ha ha.'

Hawkins's blush had not abated. I grinned at him.

'So the theory is that after Naomi went upstairs, Linda confronted Derek in a raging temper and was generally so annoying that he bashed her head in. But surely it would be more likely that *she'd* hit *him*? And where did he get the weight from if it wasn't premeditated?'

'That's what we're trying to establish,' Hawkins said uncomfortably. The coffee was making boiling noises. I squinted cautiously inside the lid and took it off the gas.

'I expect you know that Naomi had a grudge against Derek,' I pointed out. 'I wouldn't take her testimony as gospel. He told her after they'd, um, done it, that she wasn't to assume that just because they'd, um, done it, she was now his girlfriend, and she got all offended and cross and stormed out.'

'It doesn't change the fact that she saw Linda Fillman watching them.'

'No, but that doesn't prove anything either!'

I poured out the coffee. 'I don't have any milk,' I said apologetically. 'I'm sorry, I know it's important to some people. I think I've got sugar somewhere, though. Would you like some?'

Hawkins was staring down incredulously at the thick black liquid in his mug.

'Yes, sugar, I think,' I said, swiftly rifling through the cupboard for a couple of those little packets they give you in cheap restaurants which I had pocketed for just such an emergency as this. They were rather crumpled and stained by this time, but I emptied them both into his cup and threw the packets away before he could get a close look at them. Then I produced a reasonably clean teaspoon from the drying rack and gave it to him with another of my Josie-bright smiles. He stirred the coffee, looking unconvinced, then took a sip.

'God, this is strong!' he said, grimacing.

'Yes,' I pointed out, 'but you probably drink hundreds of cups a day of nasty coffee-machine coffee, which has practically no caffeine in it whatever and is full of additives. This has the same amount of caffeine, no additives and you only need to drink one cup. Much more sensible.'

'Hmm.' He sipped some more. 'Tell me about the other people who were downstairs that day.'

I sat down on the kitchen table.

'Brian's a bit of an enigma. He's a serious bodybuilder and he works as a bouncer sometimes – he never says much. You've probably found that out by now. I don't really think he killed Linda. I can't see why he should. The same goes for Fliss. I want to talk to them both, though, now Derek's been arrested, to see if they know anything else they weren't telling me before. Jeff is much more promising.' I explained about Linda's plans for the gym and the petition Jeff had been getting up. 'You could maybe go and talk to the councillors who run the leisure services, to see if Linda really was hatching something with them that Jeff might have got wind of. Also, she was nasty to him. She had a very cutting tongue and she used to wind Jeff up whenever she could. That makes him quite likely to me as a suspect – I can see them having a quarrel, Linda saying something unforgivable and Jeff whacking her on the head with a weight. There were some in the office, don't forget.'

'There weren't any traces of blood on his clothes, don't forget,' Hawkins pointed out.

'Were there any on Derek's?'

'No,' he admitted reluctantly. 'But there were none on anyone's, which is strange enough. Forensic seems to think that a certain amount of blood would have splattered. Not much, but a little. And obviously whoever did it was standing right next to her. But we searched the whole gym and there was no clothing concealed anywhere with bloodstains on it. Oh, and she was definitely hit with that weight, by the way. Which makes it much more difficult. There's always the problem of where it came from. That counts against Brewster too, you know. He could have gone into the men's gym and fetched it without, um—'

'Brian.'

'Yes, without him noticing. He says he would have seen anyone else. Felicity Brady says no one at all came into the women's gym and I've heard nothing to contradict that. And Jeff

Whatsit, Roberts, says no one took a weight from the office. Which doesn't look too good for Derek Brewster.'

He finished his coffee and put the cup down. 'That wasn't bad at all,' he admitted. 'Clears your head, doesn't it?'

I stared at him. '*You* don't think it was Derek, do you?'

He wouldn't meet my gaze. 'I don't know,' he said.

'Then why's he been arrested?'

He shrugged. 'Monroe likes him for it. Face it, he's by far the most obvious suspect. As you said yourself, the boyfriend's always the most probable one. And when that Fisher girl told us that Linda Fillman had seen them at it . . . well, there was the motive.'

'And he's black, and Linda was white,' I added pointedly.

'Yes, I don't think that hurts as far as the inspector's concerned,' he said frankly. 'But he – Inspector Monroe, I mean – really does think Brewster did it. He's not that prejudiced. And the Fisher girl's black, too, don't forget. She'll testify against him.'

I snorted. 'She didn't actually see Derek hit Linda, did she? And she's so involved she's not exactly unbiased. If you ask me she's much more likely to have done it herself.'

'But how the hell do I prove that?' he demanded. 'It's like the three wise monkeys down there in that basement – no one saw or heard anything!'

We stared at each other. I bit my lip and said anxiously: 'But you'll check out what we've been talking about all the same?' I came off the kitchen table and stood opposite him. 'And you'll talk to the people at the council—'

'I said I would!' Hawkins interrupted, his jaw set. 'If I say I'll do something, I do it, OK?'

'Good!' I retorted, staring back at him. Our eyes met across the small space between us. There was an unbearably long pause. Finally he broke it by saying in a rather strangled voice: 'So, um . . . what did you say your mobile was called?'

I realised I had been holding my breath. Letting it out, I said: 'Undiscovered Planet – well, that's what this art consultant woman called it. She came round last week, before you turned up, actually, that's why I was a bit dazed when you rang the door-bell that time. I thought it was her coming back, you see . . .'

I realised that I was rambling horrendously and tailed off. I had been staring up at the mobile, conscious that he was looking at me as I spoke. Bringing my head down, I met his eyes again. It was a big mistake. They really were very blue. I couldn't help it. I completely forgot for a moment that he was a policeman, and after that I was kissing him, and it was rather too late to think about that kind of thing.

He kissed very well by any standard. He was rather surprised at first but he made up for it as soon as he realised what was happening. In fact it was me who pulled away first. I said distractedly: 'This is a terrible mistake—'

'I know,' he said, equally fervently. 'I *live* with someone, goddamn it—'

Then he grabbed me and kissed me again, holding on to me so tightly he was nearly cutting off my circulation. It was the kind of kiss that could have led anywhere at all, and it very nearly did. I was lost, falling into space, and he was kissing me as if he hadn't kissed anyone for years and was making up for lost time: deep, arrowy kisses with a kind of raw need about them, as if he were dying of thirst. My head was spinning as if I were drunk and I was clutching at him with equal desperation, convinced that if he let me go I would tumble to the ground, my legs as weak as cotton wool.

When he finally lifted his mouth from mine and looked down at me, his eyes were so blue they looked charged with electricity and his hair was standing up where I had ruffled it, which contributed to the impression. We were both completely out of breath and couldn't say anything for a while. I was fully occupied with regaining my balance. The blood in my body was pounding round its circuit so fast I felt dizzy.

'So who's this person you live with, then?' I said finally. Sam Jones, tact personified. I removed my hands reluctantly from the back of his head.

He looked confounded and tried to run one hand through his hair, a gesture momentarily impeded by the fact that both of his hands were buried under my sweater. He looked shocked when he realised where they were, pulling them out with unflattering alacrity.

'My partner,' he said, catching his breath.

'Your *partner*?' I said. 'You mean your police partner? Or are you one of those men who call your girlfriend your *partner*, like you were in business with her?'

'Daphne's a feminist,' he said haughtily. 'She thinks the word "girlfriend" is demeaning—'

'*Daphne*? You live with someone called *Daphne*?' I said, seizing on the crucial point with all the gusto of a hungry piranha. Hawkins gave me a killing look, pulled down his sweater, which I had dragged around a bit, and looked around wildly for his jacket.

'It's on the sofa,' I said, going over and fetching it. Approaching him with the jacket in my hands, I looked up at him innocently.

'Do you want me to help you on with it?'

'Don't *touch* me,' he said, ripping it out of my hands.

'Did Daphne buy it for you? It's not very flattering, you know.'

'I've met some bitches in my time, Sam,' he shouted at me, 'but you are absolutely—'

'Thank you,' I said dulcetly.

'Now I'm going. I should never have come round here—'

'It was your idea, not mine, don't forget—'

He stormed over to the door, but I was ahead of him. I pressed myself back against it and said: 'You will check out everything we've been talking about, won't you? I mean, just because we surrendered to a moment of helpless passion, you won't forget what you said you were going to do?'

'Yes! Yes! I mean, no, I won't! Now let me out!'

His hair was still standing up and his jacket was all askew. If I had just tied him down and molested him he couldn't have looked more distracted. I wondered what he would actually look like if I tied him down and molested him. It didn't bear thinking about. Business before pleasure, alas.

'You're free to leave at any time,' I said, waving my hand ceremoniously. 'I don't believe in keeping men here against their will—'

'I mean, move aside from the bloody door!'

'What's the matter? Don't you trust yourself close to me?'

I stood ostentatiously aside. He fumbled with the locks inexpertly till I inserted a hand and turned the only one that was set. He jumped back as if contact with me would burn him. I pulled the door open. He was through it in a flash. His car was parked just outside the steps. Once he was standing by it, he seemed to regain a measure of poise.

'I'll ring you,' he said, laying a heavy emphasis on the word 'ring', 'when I know something. OK?'

'Fine.' I smiled at him sweetly. 'I can't wait.'

He glared at me. 'You've got lipstick smeared all over your mouth,' he said.

'So,' I retorted, 'do you.'

I went inside and closed the door before he realised that I had been lying. Checking myself in the bathroom mirror, I cleaned off the lipstick from around my extremely smug smile. Nothing like a little light flirtation to pick one up. I realised that I didn't yet know his first name. How odd; it's usually the other way around.

There was a half-sandwich left on the table by the sofa. Cheese and pickle. I ate it slowly. A thought had just occurred to me. Wouldn't it be ironic if, after all this effort on his behalf, Derek actually had killed Linda after all?

18

I wasn't the only person whose thoughts were running along those lines, as I discovered when I dropped into the gym later on. I was actually en route to see Derek's solicitor, Lou having asked me to talk to him. She herself had gone down to the police station, leaving Rachel to hold the fort; it was Lesley's day off, and even if she had been there she couldn't have been trusted with anything approaching actual responsibility.

Rachel was sitting in the reception cubicle poring over an account ledger, looking rather tired. I offered to help but she shook her head.

'It's not that bad. And Lou said she'd come in later.' She looked at me thoughtfully. 'You know what I've been thinking, Sam, now Derek's been arrested? Suppose he actually did kill Linda?'

'You don't really think he did it, Rachel?'

'No, no,' she said wearily. 'But you can't help wondering, sooner or later – wouldn't it be strange if . . . oh, you know what I mean, Sam.'

'Well, I've been talking to that policeman. The sergeant one.' I toyed for a moment with the idea of telling her what had happened and decided that I couldn't face her derision. It was going to be hard enough relating it to Tom. 'And he's not that convinced himself.'

'But they've arrested him!'

'I know. But from what he said I think that was more the inspector's doing. I don't know if he's having pressure put on him to make an arrest, but apparently he really does think it was Derek.'

Rachel sighed. 'Well, I don't know if there's much more we can do,' she said. 'Everything seems to be coming to a dead end.'

'I had what I thought was a brilliant idea about the fire door, but Sergeant Hawkins deflated my presumption. Still, he's going to talk to the people at the council who deal with leisure services to see if Linda did have a plan hatched with them to privatise the centre.'

'What would that prove?' Rachel was being very negative today.

'It would give Jeff a motive.'

'Oh, right.' She didn't sound too convinced.

I remembered what Hawkins had told me: that Naomi had seen Linda watching her and Derek, and duly related it.

'What a slut that girl is,' Rachel said.

'Well, you've got to admire her initiative. She caught him with his tracksuit bottoms down and took it from there, as it were.'

'Maybe it was Naomi who killed Linda,' Rachel suggested. 'If she didn't go straight back upstairs, but into the loo, and she met Linda there – imagine what a scene that would have been.'

'But where did she get the weight from? That's always the stumbling block.'

'I told you,' Rachel said. 'Everything finishes in a dead end.'

She pulled the account book back towards her. I said: 'Are you sure I can't do anything to help?'

Rachel looked up. 'Actually, there is something. I don't want to leave the front desk – could you go into the office and pull out the invoice files for this year? There should be two or three. Red ones. On the shelves at the back.'

The shelves were on the far wall, behind Lou's desk. As they were dauntingly full of red files, it took me some time to locate the right ones. They were protruding slightly from the others, as if to catch my attention, and when I pulled them out I saw why; an obstruction behind them stopped them from being fully pushed in. It was a doorknob.

I stared at it for a moment. Then, slowly, I took out the files on the shelf directly below. It confirmed my guess: first I'd found the doorknob, now here was the lock, looking antiquated but still functional. The shelves must have been built over the original door when someone had decided it was no longer necessary. Had they bothered to plaster it up or would it still open?

The main set of keys hung, as it always did, on a nail behind the desk. I rummaged through it till I came across one with an old paper label reading simply 'Back Door' and tried it in the lock, which slid open without difficulty. With one hand pressed against the files on the shelves to steady them, I turned the door-knob. The door swung open slowly. Outside was the alley that ran round the building, and beyond it a high concrete wall, stained and forbidding, windowless as a prison.

I found myself shivering with an icy chill that had little to do with the cold air outside. For a second I stood absolutely still, and in that moment I was suddenly convinced that there was someone behind me in the office. The skin of my neck was prickling in awareness; I could almost feel her presence. She had made no sound and this total silence was as ominous as if I had seen her shadow thrown before me, a weapon in her hand. It flashed through my mind that she would be calculating how long I would remain with my back turned, raising the weight she held in her hand and coming towards me with quick, soft footsteps, face contorted in a terrifying grimace of effort and intention to smash it down on the back of my head—

I swung round, half ducking, my breath panting in my throat. The office was empty, the door slightly ajar as I had left it. No sign that anyone had been there, that anything out of the ordinary had happened apart from the fact that my imagination had run away with me on a wild, paranoiac flight of fancy. I let out my breath in a rush, my heart pounding thunderously, still racing from the shock of anticlimax.

When I had given myself a little time to recover, I closed the door, returned the key to its place and picked up the files Rachel had wanted. She was deep into the account ledger and hardly noticed me till I plonked them down in front of her.

'You took your time,' she said absently. 'Weren't they where I said?'

I made some non-committal noise. 'Rachel,' I said abruptly, 'did Lou come in just now?'

She looked up at me in surprise. 'No, she's at the police station, don't you remember?'

I remembered the face I had imagined behind me, and shivered again. I didn't know why I had thought she would have wanted to catch me with my back turned to strike the blow. After all, whoever had killed Linda hadn't been that kind of coward. They had hit her full in the face.

* * *

I had assumed that Derek's solicitor, Gavin Pritchett, would be of a radical persuasion, but the address of his firm was impeccably Establishment. The office was inside a court which was larger than almost any Oxbridge college could boast and equally redolent of tradition, atmosphere and all the other adjectives used by the defenders of clubs to which only men are admitted. No traffic could enter inside; the centre of the court was filled with a sward of immaculately-kept grass. It was pleasantly quiet, and I wondered if the ivy twining up the stone walls had originally been planted as primitive sound insulation. Several obscenely fat pigeons waddled across my path, taking their time about it; they looked as if it would take a bazooka to make them hurry. Then a couple of middle-aged men who made the pigeons look positively svelte exited from a door on my left so abruptly that they would have bumped into me if I hadn't jumped aside, and strolled away without apologising, conversing in low plummy voices. One could see who the pigeons had taken as role models.

After about a quarter of an hour spent wandering along squinting at all the brass nameplates affixed by each doorway, I finally found the name of Derek's solicitors. They were on the third floor and there wasn't a lift. These people didn't need StairMasters. Once inside the office, the politically correct tinge to the practice was more obvious; as I sat half-on, half-off the exiguous tweed sofa in reception, the faces that bustled past were of most colours British nationality could boast and mainly appeared above the kind of clothes which are affected by would-be radical intellectuals – about which the less said the better. The pot plants were all pretty much dead. Maybe they were talking to them instead of giving them water.

'You can go through to Gavin's office now,' said the receptionist, displaying an impressive familiarity with her boss. I bet in most law practices in this neck of the woods they'd have fired her on the spot for calling him anything but 'Mr Pritchett, sir'.

Gavin, as I expected I should learn to call him, worked at the end of the corridor and by my calculations his room should boast a view over the main courtyard. I knocked and entered. Sure enough, the high windows in front of me looked onto green grass and ivied stone. Very peaceful. I wondered if in spare moments Gavin fantasised that he was a law don, about to give a tutorial to a group of admiring students. He probably had it even better than a don, now I thought about it; it was supposed to be so hard now to get a placement in a legal firm that students were required to perform illegal sexual practices on senior members just to get an interview.

Then I stopped speculating on Gavin's possible perks. I had just realised that the panorama out of the windows wasn't the only attractive view his room currently offered. The other one was sitting on a chair beside his desk and had her head turned to me, her face wearing an expression which could only have been described as hostile. I shrank back involuntarily. If this was what Grace Kelly looked like in a bad mood, Hitchcock must have secretly wiped the sweat from his brow in relief when she retired from the movies.

'You!' she said in a way that would have been theatrical if it hadn't been so threatening. She stood up, pushing back her chair so forcibly that it squeaked in protest.

'Do you two know each other?' said Gavin Pritchett. He was wearing a beige flannel shirt, a brown corduroy jacket and a tie which looked as if he masticated it in moments of stress.

'Yes, we do. Hello, Janice!' I said, making a heroic effort not to look guilty. 'How's Devon?'

It didn't work. I could practically hear her jaw snapping shut. Her blue eyes were shooting laser beams of rage at me. If Grace had looked half as nastily at Prince Rainier, he'd have held up his hands in surrender and promised her that she could have the crown jewels of Monaco reset any way she wanted.

'Is *this* the person who was coming to see you, Gavin?' she snapped. 'The one who's been investigating who really killed Linda?'

'Well, I assume so . . .' Gavin did not look happy. He was

stroking his chin; when he took his hand away I could see that he was trying for a goatee. So far it looked more like armpit regrowth. 'Um, won't you sit down?' he said to me, trying to gain control of the situation. 'You must be Ms Jones.'

'Call me Sam.'

Janice looked as if she knew exactly what to call me. I hoped she didn't use that kind of vocabulary in front of Devon.

'What the hell do you think you've been doing? Investigating *me*?' she exclaimed. She took two paces towards me. I managed to stand firm. 'That's it, isn't it? Hanging round outside my house, tricking me into telling you things, pretending to be so nice and understanding – how dare you!'

'Now hang on a minute,' I said, my temper also rising, 'I didn't trick you into telling me a damn thing. You did that of your own accord, remember? You didn't even need persuading!'

'Perhaps,' said Gavin feebly, 'we could all just sit down and have a cup of tea . . .'

Janice turned and stared at him. He wilted visibly and stammered:

'Um, no tea then . . .'

'Look,' I said, cutting through Gavin's nervous babble to nail Janice with a stare which I hoped, though perhaps not on her level, was as transfixing as Linda's had once been, 'if a couple of Derek's friends anticipate that he'll probably be arrested for a murder they think he didn't commit, what the hell do you expect them to do? Resign themselves and start getting him measured for his prison wardrobe? You should be grateful that a few people have bothered to try to find some evidence to clear him – that is, if you really don't want to have him stand trial.'

'What do you mean?' Her expression was a mixture of angry and baffled. 'Of course I want Derek to be released!' she said. 'Why wouldn't I?'

I shrugged. 'If you had something to hide yourself,' I suggested in a neutral tone of voice, 'it might be quite convenient for you that he's been arrested.'

The icy look in her blue eyes made me think that Grace Kelly had been wasted playing heroines. She might have done wonders with a meaty role as a psychopathic serial killer.

'Where were you when Linda was killed? Just out of

interest,' I said, deciding I might as well go for broke. After all, it wasn't my fault that she'd spilled her guts to a stranger at a bus stop.

'I was at work when it happened!' she snapped at me. 'I suppose you think *I* killed Linda?'

'You had a motive,' I said mildly.

To my surprise, she blushed lightly. Her hair was pulled back in one of her French pleats and I could see the pink flush right up to her hairline.

'What about you?' she threw back at me. 'Did *you* kill her?'

'Yes, actually I did,' I said, sitting down on the chair Gavin had indicated some time ago. 'I wouldn't have, though, if I'd known it was going to cause all this trouble.'

Perhaps my attempt to leaven the situation with a touch of humour was ill-timed. Gavin twitched visibly and Janice's lovely face froze like Grace's in *Rear Window* when Jimmy Stewart has finally managed to convince her that a murder has been committed across the courtyard.

'Joke, ha ha,' I said, trying to salvage the situation. 'I'm really very funny. I must tell both of you my blonde jokes some time. Anyway, no, I didn't kill Linda. I have an alibi. Even the police don't suspect me, OK? And if I had I wouldn't be chasing round trying to find out who really did kill her. I'm not a complete moron. I'd be keeping my head so low I'd have neck cramp.'

My effort at humour had at least had the effect of deflating Janice's anger. The blush was fading from her skin, which was usually a creamy white – Dulux would have called it Milk With A Hint Of Pink – but now seemed drained of any colour. She looked, suddenly, very tired.

'So why are you trying to find out who did it?' she said, lowering her voice to a normal volume for the first time.

I shrugged again. 'Because Lou and Rachel asked me to, originally,' I said. 'And once I get my teeth into something I find it impossible to let go. It's one of my vices.'

I thought for a moment of the Thing, remembering how long I had struggled with it before I had turned it into a mobile, unable to put it aside and start another piece of work till I had found out what it needed. I was single-minded to a fault. As for the need to know, it could be defined as a metaphysical quest, if you happened to use that sort of vocabulary. For me that was a euphemism for bloody-minded curiosity.

'By the way,' I said suddenly, the curiosity kicking in again, 'what are you doing here, if that doesn't sound too abrupt?'

'I work here!' Janice said impatiently. 'I'm a solicitor. Don't you remember I told you that while you were snooping around in my private life?'

'There's no need for that kind of comment,' I said austerely. 'I take it you recommended Derek to Gavin here when he needed a solicitor?'

'Yes. I do conveyancing mostly. Gavin's our criminal law specialist.'

I glanced over at Gavin. He was chewing on his tie. At least this obscured the attempt at a goatee. I had been going to tell him about the possibility that someone might have entered the gym through the fire door; now that was out of the question. Janice would make him repeat verbatim anything I told him ten seconds after I was gone. Aware that I was looking at him, he glanced up, his eyes meeting mine with a timid, imploring expression like that of a small furry woodland creature which has come out of its hole for the first time and feels that the outside world may on balance be a little too demanding for it. I hoped he was slightly more assertive with the counsel for the prosecution.

'Um, who *do* you actually think killed Linda Fillman?' he said, removing the tie from his mouth just after he had started speaking.

'Frankly, Gavin,' I said, 'I haven't the faintest idea.'

19

I was due to meet Tom at the Chinese restaurant later on that evening, and I was dreading the confession I would have to make. I'm not a bad liar in general, but I can't hide anything from Tom. I got there early and had a ginseng beer to fortify myself.

'What have you been up to?' he said as soon as he saw me. 'I can tell there's something.'

'Sit down first.'

'My God, what is it?' he said excitedly, plonking his behind down on a chair.

I stared at him in silence.

'Sammy, if you don't tell me—'

I took a deep breath. 'I kissed a policeman. If you must know.'

He burst out laughing. 'Jesus,' he said finally, 'you really had me going, you know? You're getting good at this. Do you remember when you told me—'

'No, Tom. I'm not joking. I really did kiss a policeman.' It was easier to say the second time.

There was a horrible pause.

'I don't believe it.'

'Really.'

'Do you have no shame, woman?' he thundered. 'Are there no depths to which you will not sink? Jesus, if it had been a priest – I could understand a priest – but a *policeman* . . .' His voice altered slightly as he yielded to vulgar curiosity. 'So, did the helmet get in the way?'

'He wasn't in uniform, you prat. I'm not completely debauched.

He's plain-clothes. Literally. His clothes are awful. And you're going to love this bit: he's got a girlfriend called Daphne.'

'No! Not really?'

'Mm.'

'Daphne,' Tom mused. 'Sounds like a head girl at school, sort of tall and strapping. Captain of the lacrosse team.'

'He has to call her his partner. She won't let him use the word "girlfriend" because she says it's demeaning to women.'

'They're terrible, those girls,' he said in a heartfelt voice. 'I had one once who made me read her entire collection of Virago paperbacks and discuss them with her afterwards.'

'You poor thing.'

'It was awful. Not the books so much as the discussions, though some of them were pretty awful too.' He shuddered. 'Better not to think about it. So tell me, was he a good kisser?'

'Mm, very. Only he gave the impression that he hadn't done it for years. I bet Daphne's one of those feminists who are anti-penetrative sex because they say it's invasive. She probably doesn't even let him put his tongue in her mouth.'

'She was like that too – the girl who made me read the books!' Tom exclaimed. 'I never told you because I thought you'd laugh at me.'

'What, she wouldn't let you put your tongue in her mouth?'

'No, prat, my willy. And not in her mouth. Jesus, I should have been so lucky. Anywhere.'

'God.' I contemplated this for a moment. 'But what's the point of men if you don't have penetrative sex with them?' I said blankly.

'Don't ask *me*,' said Tom.

'That,' I said firmly, 'is *not* what I call feminism. And I certainly consider myself a feminist.'

'Best of both worlds for us males, girls like you,' he said cheerfully. 'Ones who'll do filthy things to you in bed but don't expect you to pay for dinner.'

This was pushing things a little too far. 'That's it,' I said firmly. 'Tonight's on you.'

Tom spluttered in indignation. 'Save that for your policeman,' he said nastily. 'Don't they have expenses for entertaining?'

'I doubt it. He's only a detective sergeant.'

'But a good kisser, eh?'

'Don't be so bloody prurient! Don't you have anything interesting going on in your own life you'd like to share with me?'

He shook his head dolefully. 'You're the one having all the excitement. By the way, I thought of something the other day.' He leaned forward over the table with his best serious expression. 'Sammy, has it ever occurred to you that Mr Muscle might actually be guilty as charged? It would be a bit ironic really, wouldn't it?'

I stared at him. 'If one more person says that to me,' I said gloomily, 'I'm giving back my Nancy Drew badge for good.'

* * *

'Sam! Sam! In here!'

I had just come down the basement stairs and was passing the office. This furtive whisper snapped my head around, but I knew who was calling me even before I looked. Brian's voice, even at its lowest bass rumble, was nothing if not distinctive. He was lurking inside the office. A white sweatshirt, doubtless sized XXL, strained nonetheless across the massive curves and indentations of his chest. I walked into the office, my curiosity stirred. Brian was not a natural lurker.

'What is it, Brian?'

Instead of answering, he ducked his head and looked around for eavesdroppers, like an actor in a third-rate spy movie trying to look surreptitious.

'What *is* it?' I repeated, rather irritated.

'Something to tell you,' he mumbled.

'What?' I seemed doomed to reiterate this endlessly. 'Go on, then,' I added in more encouraging tones.

'It's Fliss.'

Not wanting to say 'What?' again, I flapped my hands around in frustration. Brian noticed this and made an effort to expand on his previous efforts at information dispersal.

'She wants to talk to you.'

'What about?' I said between gritted teeth. It was lucky for Brian he was so large; otherwise long before now some unfortunate person who had simply asked him a basic question – what time it was, let's say – would have gripped him by the ears and pounded his face against the wall in frustration at not getting anything that was recognisably an answer. Indeed, on the subject of what Fliss had to say to me Brian was as silent as the Delphic Oracle when the temple was closed. His massive contours made this mythical comparison somehow appropriate. I gathered, however, that Fliss was at her stall that day.

'Is it urgent? Should I go straight away?' I asked. I had only come in to work out; I didn't have a class to teach.

Brian nodded seriously. I thanked him, curious rather than concerned.

I would have been more worried if I had realised that he was following me.

* * *

It was the weekend and Camden was in full swing. Outside the entrance to what called itself an antique market, but I had the suspicion was more like a car boot sale, a town crier was standing, dressed in full regalia including three-cornered hat, waving a large bell about and shouting: 'Oyez, oyez!' This was presumably an attempt to impress potential customers with the authenticity of the antiques, in which case the effect would have been enhanced by his not holding a hot dog in the hand that wasn't occupied by the bell and taking big sloppy bites out of it in the intervals between the traditional cries.

I wove my way slowly through the crowds. A Goth couple passed me, one of the most perfectly executed I'd seen in a long time; both of them exquisitely emaciated, dressed in long, flowing black coats and high-heeled boots, the man in a high black hat, the woman with a black feather boa wound round her narrow neck. Their skin was as white as if they were already dead. Perhaps they were. Camden is that kind of place. There were the usual hordes of young people hanging out at bus stops and corners, pretending to be American teenagers, with the requisite dirty hair, skewed baseball caps, pieces of clothing tied loosely round various parts of their bodies and canvas boots with the laces undone. This last detail always struck me as being peculiarly moronic; I lived in hope of seeing one of them trip over a bootlace and go flying.

The smell of frying spicy food hit me from various angles as I ducked into the archway beyond the railway bridge, making my stomach rumble. Maybe later I'd get a vegetable samosa. The stall that offered hair plaiting was doing brisk business; a group of giggling French schoolchildren were queuing up to have brightly coloured strands twined in with their own shining locks. Children on the Continent definitely wash their hair more frequently. Even the boys looked like they used conditioner on a regular basis and remembered to rinse thoroughly.

Fliss was busy with a customer as I neared the stall, so I hung around until she had finished. He was one of those people who pick up everything and ask the price, even though it's all clearly labelled, and then walk away without a word of thanks.

'Fliss?' I said tentatively. She looked around and when she saw me she started with surprise. There was a wariness in her expression that hadn't been there before. She rocked back on her heels, shoved her thumbs into the front pockets of her jeans and surveyed me. With her shiny black bomber jacket and razored haircut she looked from a distance like a skinhead.

'Oh, hi, Sam,' she said with absolutely no noticeable enthusiasm.

I raised my eyebrows at this. 'Brian said you wanted to talk to me,' I said. 'At least, that's what I think he meant. You know Brian.'

'Yeah.' For quite a while this looked as if it was all she was going to say. Then she pulled the little comb out of her jeans pocket, ran it back through her hair, replaced it and said, slowly, as if coming to an unwelcome decision: 'Andy, keep an eye out, will you? Got to talk to Sam.'

This made me start. I hadn't realised that Andy, Fliss's boyfriend, was present. Looking in the direction to which she had spoken, I saw that he had in fact been in view, though hidden from the waist down by Fliss's artistic stack of leather suitcases. But he was such a fragile little thing that he was easy to overlook, especially when he was standing next to Fliss. It was probably an experience he was accustomed to, because he seemed to bear me no malice; in fact he flashed me a lovely smile and tossed his head back slightly. His golden curls caught the sun. His jacket, open slightly at the neck, revealed his collarbones, so frail they looked as friable as old ivory. Fliss smiled at him fondly.

'Hi, Sam!' he said.

'Oh, hi, Andy,' I said guiltily. 'Sorry, I didn't see you there.'

Fliss and I moved slightly to one side of the stall, sheltered by the stone wall. She adopted her usual mannish stance, one leg bent at the knee, foot resting against the wall. Her arms were folded across her chest. She looked forbidding and I didn't know what to say; I had understood that it was she who had something to communicate. For some reason I felt like a luckless subaltern forced to question a gouty old major-general.

Finally Fliss said shortly: 'Brian explain?'

'He didn't say anything apart from the fact that you wanted to talk to me.' I laid a certain emphasis on the latter half of this sentence.

'Humph,' Fliss grunted in a very major-general sort of way. 'Well. Brian thought I ought to tell you this. None of his business, if you ask me.'

I smiled politely and waited. She added reluctantly: 'Afternoon Linda died, we had a bit of a set-to. She and I.'

'How did that happen?'

'Came into the gym with her clipboard,' Fliss said, pronouncing the word 'clipboard' with magnificent contempt. 'Making notes on everything. Kept on at it till I asked her what she thought she was doing. "Rationalisation", apparently.' She looked at me. 'You know, what cuts she could make to the budget. Bloody ridiculous. There isn't anything left to cut and she knows it. So I said, if she meant privatisation she should damn well come out and say it. D'you want a cigarette?'

I shook my head. Fliss pulled a packet of tobacco and some papers out of one hip pocket and proceeded to roll up with one hand as I watched in admiration. She must have practised for ages, watching westerns on TV. I bet Andy was impressed.

'Anyway,' she went on, making a shelter with her cupped hands and lighting up expertly, 'she said was I calling her a coward, and I said well, I thought she should call a spade a spade.'

She smoked in short, hard puffs, eyes narrowed as she looked into the distance.

'Didn't go down well,' she said. 'Started calling me names. My back's broad enough – I didn't mind. But then she got on to Andy. Insulting him.' Her jaw narrowed. 'So I warned her to cut it out. More or less told her to close her mouth or I'd close it for her.'

I stared at her. 'Did Brian hear you? Is that why he said you should talk to me?'

She nodded. 'Said he'd tell you if I didn't. Like I said, none of his business.'

'How come he heard you? I thought the music was on in the gyms – I could hear it when I went downstairs.'

Fliss took a last drag on her roll-up and ground it under the heel of her boot.

'Tapes, not radio,' she said telegrammatically. What she meant was that the stereo had not simply been switched on to Kiss FM all day, as it usually was, but that they had been playing cassettes instead. In the inevitable silences between one finishing and another being inserted, the events happening in the next-door gym would be easily audible, even to someone who wasn't trying to eavesdrop.

'I didn't even notice the music had stopped,' Fliss said. 'I don't when I'm working out. Concentrating too hard. Anyway, we were shouting by that time. Wouldn't have been difficult for Brian to hear.'

'Did Brian hear Linda leave the gym?' There wasn't a way I could think of to ask delicately whether Linda had really left under her own steam, or whether she had been transported. Still, if Brian had actually heard Linda fall and Fliss subsequently carrying her out of the gym to arrange her in the women's toilets, wouldn't he have said something? Fliss gave me a long, hard look.

'Have to ask him that,' she said.

'It's nothing personal, Fliss. You understand.'

She nodded abruptly. 'Well, that's all, then.'

She turned back to the stall, having dismissed me. Andy was doing his best to talk a customer into buying not just an antique mirror but the matching set of brushes too. It looked as if he was succeeding.

Thoughtfully, I retraced my steps towards the samosa stall,

where I bought a vegetable one wrapped in a paper napkin. I stood there for a moment, blowing on the samosa to cool it down. Looking ahead of me, to my surprise, I saw Brian. He was by the opposite stall, half hidden behind a rack of T-shirts with dancing skeletons printed over them, looking not at all like someone about to buy a skeleton T-shirt but even more furtive than he had been before. And now he looked embarrassed as well.

'Brian?' I said, not yet nervous. I crossed over to where he was standing. He made what seemed to be an attempt at concealment, dodging sideways behind a rack of second-hand jeans. 'What are you doing there?'

He lowered his head and produced one of his usual grunts.

'What?' I said inevitably.

'Everything OK?' he said sheepishly.

'Of course it's OK,' I said blankly. 'What do you mean?'

He shrugged. His shoulders looked heavy enough to need a fork-lift truck to lift and lower them. The rack of jeans was still between us and he seemed in no hurry to emerge from behind it. He grunted something else I couldn't catch.

But by this time I had realised that Brian must have followed me from the gym. I looked over at Fliss's stall and noticed that from this position he would have had an excellent view of the proceedings, though he couldn't have overheard our conversation. He had been well tucked away behind those T-shirts; if I hadn't happened to stop at the stall directly opposite, I would never have noticed him there.

This thought was distinctly unnerving. I backed away a couple of paces, and this time I was the one looking around me anxiously, wanting to make sure that there were other people around. Brian seemed to realise what I was thinking and took a step forward. He narrowly missed carrying the entire jeans rack with him.

'No, no,' he said, looking distressed.

I stared at him. Next to me the stallholder said tetchily: 'Oi! No eating food near the clothes – you blind? Can't you see the sign?'

'Sorry,' I said, stepping back and looking down at the samosa, which was leaking grease into the napkin. When I looked up again, Brian was making his escape; all I could see of him was his shoulders disappearing into the distance.

I balled up the napkin and tried to throw it away, but the first three waste baskets I came to were already overflowing with litter. Slowly I walked back towards the gym, still holding the napkin. I was feeling shaken. The idea of being followed by Brian was not a relaxing one. He was just so damn big. His fists were as huge as sledgehammers – not that he'd even have to use them; if he wanted to obliterate you all he'd have to do would be to walk over you like a steamroller, leaving you flattened in his wake.

I was so preoccupied I nearly bumped into Jeff crossing the road.

'God,' I said, 'the gym must be like the *Marie Celeste*. Its entire staff seems to be wandering around the market.'

'Just popped out to get a sandwich,' he said, with the air of someone making an excuse. 'You going back now?'

'Yup.'

'Me too.' He walked along next to me. 'What have you been doing?'

'I dropped in on Fliss,' I said absently.

Jeff took it as a cue. 'Fliss!' he snorted. 'She's got off pretty lightly if you ask me!'

I looked at him. 'Do you mean about her quarrel with Linda?'

'Oh, they had a quarrel?' He looked surprised. 'I didn't know. It'd been going on for a while, anyway.'

I was baffled. 'What had? The privatisation thing only happened last week.'

'Not *that*,' Jeff said self-importantly, his chest puffing out like a pigeon swelling with gossip. 'Linda was making a play for Andy. Didn't you know?'

'Oh, come on, Jeff,' I said dismissively. 'That's ridiculous.'

Jeff looked highly offended. 'It's true! She was trying to make Derek jealous. You ask Rachel. She knows about it.'

'You're not serious.'

'No, I tell you! She was there once when Linda was flirting with Andy. Apparently Fliss was furious.'

I shook my head, not knowing what to believe. We had reached the gym now.

'It's true,' Jeff insisted again. 'Ask Rachel.'

'I'll make a note to remind myself.'

As the gym doors swung shut behind us, I made a sudden decision: to avoid finding myself alone in any part of the gym, or with just one other person present. The phrase 'safety in numbers' had lodged itself in my head and refused to leave.

20

It was early for the Freedom Arms, which didn't really get going till about nine. Once it had got going it was hard to stop, but that was another story. Tom had left a message on my machine asking me to meet him there at seven and, not wanting to disappoint an old friend, I had turned up, though what I really felt like was a quiet evening in front of the TV, pondering over the events of the day.

I was a little early, purely by accident, and I found a peaceful corner where I could sit and nurse a half of Guinness. Somehow here I didn't feel I could order anything else. A photograph of Oscar Wilde hung behind me and to my right were James Joyce and Constance Markiewicz, the latter in a dress and hairdo so elaborate it made me ashamed of my Lycra miniskirt and favourite T-shirt. Over it I was wearing my violet suède jacket, which smartened me up a bit, but I had the feeling nonetheless that Constance would not have approved.

No fire was burning tonight in the grate; that was reserved for the winter months. Still, fire would have been nice, even a fake one, to go with the wooden floor and the comfortably stained walls. This pub always made me want to go to Dublin; there, apparently, the streets were paved with pubs just like this which never closed, places where people came up and chatted to you, then invited you to parties where the Guinness flowed like the Liffey River and Bono saw you and was inspired to write a song about how you looked like the Holy Spirit fading into the mist and he'd quite like to commune with you even though he'd feel guilty about it afterwards . . .

'Hi, Sammy. Do you want the other half?'

I dragged my thoughts away from Dublin with a wrench. Perhaps I should never go there; it would probably just be a disappointment. I nodded at Tom, who returned shortly with the drinks and settled himself in. The table was in an alcove with a bench running round two sides. He looked around approvingly. A group of students had gathered on the far side of the pub, next to the piano and the sadly empty fireplace, and were making loud, raucous noises better suited to a gathering of stockbrokers, but apart from that the atmosphere was still relatively peaceful.

'So why this invitation, Tom?' I asked. 'I mean, I saw you yesterday. Are you more than usually desperate for company?'

Tom drained about half his pint of Guinness in one go. He is of Irish origin and tends to emphasise this heavily when in a group of other Irish people. I hoped he wouldn't feel the urge tonight; the accent he sees fit to adopt always sets my teeth on edge.

'This is actually for your benefit,' he said, looking smug. He was in his blue Aran sweater tonight – Tom has two or three Arans, which he rotates. I don't think they were actually in the wash when they failed to appear for a week or so, just lying fallow, because when they re-emerged they were as stained as ever. 'I've arranged with a bloke I know to come in here for a drink.'

'Who? You're not trying to set me up with someone, are you?'

'He's not your type,' Tom said firmly. 'I met him when I was labouring. I thought you might be interested in talking to him. He is,' he added with the air of someone pulling a rabbit out of a hat, 'an ex-Living Socialist. I thought he might be able to tell you something about that Jeff bloke.'

I raised my eyebrows approvingly. A shadow loomed over the table.

'All right, Tom,' it said with the authentic nasal whine of the Living Socialist. 'How's it going, mate?'

'Hi, Pegg,' Tom said urbanely. 'Pegg, this is Sam. I'll get some drinks in.'

'Pint of lager,' Pegg said concisely, sitting down opposite me. He didn't seem to have heard what we had been saying, but then Tom had fortunately been keeping his voice low. He gave me a comradely nod.

I took a quick survey of Pegg. He was very tall and equally

cadaverous, as many hard left-wingers are, despite the fact that they seem to consume huge quantities of fried food all the time. His skin, pallid and blotched, suggested that this was indeed his favourite diet. He had one of those hairlines that receded in two waves on either side of the widow's peak, leaving it marooned rather poignantly on his forehead as a reminder of past glories, though in his case the remaining hair was such a nasty shade of ginger brown that one couldn't imagine the loss of the rest could be much lamented.

From his body came that musty smell – not body odour, so much as long-unwashed clothes and hair – that again is a common sign that you are in the presence of someone on the far left. Even those who don't live in squats with no running water and no launderette within miles, and thus have no excuse for this sort of thing, seem to cultivate it as a token of commitment. His black jeans looked worn and greasy with years of wear, and the inevitable donkey jacket hung off his skeleton as if anchored there by the protruding knobs of his bones.

Tom came back with more drinks and some packets of crisps. Pegg seized on one, ripped it open from stem to stern and devoured the contents as if he hadn't seen food in weeks.

'Tom says you used to be a Living Socialist,' I said, deciding that Pegg was not a person who needed to be buttered up with small talk before you got down to brass tacks.

'Too right.' He tilted the crisp packet up unashamedly to let the last shreds trickle down into his mouth. 'But they just want to create a total hegemony of their own, y'know? I worked that out after a while. Now I'm an anarcho-syndicalist.'

'Oh, right,' I said, interested, before I remembered that I was supposed to be concentrating on the Living Socialism part. I dragged myself back to the topic in hand. 'So it's very structured then, Living Socialism?'

He shot me a glance. 'You thinking of joining, then?' he said.

I shook my head. 'Just interested.'

'Yeah, well, I wouldn't advise it. Especially not for a woman, y'know?'

'Why not?' asked Tom curiously.

'It's a really fucking sexist set-up, man,' Pegg said seriously.

'They have these levels, right? Like karate. You ever done karate?'

'You mean like dans?' I said. 'Belt colours and things?'

'Just about.' Pegg turned back to me. 'They've got seven, right? Levels, I mean. And women can't get beyond Level Three. It's a rule. And no non-working-class people beyond Five. I tell you, some pretty heavy shit goes down at the top levels. They have this house, right, in Peckham, with all barbed wire round it, kind of the Central Headquarters, and you have to be Six or Seven to be allowed in.'

'And what do they do there?' Tom said sarcastically. 'Plan military insurrection?'

'I don't know, do I.' Pegg seemed rather pettish at this gap in his information; he was clearly enjoying having such an enthralled audience. 'Probably fiddle with themselves, y'know? Point is, it's just another club, like all those rich people and TV presenters down Pall Mall that won't let women be members either. Same old shit with a different face.'

He drained his pint and disembowelled another crisp packet.

'No black people either,' he said. 'Dunno if they actually turn 'em away or if they just don't apply.'

'So you just get white working-class men with an axe to grind,' Tom summarised.

'Basically, yeah. Which is definitely not what I'm into. Some of us are trying to get a communal place together down New Cross way. All ages, colours, whatever. Trade work with other people, try to let as little money change hands as possible, y'know?'

'Wouldn't you be better off in the country?' I suggested. 'It's easier to work the barter system there. Some villages already have it going – they have their own currency and when you work for someone you earn a certain amount, which you can use to pay other people for food or whatever.'

'Really?' Pegg looked interested. 'D'you know where?'

I shook my head. 'I heard about it from a New Age guy I know. I could give you his number if you like.'

'Excellent,' Pegg said with enthusiasm. I finished my Guinness and said: 'It's my round.'

'No, I'll get them in,' Pegg said, picking up the empties. 'Same again?'

He loped off to the bar. Tom gave me a thumbs-up.

'You've made a hit there,' he said. 'I've never heard him say that much all at once, in a coherent way. He usually rants.'

I ate some crisps while Pegg was away. I hadn't wanted to get between him and his feeding frenzy. 'I'll move on to Jeff now,' I said, mouth full of Bovril taste. 'I feel I'm on a roll.'

When Pegg settled back into his chair with a fresh pint in front of him, I said innocently: 'I know someone who's a Living Socialist, actually – he works in the same gym as me. He seems all right about feminism and stuff, though, not the way you were describing them.'

'What's his name?' Pegg said instantly, taking this as a challenge. There is nothing so virulent as left-wing splinter-group internecine hatred. It always makes me remember *Monty Python's Life of Brian*, where Brian is searching for the Judean People's Front and comes across a group he thinks are it, only to be informed haughtily that they are the People's Front of Judea, and the Judean People's Front is the man sitting on the steps above them, sulking. Right-wing splinter-groups, on the other hand, seem to engage less in that kind of highly sophisticated political debate and more in bombing each other.

'Jeff Roberts,' I said, feeling like someone taking the pin out of a grenade, chucking it, then sitting back and hoping for the explosion. It came.

'Jeff Roberts?' snorted Pegg incredulously. 'Fuck, I was in the same cell as him!' I presumed he meant indoctrinational rather than police cell, but I didn't want to stem the torrent by asking.

'Jeff's no fucking *feminist*,' Pegg continued with scorn in his voice. 'He just thinks he'll pull girls that way. Sorry, women.' This merely confirmed what I had always thought about Jeff, but it was nice to hear it from someone else. 'And he doesn't, let me tell you,' Pegg added nastily. 'Pull, I mean. He's just one of those university-educated middle-class kids that put on working-class accents and pretend they grew up in South London.'

'Well, he probably had to put the accent on to be accepted by the Living Socialists in the first place,' I suggested dulcetly.

Pegg snorted. 'He's not fooling anyone and he knows it. He can shout louder than everyone else and sell loads of papers on demos but he'll still be a middle-class piece of shit. 'Scuse me.' He drank some beer. 'I've got nothing against the middle classes when they're honest about it – it's the creeps who try to pretend solidarity with the workers that fuck me off.'

I thought of all the people I knew at art school who dumped their posh, Home Counties accents after a few days and spent the rest of the three years cultivating more street-cred ones. At least Baby, with all her faults, hadn't done that; but she was so thick-skinned that it probably didn't occur to her for a minute that she needed to change in any way. The only thing she had altered was her name, which her cousin Tim had told me was really Eleanor. I had sniggered to myself a couple of times over that one.

'When you said you were in the same cell as Jeff,' I said curiously to Pegg, 'do you mean the Living Socialists split you all up into cells to organise you, and you didn't know who anybody was outside your cell? It makes it sound so terrorist.'

Pegg burst out laughing. 'Nah,' he said when he had recovered. 'Nah, that's not one of their things. They go in for big meetings with all the high-ups on the platform. Really fucking socialistic, eh? No, me and Jeff were arrested at a demo and banged up together. I nearly went mad, I can tell you – it was one of those yellow holding cells, a really bright colour, y'know, hurts your eyes after a while, and nothing in there but me and Jeff, whiny little git, going on and on. I nearly gave him a taste of his own medicine.'

He looked at my blank face. 'You don't know what I mean by that, do you? He hit someone over the head with a placard. That's what he got done for. Me, it was just the usual, y'know, bad-mouthing the police. But there were some Marxist Workers on the demo as well, and Jeff and one of them got into a slanging match about fuck knows what, y'know, the second volume of *Das Kapital* or whatever. Can't say I've read it myself.'

He paused for a swig of beer, obviously relishing the effect this story was having on us; we were hanging on his every word.

'Anyway, Jeff got really pissed off by something this guy said and he whacked him over the head with this placard he was carrying, y'know, "Troops Out" or something like that. The guy was concussed, poor sod, but that didn't stop the coppers arresting him too. Fascist pigs,' he added automatically. Some old Living Socialist habits obviously died harder than others.

I looked at Tom, whose mouth was slightly open. This was richer meat than either of us could have bargained for.

'Was the guy all right in the end?' Tom asked finally.

'Who?' Pegg said, baffled for a moment. 'Oh, you mean the guy Jeff did? Yeah, he's fine. For a Marxist Worker prat, that is.' He ate some more crisps. 'Jeff's a wanker, right, but let's not exaggerate. I mean, he's not a murderer!'

21

'I don't know what to do,' Janey was saying despondently. 'The landlord swears he's tried everything. He's put down three different kinds of poison for them but apparently they just munch it up without even noticing. I'd move if the flat weren't so lovely.'

'Their systems must be able to process anything by now,' I reflected. 'Think what you see them eating on the street.'

Janey sighed and stood up. She was very pretty, in the style of an eighteenth-century nymph: plump, soft and white like a velvet cushion with its nap worn down. Her eyes were large and her hands, piling up the dinner plates, were practically round with short little fingers, like baby starfish.

'Can I help clear up?' I said.

'No, it all goes in the dishwasher.'

'I'll go to the loo, then.'

'Good,' said Janey with surprising emphasis. 'They're on form at the moment. You'll see what I mean.'

Sure enough, as I sat on the toilet I could hear the jostling of feathers and the clicking of feet as the pigeons manoeuvred into position, followed by a series of coos and cawing that increased in volume and speed as they got on with it noisily. The ledge on which they nested had originally been intended to shelter the ventilation grate above the bathroom sink; now, of course, the grate was nearly choked up. Though only a foot-square niche, it was a popular resting place for the large colony of birds who lived in the area and spent their time waddling over the rooftops of the houses next door, standing on the edge of the guttering for minutes at a stretch, poised like figureheads, before they finally decided to dive from one window ledge to another with great heavy flaps of their wings.

The pigeons were still at it when I emerged. Janey's little sitting-room, like its owner opulent and hung with richly brocaded materials, was redolent with the rich, welcome smell of coffee. Janey looked round at me gloomily, an unspoken question in her eyes.

'Yes, they are at it again.'

'God. And now they're going to shit in there and I'm going to find dribbling dollops of black-flecked goo all down the wall next morning. Sometimes I swear they aim it right on to my toothbrush. And they've been going on the windowsill outside since time immemorial. I don't dare open the window beyond a crack. The landlord won't block up the grate. He says Health and Safety regulations are against it.'

She flopped into her chair. I was beginning to feel guilty about having broached the subject.

'Lovely dinner,' I said in an attempt to distract her. 'I wish I could cook like that.'

'You could. You just can't be bothered,' she said firmly. Her appearance, all floating scarves and necklaces and layers of embroidered clothing, together with her transcendent prettiness, combined to cloak Janey's strong will to those who didn't know her well. She was in fact an ambitious and successful TV script editor; but to look at her you'd think she was a pottery teacher at a girls' public school on whom most of the pupils, and probably some of the parents too, had crushes.

She poured out the coffee. 'All they do,' she continued, returning inexorably to the pigeons, 'is eat and screw all day long. And poo down my wall. Little bastards.'

'Ah, it's all that straight sex that's getting you down,' I said. 'Bet if they were a colony of lesbian separatist pigeons revelling in free love you'd be more sympathetic.'

Janey didn't dignify this with a reply. She merely raised her eyebrows at me and adjusted one of the rings she wore on nearly every finger.

'How's Helen?' I asked politely.

'She left me for a TV producer. Little trollop.'

'She's an actress, isn't she?'

Janey nodded. 'Always on the lookout for the main chance, that's Helen. Kurt was more useful to her career than me.'

'Kurt strikes me as being unequivocally male, as names go,' I observed.

She laughed shortly. 'Helen would have sex with a tea strainer if she thought it could get her a good part in a TV series.' She grimaced. 'Let's not talk about me, OK? What with an infestation of pigeons and my love-life going to pot again – let's talk about you instead. Tell me everything that's been going on. I need distraction.'

'Strangely enough,' I said smugly, 'I can provide you with exactly that.'

It took about an hour to recount to Janey the events of the previous few weeks. I withheld nothing from her; she was a very appreciative listener, interjecting questions when she hadn't completely understood something. At the end she took a deep breath and said: 'It's all too complicated, isn't it? If someone sent me a script like that I'd tell them to cut out a few incidents. The more unlikely ones.'

This was one of the most intelligent observations anyone had made on the subject, though I didn't grasp its significance at once.

'I have to say Jeff sounds most likely,' she continued. 'After all, he already has a tendency to this kind of thing.'

I nodded. 'But against that, you have to set the fact that he gave both Rachel and me an alibi, and he didn't have to do that. I know he's got rather a soft spot for Rachel, but why me as well?'

'No, I take your point. What was it, he said he'd seen Linda – it is Linda, isn't it? – in the corridor after Rachel had already gone upstairs to teach her class?'

'You've got a very good memory,' I said appreciatively. 'You should be a script editor or something.'

'I expect there's no doubt he actually saw Linda? He couldn't have mistaken her for anyone else?'

'Absolutely not. There's no one else who looks like Linda – apart from Lesley, that is, and she dresses and walks so differently you wouldn't mistake her for Linda for a moment—'

I broke off. Suddenly I felt my heart beating hard in my throat. A train of ideas was rushing through my head, one following the other in a neat sequence of conclusions, facts that I had never before thought to connect now snapping together into a pattern, the only one that would explain everything, everything that had happened—

Janey was staring at me. 'Sam, what is it?' she said urgently. 'Are you all right? You look like someone just walked over your grave!'

* * *

I needed to talk over the conclusions I had reached with someone more closely involved than Janey, and by a fortunate coincidence I had already made a date with Rachel to meet the next day at our café. In a reversal of our usual habits, she was early and I was late. When I walked in she was already sitting at our normal window table, reading a newspaper, shopping bags piled at her side. With a mock frown she looked up at me, saying: 'What kind of time do you call this? I could have gone round Sainsbury's twice!'

'Sorry.' I ordered a camomile tea and waited at the counter for it to be made, carrying the heavy pottery mug and saucer over to the table. Sitting down opposite her I said without preamble: 'I think I know who killed Linda.'

'What!' Rachel's eyes widened. 'You're joking!'

I shook my head slowly. 'And do you know what made me work it out? Lesley's appalling taste in clothes. Isn't that ironic?'

'I don't understand,' Rachel said with comprehensible confusion, leaning forward in her chair.

'It goes back to Jeff,' I said. 'He said that he saw Linda in the downstairs corridor that afternoon, alive and kicking, and that he was absolutely sure it was Linda because at first he thought she was Lesley until she turned her head and he caught a glimpse of her face. Which is called over-egging the pudding. No one seems to have realised how unlikely it was that Jeff should have mistaken Linda – who was my height and always wore dark clothes – for Lesley, who must be five foot ten and has never to my knowledge been seen in anything darker than pastel pink. Yes, they were both blonde, but that's their only similarity; and anyway Linda wore her hair in a top-knot and Lesley has a sort of short fluffy cut.'

Rachel was hanging on my every word.

'So then I thought of Janice. You know who Janice is, don't you? She's about Linda's height, and you could certainly take her for Linda, even if you knew the difference between a French pleat and a top-knot. Whenever I've seen Janice she's been wearing mostly black. Jeff could easily have mistaken her for Linda. But then he would just have said that he'd seen *Linda* – he wouldn't have needed to confirm it by saying that he'd thought that the woman he'd seen was *Lesley*. Which, if you think about it, is ridiculous.'

I reached over and took one of Rachel's cigarettes, feeling suddenly that I needed to smoke. 'Do you mind?'

'No, no. Go on, I'm riveted.'

I lit up. 'Besides, I had dinner with my friend Janey last night. She's a script editor and has a very good nose for the way something reads. And when I told her what had been happening, she said at once that it was all too complicated and that, if it had been a script, she would have cut out the more unlikely parts of the story. Which made me ask myself what the more unlikely parts actually were. And that was easy. Jeff told me the other day that Linda had been making a play for Andy and Fliss was desperately jealous. I didn't believe it then and I don't believe it now.'

'Hang on a minute. I still don't know who Jeff saw downstairs,' Rachel said intently.

I took a drag on the cigarette and winced at the foul taste. It was hard to believe people did this kind of thing for pleasure.

'I don't think he saw anyone at all,' I said. I looked down at my tea, which would be getting cold by now. Somehow I didn't feel like drinking it. 'I think he made the whole thing up. Then when the police asked him if he was sure that it was Linda he had seen, he fell into the trap of overdoing it to convince them. He should have kept it simple.'

Rachel was sipping her tea, her eyes fixed on me.

'So then I thought, why should Jeff have needed to make that up? Not for his own benefit – if he'd killed Linda he would have wanted as many people to be suspected as possible. The only answer is that he was innocent but wanted to help the person who was guilty. And the only person helped by his lie was you, Rachel.'

Her eyes were large and dark in the serene setting of her face. They didn't even blink as I went on: 'But you didn't have a motive – the idea of anyone killing Linda to keep the gym in the public sector was always very far-fetched. And you're not a person who is easily wound up, unlike Jeff. I don't believe this was planned, you see. No one, especially someone as clever as you are, would plan to kill someone in such a dangerous way. For all you knew, everyone else downstairs might have had an alibi and it would have been instantly obvious who the murderer was. No, this happened on impulse. And the only thing I could think of that would wind you up enough to kill Linda was the motive that's already done plenty of circulation round the gym. In all senses. Namely, Derek.'

Rachel put her cup down and sat back in her chair, still silent.

'Janice said something to me, the first time I talked to her, that didn't make sense, only I didn't realise it then. She told me that Derek had been having an affair with Linda for several years, well before Janice and Derek had met. Which, since their son Devon is five, would put it at six years minimum. But Linda only came to the gym two or three years ago, according to Fliss, so the woman Derek was having an affair with back when he met Janice couldn't have been Linda. It was you, Rachel, wasn't it? You've been at the gym for ages. I'm ready to bet that Derek is the married man you told me you were involved with. I should have picked up before on the fact that there was someone else Derek was involved with who worked at the gym. Only another instructor would have known enough to report Lesley to the Performing Rights Society. Derek guessed it was you, and he told you to lay off Lesley. But Lesley herself didn't realise that you had anything to do with it. She picked a fight with Linda instead and Linda told her to use her brains for a change, but didn't deign to explain further. Lucky she didn't – it could have confused Lesley irreparably. It's not surprising that Linda knew about you and Derek. She would, if you'd been having an affair with him for all this time. He's gone from Janice to Linda and back to Janice again with loads of affairs on the side, but you two have always been a constant, right?'

There was a long pause. It seemed as if Rachel was going to maintain the silence she had kept up to now and for a moment

I was frightened that everything I had said was just a crazy stream of wild conclusions that bore no relation to reality at all. Then, her lovely face as calm as it had been while she had listened to me, she said slowly: 'I never put any pressure on him, ever. I was too proud. I kept hoping he would leave Janice of his own accord, but he never did. And then Linda came along. She dug her claws into him and made his life a misery until he left Janice for her. I couldn't have done that, pushed at him like that, forced the decision on him so shamelessly. He'd have to want to do it enough to do it on his own. How could Linda be happy knowing that he'd just given in because she was the one who shouted loudest?'

It was eerie how her words echoed the ones Janice had used to me. But Janice had learnt her lesson the second time around; she had realised that if she wanted Derek, and she did, this was the only way to take and keep him. She had not only made mincemeat of Lesley; she had effectively seen off Rachel, too, without even knowing it.

'You didn't mean to kill Linda,' I said; a statement, not a question.

'Of course not.' She shivered as if she were remembering the moment all over again. Her brow creased and she leant towards me, intent on making me understand how it had been. 'You know what she could be like, Sam. She was spitting with rage. She came into the women's loos and when she saw me, it was as if the cup overflowed and it all came pouring out. Apparently she'd just seen Derek and that little tart Naomi in the men's changing rooms, and she couldn't stop saying: "That he'd do it here! Practically in front of me! In my gym!"'

She shivered again. 'As you've worked out, Linda knew about me and Derek. She didn't like it but she thought it better not to interfere because we'd been seeing each other for so many years. Oh, I'm sure she was working on Derek to finish with me, but she wanted to make sure of him first, stop him screwing around. So seeing him with Naomi was what you might call a setback for her.'

She looked at me, her eyes wide and clear, trying to convince me to see her point of view, to comprehend what she had done. 'I understand Derek, you see, Sam. We grew up just round the corner from one another, went to school together, everything. I think because of that he always thought I was a bit too close to home for him. I knew him too well – what he was like, where he was coming from. He was always successful with women, even when he was really small. He could wind his mother and his sisters round his little finger. His father wasn't around, and he was the only boy in the family. He could do anything he wanted with them and he knew it. To keep him, you just had to hang on and let him be himself. That's what I did, and he always came back to me.'

Her lips tightened. 'But when Linda started in on me, I completely lost it. She told me I was a fool to be waiting around for Derek. Couldn't I see, she said, I wasn't even really his type, because he preferred white girls, blondes. I was wasting my time and no matter how long I waited I'd always be his bit on the side – and more like that, much more. You know what Linda was like, Sam. She'd say anything that came into her head as long as it would hurt you. But I didn't think of that at the time – I just wanted to make her shut up. I shouted at her but she kept going; she was as unstoppable as a tank. She'd brought a hand weight in with her, and put it down on the ledge above the sink. Anyway, she was right in my face, waving her finger in front of my nose, and when she called me a stupid black bitch, that was it. I just grabbed the weight and smashed it across her face without even thinking.' She paused. 'The silence was wonderful.'

I stared at her, lost for words.

'Jeff saw me going upstairs,' she said. 'I must have had a strange expression on my face. I tried to duck my head, but he was looking straight at me and I knew he'd seen me. I stopped for a minute on the stairs to calm down and by the time I came to the top I'd got myself under control. But when Jeff heard what had happened, he knew at once it had been me. That's not the only lie he told for me, by the way. Linda took that hand weight out of the office earlier on that afternoon. Jeff said that she was meaning to ask Derek why it had been put there for mending, because it looked OK to her. That's why she was looking for Derek in the men's changing rooms. When she saw what was happening there she didn't go in, just came straight down the corridor, and she had the weight in her hand all the time. Ironic, isn't it? If she hadn't brought it with her I would probably just have punched her in the face and none of this would have happened.'

'Jeff must have more than just a crush on you to risk lying like that to the police.'

'He's in love with me,' Rachel said flatly. 'Or that's what *he* calls it. He came and told me – not quite in so many words, it was all wrapped up in flowery language – that he'd keep on telling that story to the police if I'd go to bed with him.'

Somehow this seemed the worst part of all. I knew that was absurd, but it still seemed the worst part.

'He has,' I said, 'so I assume you have too.'

Rachel nodded. 'What else could I do?'

I felt sick. I was remembering a time a week or so ago when I had been entering the main gym as Jeff was coming out, and how surprised and embarrassed he had looked to see me. Rachel had told me that he was trying to discuss a new petition with her, but she had looked tired and stressed. As she was looking now.

'How can you bear it?' I said.

'Don't moralise to me,' Rachel said sharply. 'It's my decision.'

'You and he should have synchronised your ideas better,' I said, hearing my voice come out hard, almost raucous. I hardly recognised it for my own. 'Jeff with that ridiculous story about Andy and Linda. He could see I didn't believe it, so he dragged you into it, telling me you'd been there when Linda had started flirting with Andy. He should never have involved you. And you – you sent me into Lou's office to find that back door, didn't you? I only realised later that it was a strange place to put this year's files. They should have been in chronological order at the top, but instead they were underneath the others, jammed by that doorknob so I couldn't miss spotting it. By that stage you must have been trying to cast suspicion on anyone you could. Did you know Lou had gone into the office for a cigarette during the period in which Linda was killed, or were you just lucky?'

Rachel shrugged. 'She often popped in there for a fag. It was worth a try. I didn't think you'd really suspect Lou, just be thrown off the track for a while.'

'For a while I was, until I remembered that the police had already checked the fire alarm. Lou might have switched it off but she didn't have the opportunity to switch it on again – you were in the crèche with all your students. So then I started thinking about who had directed me to the most unlikely theories. And it was always you or Jeff.'

She was silent. I stubbed out my cigarette, changing tack. 'And what do you plan to do about Derek, now he's been arrested?'

'That's his problem now,' she said, and her eyes were as hard and flat as black stones. 'I was there when Janice came in to pick him up and they all started playing happy families. He saw me standing there and he looked right through me like he didn't know me, the bloody hypocrite. At first I was terrified he'd be arrested – now I don't give a damn any longer. He can get himself out of it. It's his mess as well as mine.'

'But he's busy protecting you, don't you realise? That's why he's refusing to talk – not to protect Naomi, but you. Does Derek know it was you who killed Linda, or is it just a guess?'

'He guessed. I didn't tell him anything, though. He's got no proof. But he knows.'

'He's a bad liar,' I said. 'So he's just keeping his mouth shut and protesting his innocence. That kind of thing could get him convicted. Everyone will see there's plenty he's not telling.'

Rachel stared at me, her jaw set with anger. 'He pushed me too far,' she said. 'Too many times, too many promises I didn't even ask him for—'

'If you'd fought for him at the time maybe none of this would have happened,' I said. 'If you'd put up a fight when Janice came along he'd have stayed with you. It had all been building up for years and something had to give—'

'He would never have stayed with me,' she said, every word biting like acid, 'because he was never with me. He always kept me in the shadows.' She pushed back her chair. 'I'm sorry you found out, Sam,' she said. 'I really liked you. I still do.' She paused, and for a moment her voice softened. 'I wish I could make you see my point of view. Can't you understand what I've been through, what he's made me suffer?'

Her eyes were fixed on me, pleading, waiting for a sympathetic response. When it became clear that I wasn't going to reply, her expression became angry, offended, and she snapped: 'But it doesn't change anything – that you've found out, I mean. You'd better understand that, if nothing else.'

'What do you mean?' I said, feeling suddenly very cold.

She shrugged. 'You haven't got any proof,' she said. 'Jeff will never change his story now. He's mad about me. Like I said, Derek will just have to take his chances.'

She stood up and horribly, banally, picked up her shopping. She was so self-controlled that she could even remember such a detail at a moment like this. She looked absolutely ruthless, like an angel of death for our times, only more frightening by virtue of the carrier bags in her hands. The everyday is the greatest horror of all: the sight of your friend's face changing, setting into a vengeful mask behind which the person you once liked has been lost, consumed entirely by their own worst emotions.

In a flash I relived the moment when I had thought Lou was behind me in the office, about to kill me as Linda had been killed, and I remembered the terror I had felt on turning round, afraid not so much of the weapon in her hand but the intention to kill that I would see in her face. Rachel had made me suffer that twice, the transformation of a well-known face into that of a murderer and she wasn't even repentant. I shouldn't feel such an ache of loss for her friendship. But I did. I did.

I watched Rachel leave the café with a sense of utter hopelessness. I had reached a triumphant solution and it was a dead-end street. I had lost a friend and gained absolutely nothing.

And Derek was still in prison.

22

The events of the rest of that day are best left blurred around the edges, which, after going home, chipping my heavily frosted bottle of vodka out of its resting place in the freezer and wresting off the cap, is very much how I experienced them. There were a couple of phone calls but I left the answering machine switched on, and with the TV and stereo going full blast I couldn't hear a word of what was being said. I didn't try very hard, either. I was feeling distinctly misanthropic.

At about ten o'clock, in a sudden fit of hunger and self-pity, I ordered a takeaway pizza. If Ray Milland in *The Lost Weekend*, having reached the halfway mark on his third whisky bottle, had decided that what he needed was a four-cheeses pizza with garlic and sweetcorn, he couldn't have slurred his order into the telephone receiver with more gusto than I did. However, by the time the doorbell rang forty minutes later I had forgotten all about the pizza and flung open the front door in a rage at being interrupted in the middle of some late-night sitcom, snarling so extravagantly at the delivery boy that he practically gibbered in fear. Then of course I had to tip him extra.

Faced with the large, extravagantly reeking white pizza box – why on *earth* had I ordered extra garlic? – the appropriate gesture for someone suffering tortures of the soul would have been to cast it aside, disgusted with her animal appetites. Naturally, I ripped open the lid and polished off the pizza with lightning speed, hardly bothering to chew before I swallowed. I regret to add that I didn't brush my teeth before I went to sleep. Though, since I didn't actually go to bed, but passed out on the sofa, there was at least some excuse for that.

I awoke, predictably enough, at five in the morning, with a terrible thirst, not to mention the toxic fumes of garlic which spiralled out of my mouth like a fire-eater's best effort when I opened it to drink some water. Slumping back on the sofa, I closed my mouth to avoid asphyxiating myself in my sleep and passed out once again. Unfortunately I had neglected to position myself carefully enough to take account of my sofa's well-known eccentricities and in the morning discovered a neat circular imprint on my cheek from one of the springs, which had for some years been trying to make a break for freedom.

The state I was in the next day is best glossed over, apart from the fact that my fugue from reality was a continuing success; the previous night I had been trying to avoid having to think about anything at all, and in the morning I was no better equipped for anything beyond the task of sluicing my mouth out thoroughly enough to remove the impression that a couple of heads of garlic had crawled in there overnight to die. I took some Solpadeine, of course. If I had a religion, this was the one: I worshipped at the shrine of Saint Solpadeine, Lady of the Migraine, patron saint of nasty throbbing headaches, every capsule containing a droplet of her sacred blood . . .

After a while I made myself get dressed and put up my hair, on the principle that it would make me feel better. Fortunately the studio was still relatively tidy from my big cleaning jag of the previous Sunday, so at least I wasn't able to depress myself further by the reminder of how filthy and uncivilised I was. Then I lay down on the sofa again and made myself be very still. It helped, a little. Time passed, slowly.

At about two o'clock in the afternoon, the doorbell rang. I was pretty sure that I hadn't ordered another takeaway pizza but by now I was in recovery and getting hungry again, so optimistically I dragged myself off the sofa and put my eye to the spyhole. Then I wished I hadn't.

Felice Bortshe, Duggie Sutton and Mr and Mrs Ashley were ranged down my steps, in that order, as if they had previously decided on some rough scheme of precedence. For a moment the idea flashed through my head of sneaking back to the sofa and lying low till they went away, but Felice happened to be staring straight into the spyhole as if she knew I was there. By some trick of the lens her eyes seemed to be looking directly into mine and, weak and enfeebled as I was, I could not oppose my will to hers. Dutifully I opened the door.

They flowed in like a tidal wave, Felice, of course, leading the way. Her manner was that of an anthropologist conducting a group of travellers on a guided tour through the habitat of some fascinating but primitive tribe.

'Sam, darling, you got my message, then?' she cried, gripping my hands and kissing me at the same time. Her perfume swirled around me and settled. I would have to take a bath later. 'Great! Betty, Jim, come in, don't be shy. Isn't it just exactly as I described it?'

She waved her hand in an encircling gesture. It was obvious that she meant the studio itself, rather than the mobile.

'And Sam sleeps up on the platform there – see the ladder? So New York, isn't it?'

'Interesting neighbourhood,' Jim Ashley said to me drily. 'What with the prison and all.'

'You must have come through Holloway,' I said. 'I see you've picked up the English technique of understatement.'

He grinned. I assumed that was what he was doing; what actually happened was that the hard set of his jaw relaxed and little lines appeared at the corners of his eyes. Jim Ashley was my idea of what all those strong and silent heroes of romance turn into as they get older. Betty, alas, was probably the female counterpart. She was exclaiming: 'Why, the prison's a while back, Jim! It's not like Sam here lives right next door to it!'

She smiled at me, the artificially stretched and painted mask of her face at odds with the friendliness of her character. Her hair was as pouffed out as it had been at the party; on close inspection it was clear that there wasn't that much of it, but that each separate strand was held in suspension from its neighbours by some form of super-lacquer which sealed it there as effectively as glue. I wondered what on earth she did with it at night. The lacquer looked as if it would only be removed by some form of industrial solvent.

I felt it incumbent on me to offer some form of hospitality.

'Would you like some tea?' I said, hoping they would feel it incumbent on themselves to refuse politely. I was pretty sure that I had used up all my sugar packets on Sergeant Hawkins.

The offer went down very well. Felice, still the anthropologist, clapped her hands together as if I had performed a particularly clever trick and said to the Ashleys: 'What did I say! So *traditional*! It's like the national drink – the first thing Duggie always says to me when I drop into his gallery is: "Would you like a cup of tea?"' She smiled at me dazzlingly. 'No, thank you, Sam. Not for me.'

The Ashleys shook their heads too. I looked over at Duggie. He was standing underneath the mobile with his head tilted back, and seemed to be dressed exactly the same as he had been the night of his party, even down to the fob chain across his waistcoat. The tweed jacket and corduroy trousers looked comfortably lived-in; Felice would doubtless call it the classic English gentleman's style. He seemed to be paying little attention to what she was saying. Somehow I had the impression that this was their modus vivendi.

'The mobile!' Felice said, following my gaze. She clicked towards it, taking little steps because of her short, tight skirt. Behind her went Betty Ashley, but Jim chose to stay where he was, near the door. I had already pegged him for a sensible man; that way he got a better view of the mobile and he didn't have to crick his neck.

I hadn't yet rigged up the supporting wires for the Thing, but there was little breeze today and it was hardly moving at all. Duggie walked back from it, eyes narrowed, his corduroy trouser legs rubbing against each other; for some reason the sound set my teeth on edge. This was terrible. I found myself looking round surreptitiously for the empty vodka bottle, unable to remember whether I had thrown it away last night or if it was still lying by the sofa, shrieking 'Alcoholic!' in a thought bubble above its head. I couldn't see it from where I was standing and I didn't want to move and call attention to myself.

Suddenly I was swept by a horrendous wave of embarrassment at being present while four people surveyed my sculpture in thoughtful silence. I felt as if I myself were hung up there, naked and hung-over on a piece of chain, and they were all staring at me assessingly. How did beauty contestants bear it?

Duggie took a deep breath and let it out slowly between his teeth with a kind of whistling sound. This seemed to be a signal of sorts to Felice, who cast a swift glance at him and said to Betty: 'Powerful, isn't it? It's called Undiscovered Planet. I love the sense of the unknown! Don't you just feel the excitement of discovery, like a new comet being created in immense black space, whirling in a void, waiting to be found . . .'

There was quite a lot more in this vein. I tried not to listen. If I did I would have to crawl under the sofa in embarrassment. Perhaps I would find the vodka bottle down there. By mistake I caught Jim Ashley's eye, which was unreadable. Betty was nodding her head eagerly to Felice's rhapsody. Her hairstyle seemed to be able to take this kind of thing without batting an eyelid; it made Felice's auburn sweep of hair look positively relaxed. Betty was wearing tailored trousers and a silk sweater, a smart beige coat and shiny white trainers. The effect was schizophrenic.

Duggie seemed to have come to some verdict on Undiscovered Planet; he wandered over to me, and without examining the sculpture further kindly distracted me by asking where I had studied and making general conversation about art school. Felice in the meantime was over at the kitchen table, rifling through my sketches for Son of Thing and spreading them out for Betty.

'Jim, honey,' his wife called, 'come and look at these, won't you?'

Her husband proceeded magisterially over to the table and stood over the sketches, his arms folded. Duggie beamed at me. His manners were so good I couldn't tell what he was thinking.

'Are those sketches for work in progress, darling?' he said. 'More of the same or a new departure?'

I cleared my throat. This was probably the moment where I was supposed to launch into some Felice-like spiel about Son of Thing, but for the life of me I couldn't do it.

'Er, it's going to be quite like that one, really,' I said rather helplessly. 'Only bigger,' I added hurriedly, remembering Felice's enthusiasm for large mobiles on her last visit. 'Much bigger.'

Duggie was nodding.

'Good, good,' he said. 'You don't want to chop and change too much, it's too confusing. May I look at the sketches, darling?'

Without waiting for an assent, he drifted over to the table and cast a quick eye over the drawings, which Felice was just stacking back into a pile. I noticed with horror that the empty vodka bottle was lying on its side in the middle of the table. Duggie reached out a hand and stood it up. I caught Jim Ashley's eye again. No doubt about it, that expression was definitely a grin. Sardonic bastard.

'Well,' said Felice briskly, 'I think we've seen all we came to see, don't you?'

She turned to the Ashleys.

'Oh, it's lovely,' Betty said happily. 'And so unusual! Though Lord knows where you hang something like that if you don't have all this space,' she added, smiling at me.

Next to her Jim shifted. 'Didn't you say something about dinner tonight, Felice?' he said unexpectedly. 'Perhaps Sam here would like to join us and we could talk about it then.'

Felice directed a hard stare at me. Refusal was out of the question. I said that I would love to come to dinner, and was told to meet them at eight at L'Orange, which made me blink. I might even have to iron something to wear. They streamed out through the door, all smiles. Duggie hung back for a moment.

'Well, darling, I think you might even have a sale,' he said. 'I expect you haven't got the faintest idea about what you were going to ask? Price-wise, I mean?'

'Oh my *God*—' I said, panic-stricken.

He seemed to have anticipated this reaction. 'Don't worry, that's what I'm here for. I think we should talk about representation, don't you? Why don't you pop into the gallery tomorrow morning about twelve-ish and we can go over the paperwork. You know where it is, don't you?'

I nodded. It was all I could manage. He blew a kiss in my direction and floated out through the door, saying: 'Until *ce soir*, then, sweetie.'

I stared after them in disbelief. Then I turned and looked at the Thing. It was impossible to imagine anyone actually wanting to buy it. I didn't much want to sell it, either. We had been through a lot together and it would feel like selling a friend. The Thing swung slightly in the air, sturdy as always, but now it had a rather malevolent expression. It hadn't looked so sulky since it became a mobile. Somehow I didn't think it wanted to be Betty Ashley's undiscovered planet.

* * *

Realising that if I stayed around the house I would start worrying about what to wear to a restaurant as smart as I knew L'Orange to be, I pulled on my leopardskin coat and headed out to the gym. I didn't know why. Perhaps I wanted to talk to Lou. I'd see what came to pass when I got there.

As it happened, Lou was out at a meeting with the Deputy Head of Leisure Services at the council and wouldn't be back for a couple of hours. I hovered around indecisively in reception, wondering whether to wait for her.

'Look at this!' Lesley said to me as wide-eyed as if she had just made an important discovery, holding up a copy of a women's magazine. 'It's some photos of Michael Jackson as a little boy and what he looks like now. You've got to admit there's a difference! I'd say he'd definitely had plastic surgery, and don't you think his skin looks paler, too?'

I stared at her in wonderment. 'It's just a trick of the lighting, Lesley,' I said gently. 'They can do amazing things these days with halogen lamps.'

She crinkled her brow. 'Really?' she said, poring over the magazine. 'Here it says he has a rare skin condition.'

The doors swung open and a pregnant woman entered, her stomach swelled out majestically like a sail in the wind. Her hair was corn-rowed at the front and massed at the back of her head in an intricate arrangement of loops and plaits. She would have made a wonderful ship's figurehead.

'Can I help you?' said Lesley, putting her magazine down.

The figurehead gave her a withering stare. 'Well, you can sell me a ticket for the stretch class,' she said.

'The stretch class,' Lesley mused, poring over the timetable, her pretty brow furrowing slightly. 'There are two starting shortly, the mums-to-be yoga and the Stretch and Condition—'

'Which class,' cut in the figurehead coldly, 'do you *think* I want to attend?'

Little did she know that her choice of verb and Lesley weren't always compatible. Lesley simply favoured her with a big, blue, uncomprehending stare and said: 'Well, it's the same price anyway unless you have a concession.'

Painstakingly, she stamped out a ticket.

'*Thank* you,' the figurehead said pointedly. 'Perhaps you could help me with something else?' She made this sound about as unlikely as the possibility of Lesley – or anyone, for that matter – having finished and understood *A Brief History of Time*. Flicking a glance over her shoulder, she included me in the request, clearly considering Lesley a broken reed. From her capacious bag she pulled out something black and woolly.

'I must have picked this up by mistake the last time I was in here,' she said, 'though God knows how. As you can see, I wouldn't exactly fit into it at the moment. Could you find out who it belongs to and give it back to her with my apologies?'

She held it up for inspection. It was a cropped knitted sweater with a high neck and a big ribbed welt at the bottom. I recognised it at once.

'Oh!' Lesley said. 'That looks like something of Rachel's to me, don't you think, Sam? She wears a lot of black. But then, so do you—'

By that time I was already removing the sweater from the woman's hand with my best charming smile.

'Thank you so much,' I said. 'I've been looking for it everywhere! What a coincidence that you should have brought it back when I was here! I thought I had left it in the crèche,' I added, as casually as I could manage. 'I was working in there last week. Is that where you found it?'

'Actually,' she said, frowning slightly, 'I can't think what happened. I certainly don't remember picking it up. I just found it at the bottom of my bag and worked out what must have happened. I'm really very sorry – you must have been going mad trying to find it.'

I smiled forgivingly. 'No problem,' I said. 'Would you mind telling me what day you think it might have been? Just out of interest?'

'Oh, it would have been the day that woman was found dead,' she said at once. 'I haven't been back since. And usually I'm quite organised. I wouldn't have walked off with someone else's property if I hadn't been distracted.'

She smiled at me. 'I'm really sorry,' she said again. 'I can't think why I would have put it in my bag. But I must have, obviously. And you're right, I must have picked it up in the crèche, because I went straight in there and didn't come out till they sent us home again.'

I was holding the sweater as carefully as if it had been the baby that was currently swelling out her stomach. I had only cast it the most cursory glance, but I was quite sure that down the front I would find a few splashes of blood. Linda's blood.

'Really,' I said, 'there's no need to apologise. None at all.'

23

It was cold and draughty in the big room with the newly mopped floor. I thought that I should have brought a jumper and then shivered, more at the association of ideas than the chill in the air. The orange moulded chair was hard and uncomfortable. High design and low design have that in common; they don't make seats you're happy to sit on. It's bourgeois taste which produces nice comfy armchairs you can curl up in.

But what did I expect in the way of creature comforts from a prison?

The far door opened and she came in, a warder behind her. The latter was the opposite of what I had anticipated, slight and pretty. They walked over to me with no apparent haste, the warder still following, quietly efficient, not taking her eyes off the prisoner. In the world outside, time was a commodity. Clearly within these walls the same rules did not apply.

Rachel sat down opposite me. The warder politely waited for her to pull up her chair to the table before reciting the list of rules governing our conduct. She had a pleasant voice and almost managed not to sound as if she had said these words a thousand times before. Then she stepped back a few paces, folded her hands and went still. I was reminded of the Greek nymph who was turned into a tree. What was her name? Oh, that's right. Daphne.

The prison uniform had done nothing to mar Rachel's beauty. Her hair was pulled back to her nape in a thick plait, throwing the delicate bones of her face into relief. Her neck rose from the ugly collar of the uniform with exquisite grace. Rachel could only be a Monday's child. Everyone here must be in love with her.

She was clearly waiting for me to speak. After all, it was I who had wanted to see her. I had some words prepared but they failed me now. Finally I said lamely: 'I wanted to see if you were – if there was anything you wanted.'

She looked straight at me. Only her eyes moved. Her body was as motionless as that of the warder. It was as if, once inside this place, its more intelligent occupants learnt a kind of composure to allow them to cope with the boredom, the endlessly repetitive routine of each new day; a way of pushing everything to one side and staying within themselves, unaffected by what was going on around them. Rachel seemed much further away from me than the mere width of the Formica table between us. I had a vision, like an acid hallucination, of the table stretching suddenly away to the far wall of the room, with Rachel a tiny figure in the distance whose voice, strangely, still reached me with perfect clarity.

'You came to try to feel less guilty, Sam,' she said. 'Well, do you?'

'Not right now,' I said. 'But I can't help that.'

'No, that's all past now. You made your choice.'

I leant forward. 'I did what I had to do,' I said, my voice sounding as unconvincing as I felt. At that moment I despised myself.

She shook her head, very slowly. She had kept herself so still that even this small movement was a shock.

'That's not true.' Her voice was distant, as if we were discussing two other people we hardly knew. 'It was no business of yours.'

'You made it my business at the beginning. You asked me to get involved.'

'What was between me and Derek was nothing to do with you.'

'I couldn't let an innocent man be charged for a crime he didn't commit!' I protested. I heard my words reverberating with much embarrassment. They sounded like something out of a cheap true-crime novel.

'He wouldn't have been convicted,' Rachel said, lips closing tight after the words as if this were the only fact she regretted.

Her good looks gave an unreal quality to the conversation, as if she were an actress more photogenic than the real-life person she was playing. She wore no make-up, and somehow managed to look as if she had been carefully made up in a trailer at five o'clock that morning to give precisely this impression.

'How can you say that with such confidence?' I demanded, finding a welcome release in anger.

She simply shrugged.

'So you meant what you said to me before, that Derek would just have had to take his chances? You wouldn't have come forward, even if it had gone to trial? Or if it looked like they were going to convict him?'

Her lips curved in a humourless smile. 'I'm not going to make you feel better about what you've done, Sam. I won't answer that.'

There was a moment of dead silence. Rachel, as she had a knack of doing, had put her finger on what was for me the crucial point. I still didn't know if I had done the right thing. And what had I expected to achieve by coming to see her – that she would pat my hand and tell me it didn't matter?

'I'm not the one whose conscience should be troubling me,' I retorted, unwilling to let her have the upper hand.

Her response was something of a surprise.

'I don't know what you mean,' she said sweetly, her dark eyes large. 'I haven't done anything wrong. OK, I had an affair with someone who already had a girlfriend, but it wasn't as if he was even married . . .'

'What the hell are you talking about?'

'Haven't I made myself clear?' She stretched her arms out in a display of elaborate nonchalance which was meant not to take me in, but impress me with her self-composure. 'I haven't done anything wrong.'

I stared at her, momentarily lost for words. She gazed back at me. 'That's not the view the British legal system seems to be taking,' I said finally. 'I thought you'd signed a confession.'

She folded her hands in her lap again. 'Under duress,' she said simply.

'Don't be a fool, Rachel. Didn't you have a solicitor present?'

'Not till later.'

'You're going to challenge the confession?' I said incredulously.

She nodded. 'But I'm not going to deny my relationship with Derek,' she said.

'You couldn't,' I pointed out. 'Lou knew about it.'

Her eyes narrowed slightly, but she continued talking as if the interruption hadn't happened.

'I knew that signing the confession would be a way to get him out of prison. I wasn't thinking straight. They intimidated me.'

'Oh yes, you're such a fragile, defenceless little thing. Well, I'm glad I'm providing you with an audience to try this story out on,' I said sarcastically. 'What about Jeff? Have you thought of that? Do you still think he'll lie for you under oath?'

There was a self-satisfied, amused expression on her face by way of answer. She leant back in the chair, crossing her legs.

'What about the bloodstains on the sweater? Your sweater?' I pressed her. 'And who put it in that woman's bag, if not you?'

Her face remained amused. 'Someone put the sweater on to protect their own clothing and then discarded it,' she said.

'The only people who could have put on that sweater would have been Fliss or Naomi, and it would have been a tight fit on either of them,' I pointed out, adding sharply: 'What a shame for you that you can't try to incriminate Derek that way.'

She became as withdrawn and still as she had been at the start of our conversation. 'Do you have anything left to say?' she enquired coolly. 'Because I'm getting rather tired of this. I've been interrogated enough already.'

'No. Nothing at all.'

I pushed back my chair. It squeaked horribly on the floor. For the past twenty minutes I had been concentrating so hard on the ugly chipped blue Formica table and the part of Rachel I could see above its surface that when the warder swam into my line of vision I started with surprise.

'Ready to leave?' she asked in a sympathetic voice.

I stood up.

'Yes,' I said. 'You could put it like that.'

* * *

In cheap crime novels, when you come out of prison the brightness outside hurts your eyes. That morning I would have been grateful for the cliché. It was noon, but the skies were the colour of grey flannel and had loosed a torrent of rain that by the force of its descent seemed to be enjoying itself tremendously. At least something was.

I hadn't brought an umbrella. Nor had I brought the van, God knows why. Something about not wanting to drive while emotionally distressed, not that they can test for that yet. I stood on the stone steps squinting gloomily out through the stream of water pouring down from the lintel. At least I was wearing my raincoat. Maybe I should wait for the storm to let up. But it could easily last for a couple of hours now it had got into its stride, and I didn't particularly fancy hanging around the main entrance to a prison for even half that time, like an ex-con not quite ready to face the outside world.

A car pulled up in front of the steps. I eyed it enviously. It would at least be dry in there. The passenger door swung open but no one got out. Then the driver leant over the passenger seat and started gesticulating. I looked over my shoulder; there was no one behind me.

'Will you get in the bloody car?' he was shouting, or something along those lines. The rain was making a tremendous din.

It was Sergeant Hawkins.

I didn't want to look too eager for his company, so I strolled down the steps rather than running and got myself wetter than I need have done as a result. He cast me a scornful look as he pulled away.

'If I'd known you didn't mind the rain I wouldn't have bothered to offer you a lift,' he said, turning out of the car park.

'You were going to offer me a lift anyway,' I said, unable to resist the temptation to be a smart-arse. 'You must have been waiting for me. It was you who got me in to see her, after all.'

'Don't flatter yourself,' he snapped. 'Anyway, why didn't you drive on a day like this?'

'Oh, you must have seen my van wasn't in the car park. Very good. Maybe I didn't drive because I knew you'd offer me a lift. Thought of that?'

He didn't bother to answer; he was busy negotiating a nasty roundabout. He drove very well.

'Do you have one of those clip-on lights that make a noise?' I asked, trying to wring some of the rainwater out of my hair.

'Don't be juvenile.' He backed the car into a parking space so fast I hardly had time to think up a response before he was turning off the ignition.

'Where are we? The nick?'

I looked out of the window. It wasn't the police station – not unless its frontage was disguised as a public house called The King's Head and Artichoke. Hawkins was already getting out of the car. I thought about making another wisecrack, and then a great weariness descended on me suddenly and I followed him into the pub and didn't say anything at all apart from a meek request for a double vodka when asked.

He looked at me sharply. 'Are you OK?'

I shrugged, seeing no point in answering.

'I didn't think it was a good idea for you to go.'

'I had to.'

The drinks arrived. I downed mine almost in one gulp, feeling his eyes on me.

'Is that your usual choice of anaesthetic?' he said.

'Whisky gives you a worse hangover,' I said, looking pointedly at the contents of his glass. He put a stop to that by finishing it off.

'I take it things didn't go too well in there,' he said.

'No better than you'd expect.'

I didn't want to tell him that Rachel planned to deny her confession. He'd find out in good time. And though I had nothing against him, somehow I felt that I'd already told him more than enough. There was a bitter taste in my mouth that didn't come from the vodka. I hadn't previously seen myself as a police informer and I didn't much like the new unimproved me.

'Same again, please,' I said to the barman, who was hovering nearby. Hawkins opened his mouth to speak but by that time the barman was already busy at the optics. I raised my eyebrows at this alacrity.

'Do they know who you are?' I said curiously. 'I've never been served so fast at lunchtime in my life.'

'A few of us come in here quite a bit,' he admitted. 'It's not far from the station.'

'I assume Daphne's not a regular, then,' I said nastily. 'Otherwise you wouldn't have brought me here.'

Fortunately at that moment the drinks were put in front of us, saving me from venting my anger on Hawkins any further. It wasn't his fault the way things had gone. Nor was the fact that I still found him attractive and was annoyed with myself as a result.

'Are you going to drink that,' he said between his teeth, 'or do you just intend to stand there in your flasher's mac and take all your grievances out on me?'

'Why not both? And it's not a flasher's mac. Flashers don't wear black PVC; they don't want to call attention to themselves before they do the deed.'

But I picked up the glass and started drinking. My head felt as cool and calm as a vodka bottle in a freezer; the alcohol wasn't getting through to me. Yet. We drank in silence, Hawkins staring straight ahead. I was very grateful for his reticence. I could think of nothing worse at this moment than someone sympathetically trying to persuade me to talk things through, and mercifully he seemed to understand the way I felt without having to be told.

I looked at his reflection in the mirror behind the bar. The sprinkling of rain on his hair had smoothed it down a little, which rather suited him. His eyes looked very blue and his mouth was fixed in a straight line. That probably meant he was cross with me. So did the square set of his jaw. He was wearing one of those trenchcoats that look ridiculous on any man who isn't tall and broad; since he was, it showed off the width of his shoulders very well. It suddenly struck me how adult he looked. Well, he *was* an adult. He had a proper job, plenty of responsibility, a girlfriend, and probably a mortgage. He also had very blue eyes. I wondered what the hell he was doing drinking whisky with me at lunchtime.

'Shall we go?' he said, cutting through my meditation. He put his glass down. I followed suit, my hand perfectly steady. He paid the reckoning with such an air of decision that I didn't argue and offer half. We went outside and he unlocked the car.

'Should you be driving with two double whiskies inside you?' I said as I got in.

He switched on the windscreen wipers. 'Absolutely not.'

It was only a short drive to my studio.

'Well, thanks for the lift,' I said, getting out. 'You won't mind if I run inside? It's wet out there.'

I didn't wait to hear what he had to say, just shut the car door and dashed up the front steps, fishing the keys out of my pocket. I had an overwhelming desire to be alone, even if it wasn't going to be particularly good for me. I unlocked the third lock, shoved the door open and went in, kicking it to behind me. But it didn't shut, or I didn't hear the sound of the Yale snapping into place. I swung round.

Hawkins was standing in the doorway, one large hand holding the door open. Our eyes met. He came into the room, kicking the door shut without taking his eyes off mine. The sound of the lock clicking to seemed to come from another dimension.

I pulled open the belt of my raincoat and started to unbutton it.

'What are you doing in here?' I said, managing a creditably detached tone of voice. 'I thought you were under the impression that I was the Antichrist and the Whore of Babylon rolled into one, and that you would never willingly be left alone with me again? Or that's what you gave me to believe last time.'

He said something that didn't come out properly. Then he cleared his throat and said again, louder: 'That's exactly what I wanted to talk about. The pub wasn't really private enough for that kind of thing. I wanted to say that it can't happen again.' His feet were slightly apart in the classic policeman's stance. It probably made him feel more confident. I half expected him to clasp his hands behind his back and rock backwards and forwards slightly.

Taking off my raincoat, I draped it over a chair to dry. 'That's right,' I agreed blandly, 'you live with someone and I'm certainly not looking for that kind of set-up. Look at this place: how could I ask any respectable man to share it with me? And you're *very* respectable. I don't think our leisure habits would coincide.'

He shifted slightly. 'Well, yes. Indeed. I think we should just forget that . . . that it ever happened. After all, it didn't amount to very much – if we're putting things into perspective . . .'

This remark sealed his fate. Besides, I noticed that he was making no move towards the door.

'Come upstairs for a minute,' I said amiably. 'I want to show you something.'

He followed me dutifully up the ladder. When he had pulled himself over the edge, and was standing on the sleeping platform, I gestured around me.

'Do you know what this is?' I said. 'This is where I sleep. Now, let me just run through the facts. You've inveigled a meeting with me, taken me to a pub and plied me with drink, driven me home, come uninvited into my home to tell me that you don't want to kiss me again, and now you're to all intents and purposes in my bedroom. Quite frankly, any jury would acquit me without leaving the box.'

'Acquit you of what?' he said sternly.

'Look,' I said, kicking off my shoes. 'We're going to play a game. I haven't worked out the name yet, but it goes like this: I take off all my clothes and then you have to kiss me wherever I tell you to. How does that sound?'

I don't usually feel weak and feminine, but he took me by surprise. I hadn't imagined that a policeman could have so much initiative. He kissed me so hard I saw stars, and not of the romantic kind.

'Jesus, Hawkins,' I said, wrenching my mouth free for a moment, his hands so tight on my bottom I could hardly lean back enough to look at him, 'I haven't said "Start" yet—'

'Shut up, you little wretch,' he said, his eyes blue as lightning. 'And if you're going to take your clothes off, you've got thirty seconds before I rip them off you. Get started.'

Reluctantly he let me go, presumably to assist this process. I opened my mouth to say 'How macho!' admiringly. Then I looked at him and for some reason thought better of it. Maybe it was the size of his shoulders in the trenchcoat. Instead I began unbuttoning my jeans. It seemed the best place to start.

And I didn't hurry. I might be a little drunk, but this ripping-clothes-off-idea of his sounded like fun.

24

Lou was crying again. I was used to it by now. I didn't know, and I was sure she didn't, what proportion of her tears were from relief or from sadness. She had lost some weight; her clothes were hanging off her. It couldn't all have happened in the few days since Rachel was arrested and Derek released. I hadn't noticed over the past couple of weeks that she had not been eating anything. It didn't really suit her; I hoped that she would recover her spirits, and the stone she must have shed, now that the worst part was over. She had lost the pomp and majesty that were her hallmarks.

Wiping her face with a tissue, she looked up at me.

'I'm sorry, Sam. I shouldn't be doin' this. It's partly 'cause I'm happy, you know? Seein' him walk back in that door, lookin' just the same—'

This was the first day Derek had resumed his classes at the gym. It was true; being arrested seemed not to have affected him at all. He was his usual relaxed self.

'But then to think of Rachel in that place – no matter what she's done. I hate to think about it.'

Lou had got a hold of herself now, and was sitting up straighter.

'Doesn't bear thinkin' about,' she repeated, shaking her head. 'What did she look like?'

'Lovely as ever.'

'She angry with you?'

I nodded.

'Of course, stupid question . . . Did you tell her it was me who really did it, Sam? Ain't fair you should have to bear the brunt of it.'

I shrugged, avoiding the question. 'It doesn't matter now.'

'Yes, it does. It was me rang that policeman and told him about her sweater, not you. It was me got that pregnant woman's name and address for him from the files.'

She looked hard at me, fully recovered now. 'It ain't your fault, Sam. We did the right thing, and when I say "we" I really mean "me". If I can take the weight of that, you can too. There wasn't anythin' else we could do. You know that as well as I do.'

Reluctantly I nodded. It didn't make me feel any better, but then nothing would do that. There was a knock on the door. It opened before we could answer, which had always been Derek's style. Things were certainly getting back to normal.

'Came to see how everything's going,' he said. 'And I wanted a bit of privacy to thank you two girls for all you've done for me. Lou—'

He came over to her and hugged her in the chair. She looked as if she were about to cry, but swallowed the tears back womanfully.

'And Sam—'

He was about to kiss me but I put out my hand instead, which he shook firmly.

'I don't know how to thank you,' he repeated.

Lou snorted. 'Thank us for doin' what you couldn't do for yourself. Or *wouldn't*,' she added pointedly.

Derek shook his head. 'I couldn't do it, Lou. I couldn't turn someone else in.'

'Lucky for you I didn't have those scruples,' Lou said. 'Sam here's sufferin' a bit as well. Not to say I'm not. I cared about that girl. I just have to keep remindin' myself that she wouldn't have raised a finger to help you.'

Derek looked uncomfortable. 'We don't know that for sure,' he said. 'She might just have been waiting to see what would happen. I don't blame her for that.'

'Sam? What do you think?' Lou said right at me.

I dropped my eyes and said nothing.

'I treated her very badly,' Derek said, looking sheepish. 'I can't blame her for being angry with me. Or with Linda.'

A little shiver ran over me at the mention of Linda's name, and I noticed that even Derek had pronounced it carefully. It was as if none of us wanted to say Linda's or Rachel's names out loud, as if it would keep the curse of violence and murder on this place instead of letting it drain away in the aftermath of Rachel's arrest.

'I hope you're goin' to behave better now,' Lou said. 'Be a good boy. Settle down with that nice Janice and raise your boy. I always liked that girl, and Devon's the spittin' image of you.'

A big grin split Derek's face at the mention of his son. 'Don't I know it! He's already up to every trick in the book. Yeah, I'm moving in with Jan. We might even get married.'

Lou nodded approvingly. 'Glad to hear it. Well,' she said rather magnificently, flicking a switch on her computer, 'don't you two have nothin' better to do than hang around here? Classes to teach or somethin'?'

Lou's timing was perfect; we were both grateful for the dismissal. I stood up and made for the door, Derek close behind me. As we left the office he said in my ear: 'Come into the crèche a minute, Sam? I'd like a word.'

I went across the reception area and into the crèche, though reluctantly. I thought that Derek wanted to talk about Rachel, perhaps ask me how she had looked, and I was bracing myself for the prospect. Instead he said, leaning against the wall, legs crossed at the ankles, arms across his chest, in one of the casual positions only someone as good-looking as he could get away with: 'I've got what you might call a message from a friend.'

I stared at him. 'What are you talking about?'

'It's Brian.' Derek was grinning evilly. 'I know this is a bit school-playground stuff, you know – Miss, my friend fancies you . . . Anyway, Brian does. Fancy you, I mean. But you know how shy he is. I offered to sound you out to stop him making a fool of himself when he tries to ask you to go to the pub with him and can't get the words out properly.'

I stared at him incredulously.

'So what do you say? Yes or no?' Derek was enjoying this tremendously.

'But—' I felt my brow creasing in bewilderment. 'I've got it all wrong – I thought Brian didn't trust me! He arranged for me to go and talk to Fliss, at her stall, and then followed me and spied on us. I thought he was checking me out!'

'No, no.' Derek's grin was even more devilish now. 'You got it the wrong way round. He thought Fliss was the guilty party. He was making sure she didn't get it into her head you were a danger to her and whack you over the head with a piece of her bric-à-brac. He was keeping an eye out to make sure you were safe. Having what you might call a personal interest in your welfare. And from what he's told me, he's been doing it ever since. Following Fliss, not you, I mean. He knew he'd already freaked you out when you caught him in the market.'

'My God, I never thought of that.' I started to giggle. 'Poor Fliss. Has he been dogging her footsteps?'

'Yeah, she's pretty pissed off with him,' Derek agreed. 'But don't keep the poor guy in suspense, eh? What's it to be?'

I fumbled for an answer. 'I'm actually seeing someone at the moment,' I lied feebly. 'But I don't really think of Brian in that way . . .'

'Gotcha. No need to say any more. Poor bloke'll cry into his pillow for weeks. Well, in that case—' He tipped himself off the wall and strolled over to me. 'What about having a drink with me this evening? I don't want to poach on a friend's territory, but if there's no chance for him . . .'

He was standing very close to me. In a leisurely, unhurried way he raised his hand and lifted a lock of my hair, smiling down at me with complete confidence.

'I haven't forgotten that night after the club, Sam,' he said. 'You're really something. And you know the score, right?' He trailed one finger down my cheek. 'Just because I'm with someone else doesn't mean I can't enjoy myself every now and then. You understand that. You know how to enjoy yourself too . . .'

I removed his finger before it could go any lower than my jawline, resisting the urge to bend it back sharply.

'No thanks, Derek. Though I'm flattered. But once was enough. No hard feelings, eh?'

I swivelled on my heel, but he wasn't going to give up that easily. I felt his large hands close on my shoulders, and he said from behind me, leaning so close his breath was warm against my ear: 'What's wrong, Sam? Don't tell me you didn't have a good time before. Is it Jan? You don't have to worry about that. She understands me, I promise. There'll be no comeback. Come on.' He bent to kiss the back of my neck, very sure of himself. 'Let yourself go . . .'

I pulled myself free and twisted my head back to look him in the face.

'Shrink down your ego, Derek,' I snapped. 'Once was enough. You're not my type. I don't like my men smooth, OK? I like them rough and ready. And you may have a great pair of gluteals, but you still don't fit the bill.'

I'd never seen Derek look so cross before. One would almost think that, as far as he was concerned, rejection was much worse than being arrested.

'So what's this guy of yours like, then?' he snapped, putting a nasty twist on the words. 'Rough and ready?'

'Absolutely,' I said sweetly. Then I walked out of the crèche, letting the door bang shut behind me, and left the gym without looking back.

Springtime finally seemed to have reached the heart of London; the sun was beating down on my head enough for me to tilt it back and catch the rays on my face, the warmth like a promise of better times to come. All at once, I realised that I was free for the first time since Linda had been killed – no responsibilities to bear but my own, and God knew those were few enough. I strolled up towards Camden, light-headed, whistling under my breath.

Catching a glimpse of myself in a big mirror in a shop-front, I stopped for a moment to check myself out. Not bad for a policeman's moll. Then I realised that this was Satins, the hairdresser's where Naomi's friend Cath worked. The door stood open, taking advantage of the warmer weather. I put my head round it; Cath was sitting at the reception desk, looking bored. Her hair was in bunches and she was fiddling listlessly with one of them.

'Hello!' she said when she saw me. 'How's tricks?' She lowered her voice and looked around with an air of importance. 'I heard they caught that girl who did the murder. She was keen on Derek, right? No way he wasn't mixed up in it somehow. I could've told them that.'

'*Cherchez l'homme.*'

'You what? Oh yeah, right. Anyway,' she went on, 'you come to get your hair done, then? Still thinking about having it bleached? Be a shame, in a way.'

I shook my head slowly. 'Thanks,' I said, 'but I think I'll leave it.'

'You sure?'

'Definitely. The more I think about it, the more I realise that there are too many blondes in the world as it is.'

I waved at her and left the shop.

I should go home: I had work to do. It had turned out that Betty and Jim didn't want the Thing. They wanted Son of Thing and they wanted it big, even if they seemed rather vague about where they were going to put it. I ought to start working out if I could actually build something roughly corresponding to the sketches I'd made. It was worth my while to try, anyway; Duggie, who was now my dealer, had worked out a pleasantly healthy remuneration.

My thoughts returned for a moment to the gym. Cath had put her finger on it: Derek was an *homme fatal*. Women would be fighting over him for the rest of his life, and he knew it. If he realised in whose favour I had turned him down he would be livid.

My encounter with Derek had brought Hawkins back into my mind. I couldn't help grinning as I thought of him. Would he dislike being described as rough and ready? Well, it wasn't really fair to judge a man by the initial skirmish.

But if there was to be a second, I'd make damn sure he took his raincoat off first.

ALSO BY LAUREN HENDERSON AND AVAILABLE IN ARROW